"Grr," Joe replied.

"I'll take that as a no, though you really need to relax. A big guy like you, out in the heat, veins bulging in your forehead like that... One of these days you're just gonna go *splat*. I've seen it happen." She made a *tsking* sound as she shook her head.

"My blood pressure is fine and none of your business."

Incredibly she laughed. Then rubbed her hand across her mouth as if to make her smile disappear. It did, but her eyes still danced. "That growling—it works for you?" she asked.

"Up till now."

"I'm sure it's frightening when you're all padded up. But you aren't going to tackle me, are you?" She tilted her head. "Besides, my father was a cop. I know some tricks."

She winked, and Joe's blood pressure went up a notch. She had nice eyes. He'd always been partial to green.

"There aren't enough tricks in the world to stop me, sweetheart."

"That 'sweetheart' thing work for you, too? Or do women knock your teeth down your throat?"

It was his turn to smile. "See any teeth missing?"

"Grr," she said.

Dear Reader,

Although I was brought up in a family of girls, I now live in a household of men. Sometimes when they're talking about "boy stuff" I feel as if I'm the only human on the planet Zoltan, but it makes for a fascinating life.

With two sons heavily into Little League and a husband who is a coach, I spend most of the summer sitting in the bleachers. I get a very good tan and have a lot of time to daydream.

During one of my midsummer "what-if" games, I came up with the idea for *Mother of the Year.* What if a mother of three boys and the father of a teenage girl meet, and despite the fact that they see each other as the worst possible example for their children, they fall in love? Then they discover that sometimes what you think is true isn't true at all, and love, wherever you find it, is a gift worth sacrificing just about anything for.

I would love to hear what you think. Write to me at P.O. Box 736, Thiensville, WI 53092, or check out my Web site at http://www.eclectics.com/lorihandeland/.

Lori Handeland

MOTHER OF THE YEAR
Lori Handeland

HARLEQUIN®

TORONTO • NEW YORK • LONDON
AMSTERDAM • PARIS • SYDNEY • HAMBURG
STOCKHOLM • ATHENS • TOKYO • MILAN • MADRID
PRAGUE • WARSAW • BUDAPEST • AUCKLAND

ISBN 0-373-70922-6

MOTHER OF THE YEAR

Copyright © 2000 by Lori Handeland.

This edition published by arrangement with Harlequin Books S.A.

® and TM are trademarks of the publisher. Trademarks indicated with
® are registered in the United States Patent and Trademark Office, the
Canadian Trade Marks Office and in other countries.

Visit us at www.eHarlequin.com

Printed in U.S.A.

For Pam Hopkins, my favorite agent, and Kim Rangel,
who thought this book sounded "super."

CHAPTER ONE

ATTENTION!
ALL MALES IN THE VAUGHN HOUSEHOLD
THE RULES FOR THE UPCOMING SUMMER SEASON
ARE AS FOLLOWS:

1. THERE WILL BE NO MORE HOT WHEELS IN THE BATHROOM SINK
2. TOOTHPASTE IS NOT TO BE USED AS FINGER PAINT
3. SUBMACHINE GUN NOISES ARE NOT ALLOWED BEFORE 7:00 A.M.
4. BROTHERS ARE NOT ENEMIES AND SHOULD NOT BE TREATED AS SUCH

EVIE VAUGHN CHEWED on the cap of her pen and surveyed the paper in front of her. Had she forgotten anything?

She chewed harder and shook her head. No, the list looked good. Not too many items, but enough for the summer season.

Evie smiled to herself, doubting that other mothers divided their years into seasons—but the process worked for her. Her job as a high school physical education teacher and extracurricular coach made her think in terms of seasons. It was a division she understood, as did her three sons.

Evie stood and anchored the paper to the refrigerator with a magnet. Sounds of a war in the making drifted from the twins' bedroom. She glanced at her watch—6:55 a.m. Rule number three definitely needed enforcement.

"Mom! He started it." The shout greeted her as she entered the first bedroom off the hallway. Danny, her youngest son by four minutes, his carrot-colored hair sticking up in numerous cowlicks, made a beeline for her leg. Yanking on her sweat suit, he turned an entreating gaze upward. "You don't like it when we make war, and I told him." He pointed a semi-grimy finger at his identical twin, Benji, who ignored them both as he blasted all the bad guys into another dimension with his own slightly cleaner finger.

"Boys." Evie disengaged Danny's fingers from her leg one by one. "The new list of rules is on the fridge." Groans replaced the machine-gun sounds as the twins clutched their middles and fell to the ground. "Adam!" she called. "Take your brothers into the kitchen and read them the new rules."

"I'm not dressed," her seventeen-year-old shouted from his room.

"Then get dressed. In ten minutes my car leaves for school."

She looked down at her sons, who were still playing dead on the floor. One still had on his Batman pajama bottoms; the other wore only Ninja Turtle underwear. With one week left before summer vacation, you would think they'd be used to getting dressed in time for school. She'd heard them arguing over cereal choices before the sun shone. What had they been doing since?

Evie shrugged. She'd been too busy getting ready for work to notice. As long as no one was crying or bleeding, she counted herself lucky.

"Ten minutes, boys," she repeated. "And you'd better wash those hands, too." She turned away, mumbling, "I know I gave them a bath last night. How did they get dirty between then and now?" As she returned to the kitchen, the frantic scrambling sounds that followed assured her all three boys were racing to get ready.

Picking up her coffee cup, Evie leaned against the counter and took a moment to calm down. Every morning was the same—a flurry of activity to get out of the house and to the school on time. Raising three boys alone wasn't easy, but she did her best.

The death of her husband six years ago had made Evie's dream of a teaching degree a necessity. With the help of her parents, and the money from a small insurance policy, she'd earned her degree at a college near her home of Newsome, Iowa.

When she was offered the position of high school physical education teacher in Oak Grove, a few hours east of Newsome, she'd jumped at the chance. Her boys would at last have a stable home in a good community, free of the memories of their father—his life and his death.

With one dream realized, Evie found a new one. She wanted her children to have college diplomas. If she could land a varsity coaching position, she could put away enough money to send the boys to college. The events of the coming summer would make or break her dream—

The sound of stampeding elephants in the hallway interrupted her thoughts. The elephants materialized into boys as the twins skidded into the kitchen, followed closely by Adam—tall, wiry and as dark haired as Evie herself.

She smiled over her coffee cup as the two youngest stood in front of the refrigerator, their faces scrunching up in concentration as they tried to read her note.

"The," Benji said.

"All," Danny added.

Adam ignored them both and read the rules, putting a hand on the shoulder of each brother as they started to argue.

"But Mom, we *have* to put the Hot Wheels in the sink after we play with them in the tub, so they can drool off," Danny stated, somewhat cleaner hands planted on his hips.

"What does *em-eny* mean?" Benji asked, snatching his backpack from a chair.

"*Enemy,*" Evie corrected automatically. "It means I'm sick of the fighting. You're seven years old and in the first grade. I think you can try to get along with your brother."

Adam snorted. "Right, Mom. That'll never happen. They were born to beat on each other."

Evie grabbed her duffel bag and handed Danny his backpack as she herded her three sons out the door. "I just don't understand why you all can't be nice to one another. I never had a brother or sister. I would have loved one."

"That's the problem, Mom. You don't understand. They *like* to fight."

Evie sighed. Adam was right. Benji and Danny lived and breathed conflict. But if anyone outside the family so much as glanced at one of them cross-eyed, they defended each other zealously.

"Can I drive?"

"Huh?" Evie gaped at Adam. He smiled, and her heart skipped a half beat. When he turned on the charm, Adam was the spitting image of his father, a fact that caused her no small alarm. While alive, Ray Vaughn had made countless lives miserable, her own and her sons' at the top of the list. He had used his good looks and charm to get his way, regardless of the consequences.

"Mom?" Adam asked. "Are you all right?"

His eyes, warm, brown, concerned, peered into hers, and Evie relaxed. Adam resembled his father only superficially. Ray had died before he could totally ruin his sons, and Evie had spent the past six years fixing the damage he had managed to accomplish.

"Sure," she said, and tossed Adam the keys.

Because of the size of Oak Grove, driver's edu-

cation was just offered once a year. Therefore
Adam, despite being seventeen, had gotten his
driver's license only a week earlier. Evie still wasn't
used to the change. Her throat tightened as she
watched him shepherd the twins into the back seat,
then climb behind the wheel. Somewhere along the
way he'd become a young man—and she'd been too
busy keeping the family afloat to notice.

Blinking back the unaccustomed wetness from
her eyes, Evie got into the battered Ford station
wagon. The twins were already arguing about who
had fastened his seat belt first. Evie tuned them out
and concentrated on the road.

The high school stood on a flat stretch of land just
a few miles from their house, with the grade school
and the middle school on either side. Adam dropped
the twins off at the front door of Oak Grove Ele-
mentary, and the two raced inside without a backward glance. Then he made the short trip to the high
school teachers' parking lot and pulled into Evie's
assigned space. He handed her the keys with a grin.

She smiled back and was about to compliment
him on his driving, when a flash of red at the corner
of her vision made her turn her head. A car skidded
into the lot. Before she could warn Adam, he opened
his door to get out, and the vehicle—an expensive,
foreign sports car—scooted into the parking space
next to them, slamming into the door.

Evie instinctively grabbed for her son, but he
shook off her protective hand and stepped from the

car. She jumped out her side and hurried around to survey the damage.

"Oh, no," she breathed as she took in the mangled driver's door, which tilted crazily, held only by one bent hinge. She winced when she considered the price of a replacement compared with her insurance deductible.

Then the door to the offending sports car opened with a *whoosh* of expertly oiled hinges, and Evie's head snapped in that direction. "I'll handle this," she said to Adam, shushing him when he would have argued.

She stomped around the back of the red car and stood there, foot tapping in impatience, while she waited for the owner to make an appearance.

Tennis shoes the size of small boats hit the ground. Evie stared at them in amazement as the rest of the body followed. Her gaze traveled up, up, up along the black jeans and body-hugging black T-shirt, until she met the eyes of the giant in front of her—ice blue framed by bronzed skin, short, silver-blond hair belying the youth of the face.

Evie couldn't stop staring. She'd never seen such a large man in her life—or one so striking. Even though she was petite and used to looking up to most people, this man made her neck ache.

He stalked to the front of his car. Evie followed and watched as he bent over and squinted at the damage, which appeared minor from her point of view, then slowly straightened and returned to stand in front of her.

"What are you kids doing in this lot?"

Evie frowned. "Excuse me?"

The man sighed irritably and slammed his car door. Evie jumped at the sound. "*This* lot." He pointed at the sign directly in front of her car. "The *teachers'* and *visitors'* lot. Shouldn't you kids park somewhere else?"

Evie stifled a laugh, certain this giant would not be likewise amused. This wasn't the first time she'd been mistaken for a student. When she wore her sunglasses, as she did now, the telltale lines around her eyes were hidden, creating a more youthful appearance.

"I think you've made a mistake—" she began.

"No, you have, honey. And your boyfriend, too." He glared at Adam, who stared back without flinching. "Did you just get your driver's license, kid?"

Evie's amusement died at the man's condescending tone—and she had never taken well to being called "honey" by a stranger. She silenced Adam with a wave of her hand and stepped in front of the mountainous man.

"Listen, mister, you're the one who came tearing in here about fifteen miles over the speed limit. This is a school zone. And *you* hit *our* car. So if anyone should be asking about a driver's license, it's us."

The man looked down at her, and Evie could have sworn she saw a flash of amusement in his cool blue eyes before he frowned and stepped past her to assess the damage. The sight of their demolished door deflated his anger, and his shoulders moved on a silent sigh.

"Hell," he muttered, and reached for his wallet. Turning back to them, he ignored Evie as though she didn't exist and pulled out several bills, which he handed to Adam. "I'm sorry about the car, son. She's right. I should have been more careful. But let me give you some advice. You've got to stand up for yourself in this world. Don't ever let a woman do it for you. Once you lose control in a relationship, it's tough to get it back." After a wink at Evie, who stood speechless, he walked into the school.

"Of all the nerve," Evie sputtered. "Who does he think he is?"

Adam laughed. "I don't know. But he thought you were my girlfriend."

Her son's continued laughter drew Evie's attention away from the school. "Hey, it's not *that* funny. I'm only thirty-five."

Adam eyed the money in his hand, and the laughter stopped. "Mom? Am I seeing what I think I'm seeing?" He held out the bills.

Evie took them and gasped. Five crisp, new, one-hundred dollar bills lay in her palm.

She looked from her son's wide eyes, to the fire-engine-red car, to the front door of the school. Then she crumpled the bills. "Who is that guy?"

JOSEPH SCALOTTA, known as "Joe" among his friends, "Iceman Scalotta" to football fans across the United States and "Wild Man" in too many newspaper stories, entered the central office of Oak Grove High.

The school secretary glanced up from her computer. Her smile froze when she saw the size of the man on the other side of the counter. "M-may I help you?"

"I hope so. I'd like to register my daughter for school in the fall. We've just moved here from Chicago."

The woman nodded and began to gather the appropriate papers. She came to the counter and tossed them toward Joe from a distance of three feet. He slammed his palm down on them before they could skid off and scatter over his tennis shoes. The secretary gave a startled little shriek at the *thump* his hand produced when it connected with the Formica countertop, and scurried behind her desk.

Joe stifled his irritation. Why did people in Oak Grove treat him as if he were a monster? Didn't they grow big, strapping farm boys in Iowa anymore? Obviously not, from the way everyone gaped at Joe's height and breadth.

The only person not intimidated by him had been that teenybopper in the parking lot. *She'd* stood up to him. She'd even stepped close and tried to argue. Funny, now that he thought about it, she hadn't smelled like a teenager—teenage girls wore too much perfume—or looked like the ones he was used to seeing—they used too much makeup.

No, she'd smelled like summer air and Ivory soap, and her face had been attractive in a fresh-scrubbed way. Maybe he should find out her name so he could introduce her to his daughter. Heaven knows, Antonia could use a friend with some spunk. Toni was far too quiet and eager to please. Even though he, too, had been at fault, Joe blamed a lot of Toni's problems on his late ex-wife. The woman had been a pain in the—

"Sir?"

Joe snapped out of his reverie to see the secretary hovering nearby. He tried smiling at her, but stopped when she inched back. He should have known better. He'd used that smile often on the opposition—with the same effect. He wasn't called "Iceman" for nothing.

"When you're through with those papers, you can go down to Mrs. Vaughn's office. Room 123. She'll be your daughter's adviser for next year."

Joe picked up the forms. With a nod to the secretary he left.

This domestic stuff confused him, but with his ex-wife's death he now had custody of their sixteen-year-old daughter. His status as a pro player with a degree in physical education had brought numerous offers for coaching jobs all over America, and now that he was done with football he wanted to use the degree he'd worked so hard to obtain.

His mom had always said he was a born teacher, just like his father, who had been a high school principal. When people needed a hand, Joe was the one who helped—be it in baseball, football or algebra. He was the one who showed everyone else how to do things, and he had a lot of patience. He liked kids, and he loved coaching. He planned to make the most of this opportunity.

He'd picked the job at Oak Grove Community College because he wished to raise his daughter in a town reminiscent of the one he'd spent his youth in. The money wasn't too good coaching at this level, but then, money wasn't one of Joe's problems. He'd made scads in pro ball, and he had invested it well. What he wanted right now was to give his daughter the stable home she had never known. The kind he'd grown up in. The kind he himself craved again.

Room 123. Joe paused in front of the door and read the name plate: Mrs. Evelyn Vaughn. Physical Education.

He reached for the doorknob, only to have it spring away from his hand. Before he could move, a tiny Fury of a female barreled straight into his chest.

"Oh!" she gasped, and stumbled backward. Her arms flew out as she struggled to keep herself upright; papers and books scattered in every direction.

Joe caught her by the elbows, hauling her upward until her toes dangled above the floor.

"Hey! Put me down!" She windmilled her feet, catching him in the knee.

"Ow!" Joe set her on the floor with a *thump*. Leaning over, he rubbed his kneecap, then bent farther to collect the books and papers she'd dropped. "I was just trying to keep you from falling on your can," he said. "The least you could do is say thank-you." Joe glanced up, then straightened. The Fury was none other than the girl he'd met in the parking lot.

"You." Her mouth twisted into a grimace, as though she'd just stepped ankle deep in a swamp. She snatched her books and papers from his hands and rearranged them in her arms as she continued to frown at him.

"We meet again." He nodded at the door. "Is she your adviser?"

"Who?"

"Mrs. Vaughn. I suppose she's one of those iron-maiden teachers—as wide as she is tall, with steel-gray hair and thighs like thunder." He paused, re-membering teachers from his past. "She's probably a widow—nagged her husband to death before they'd been married five years—and teaches kids since she doesn't have any of her own. I want Toni to like it here." He squinted at the girl. "Don't you ever take those glasses off?"

"Not when I'm on my way outside. Who's Toni?"

"My daughter. She's going to start school at Oak Grove in the fall. I think you might be about her age."

"Think again."

"You've got to be close if you're at this school. She could use a friend. What's your name?"

The "girl" yanked off her sunglasses to reveal annoyed hazel eyes. "I'm Evie Vaughn." Her frown deepened the faint lines of life surrounding those eyes. "The iron-maiden widow."

CHAPTER TWO

"OH, OH," THE MAN MUTTERED.

"Yeah. Oh, oh." Evie grabbed the papers from his hand and scanned them quickly. "Well, Mr. Scalotta, I can only hope your daughter has better manners than you do, or I suspect we'll be seeing a lot more of each other."

He scowled. "My daughter is wonderful. The sole problem I see is that she thinks she has to be perfect. She wants everyone to like her. That's a normal teenage thing, isn't it?"

Evie raised her eyebrows at the hopeful tone of his voice. He was trying to convince himself as much as he was her. "Of course. Now, if you don't mind, I have a class to teach." Evie turned away.

A hand on her arm stopped her. She looked down at the offending fingers, then up at their owner. Taking the hint, he set her free, but Evie could still feel the imprint of that hand. Gritting her teeth, she purposefully ignored the shiver of awareness. She knew where such mindless attractions led—straight to disaster.

"Did you want something else, Mr. Scalotta?" The chill in her voice warred with the heat of her body.

"Joe."

"Excuse me?"

"My name is Joe. My father is Mr. Scalotta."

"You're a parent. I'm a teacher. I see no reason for us to start calling each other by our first names."

He shrugged, the easy movement stretching the taut black cotton across his chest. She'd always enjoyed the sight of a well-built man in a T-shirt. Evie yanked her gaze from the intriguing view and met his eyes, startled again by the light color against the bronze of his face.

"Suit yourself, Mrs. Vaughn. I wondered if you could spare a moment to discuss Toni. Advising is part of your job, isn't it?"

"Yes. A part. But right now my job is teaching freshman phys ed, and if I don't get outside, they're likely to start without me. Believe me, Mr. Scalotta, we don't want twenty freshmen having a gym class alone." She shook her head. "It wouldn't be pretty."

A chuckle slipped from Scalotta's lips, and from the expression on his face, the spark of humor surprised him as much as it surprised her.

"No, I can't imagine that it would. Something like the first day of training camp with a team full of rookies."

Evie stared at him blankly.

"Football, Mrs. Vaughn. I used to play football. I'm afraid I have the habit—annoying, or so I've been told—of likening life to the playing field."

"Football," Evie repeated. "Professional?"

"Yeah." He gave a half smile. "I guess you don't follow the game much. I used to be pretty good."

Suddenly she remembered those eyes, that hair, the size—but, of course, he'd never looked this big on her small television set. "Joe Scalotta." The name burst from her lips. "Holy cow! You mean you're that Scalotta? Defensive lineman? Pro Bowl six years running? The Iceman?"

"You do follow the game."

"I'm a high school physical education teacher. Of course I follow football. If not because I like the game, which I do, but because I don't want to appear like a moron to my students."

"Good point."

"That explains how you can throw hundred-dollar bills around like paper. You left before we could give your money back."

He frowned. "I don't want it back. Get your car fixed."

"We have insurance."

"We?"

"Me. My family."

"Ah…your husband, and you, and whoever that was with you this morning."

Evie stifled a smile. "Definitely not my boy-friend. And I don't have a husband. He died."

"I'm sorry."

"Yeah, well, I don't need your money."

"Take it. I was at fault."

Evie hesitated. Actually, she did need the money. Badly. She had no extra cash for a new car door—

and she could hardly drive without one. "All right." Swallowing her pride, she nodded. "Thank you."

He acknowledged her thanks with a shrug of one large shoulder. "I suppose you should get to class before all hell breaks loose. I'll just give you a call about Toni."

Evie bit her lip. The thought of any more encounters with this man unsettled her. An ex-professional football player, no less. Top of the macho hill. Absolutely bad news—especially for Evelyn Vaughn.

Just her luck she hadn't experienced such an instantaneous attraction since she'd met Ray—and with that memory to guide her, she should run for cover like a scared rabbit. But Evie couldn't run from Joe Scalotta, and she couldn't hide, either. From the looks of him, he'd find her wherever she went.

"Sure, call me and we'll discuss your daughter. I'd be happy to help in any way I can." With a sharp nod Evie walked away, not pausing until she reached the relative safety of the softball diamonds.

As she set about putting order to the pandemonium around her, Evie couldn't keep her mind from returning to Joe Scalotta. Despite her best intentions, she wondered when she would see him next, and where her dangerous attraction for the wrong type of man would lead her this time.

JOE DROVE HOME, his mind filled with Mrs. Evelyn Vaughn. She was exactly the type of female he should avoid: bossy, opinionated, a career woman. He needed a settling-down kind of woman—someone who would take care of Toni the way the girl had never been taken care of. Someone who could understand his daughter. *He* certainly couldn't.

Joe yanked the wheel to the right and turned into his driveway. The house, a colonial situated in a quiet suburb of Oak Grove, was much too big for the two of them. But the place reminded Joe of his childhood home in rural Missouri, where he'd lived happily with his parents and three brothers, and he'd been unable to resist.

"Toni?" Joe called as he came in the front door.

"In here."

He stepped into the family room and found his daughter exactly as he'd left her—watching game shows on the television. Joe couldn't remember spending any childhood free time watching TV when the sun shone, but then, he'd had three brothers to play with. Toni had only him.

She looked up from the screen. "Hi, Joe."

"Hi." It hurt every time she called him "Joe" and not "Dad," but once she'd turned twelve, that was what she'd done. He had no idea why, and he didn't know how to ask. Or maybe he was afraid to. He'd rather face a 350-pound offensive lineman than have his daughter tell him he was such a terrible father that she couldn't bring herself to address him as "Dad." Joe hoped to change her mind—but once again, he wasn't quite sure how.

"You been sitting here since I left?"

Dismay flickered over Toni's face, and Joe wanted to smack himself. She'd taken his question as a criticism, when all he'd meant to do was make conversation. She stood. "I'll have a shower and get dressed."

Joe wracked his brain for a way to get through to her. "Why don't we go out to lunch. I'll tell you about your new school."

Toni hesitated, almost as though she were going to refuse, then she shrugged, nodded and left the room. She pounded up the stairs; seconds later the shower hissed. Joe wasn't sure whether he should be happy she'd agreed to go or dismayed she'd agreed only to please him.

He sat on the couch and stared at the happy people on the television screen, who had just won a trip to Tahiti for spelling a word he had never heard of. What was he going to do about Toni?

Since Joe and his wife, Karen, had split up over ten years earlier, he'd seen very little of Toni. During the season, he'd been on the road with his team. In the off-season, there'd been days here and there—a weekend, a holiday—typical of a divorced father's visitation rights. Now his little girl was a young woman, and he had no idea how to be a father to her.

The death of her mother from cancer right before Christmas had devastated Toni. Even though a nanny had cared for Toni since birth, Karen had still been Toni's mother, and her death continued to haunt the teenager.

Karen had been a corporate headhunter, a perfectionist, a career woman with the mothering instincts of a python. Joe never should have let her have custody of Toni, but what would he have done with a little girl on the road? Joe sighed. He could feel guilty for the rest of his life over something he could not change, or he could set about making things right between his daughter and him.

Joe stood when Toni came back down the stairs. He would just have to show her that things were different with Dad. She did not need to be perfect. He loved her just the way she was. He would erase the tension from her smile, the wariness from her eyes and the sadness from her face. He just had to figure out how.

Toni entered the room. She looked like a picture Joe had once seen of his mother as a young girl— all long coltish legs and sleek blond hair. Her skin tanned easily, like his, but her eyes were warm, Italian brown instead of Joe's light blue, a throwback to a nearly forgotten Norwegian ancestor.

Joe ushered her out of the house and into the car. A short, silent ride into town followed.

They lunched at a nearby café, sitting at a table outside beneath the late-May sunshine. Joe bit into his Reuben on rye, then watched as Toni took tiny bites of a turkey on white. To him it didn't seem that she ate enough, but what did he know? He was used to dining with football players, and they definitely ate more than sixteen-year-old girls. The books he'd read about teenagers all said the same thing—don't make an issue out of nothing. Save your breath for real problems. Joe's dilemma was that he saw a "problem" wherever he looked.

"What do you want to do this summer?" he blurted to keep himself from another round of silent questions and guilt.

Toni popped a piece of the sandwich into her mouth, leaned her chin on one hand and chewed as she thought. Then with a shy smile she said, "I'd like to play baseball."

"Huh?" Joe hadn't expected that.

"I'm pretty good. I was on the team at home." Flushing, she sat up straighter, putting her hands into her lap. "I mean, where I used to live. I saw in the paper that Big League practices begin this weekend. I'd like to go."

"Your mother never said you played."

Toni took another bite. "She traveled a lot."

"Yeah. We both did." He tried to look into his daughter's eyes, but her attention was occupied with pushing her food around on her plate. Once again, he didn't know what to say except that he was sorry—and he figured she'd heard that enough from him already.

"I'll drive you to practice. I'd love to see you play."

Toni eyed him and grinned. It was the first real smile Joe had seen on her face since he'd taken her away with him. Joe smiled back.

Maybe, just maybe, they could make this work.

THE MORNING OF league practice arrived with the threat of a downpour heavy on the air. But by ten o'clock the sky had filled with sunshine—an ideal Iowa spring morning—and the baseball diamonds behind the high school had filled with kids.

Evie arrived precisely at ten. She'd wanted to be at the field at least half an hour early to watch the players warm up, but Danny had lost his shoes, then Benji had found them but neglected to tell the rest of the family. She'd spent a frantic fifteen minutes with her head under every piece of furniture in the house, before Adam had pried the shoes loose from behind his brother's back.

She dropped the twins off at the T-ball practice for seven-year-olds, waved at the father who was brave enough to referee, and hurried over to where the Big League hopefuls awaited her on the field.

In small-town Oak Grove, Little League, Senior League and Big League baseball dominated the spring and summer months. Boys and girls ages six through eighteen could participate. The games were as much a social event as an athletic activity, and when a team had the potential of going to the championship—the way Evie's did—interest skyrocketed. Already a majority of the onlookers had gathered to watch her players.

Evie drew in a deep breath. She'd been virtually assured of the boys' baseball varsity coaching position next spring if she could take her team to the Big League state championship. The coaches of the boys' teams received higher salaries because of the larger number of participants and the larger number of fans at the games. Evie wanted that money for her sons. College was expensive these days.

Last year her team had missed the championship by one paltry game. They *would* go this year if her luck held—and if she could find a decent pitcher.

Evie squinted against the morning sunshine and surveyed the boys waiting for her attention. How was she to find a new star player in a town where all the kids on her team this year had played for her the year before? Sure, she had younger players she'd drafted last month, but she knew what she had—and no one could pitch.

Sighing, she walked forward. Too bad she couldn't entice some of the girls she'd coached during their junior high years back into the game. Though Big League was open to both sexes, by the time the kids were juniors and seniors, the girls had gone on to other interests. She would just have to train a younger player, mold him into what she needed and pray for the best. She was a coach—a darn good one. She could conquer this obstacle. She would. Her dream of sending her sons to college depended upon it.

''Good morning, boys,'' she called.

'''Mornin', Coach Vaughn.''

''Excuse me?''

Evie paused in the midst of dumping a bag of baseballs onto the ground, her gaze searching the crowd for the owner of the voice. ''Who said that?''

''I did.'' A tall blond girl stepped through the

herd of boys. "I just wanted to let you know I was here." She shrugged and glanced around sheepishly. "You said 'boys' and well..." Kicking at the grass with the toe of her baseball spikes, the girl avoided Evie's eyes. "I'm not a boy."

"No." Evie smiled. "I can see you're not." Evie couldn't remember this girl from earlier years, but then, they changed so fast. "I take it you'd like to play Big League?"

"Yeah. I was told to come to your team 'cause you were short a player, and I missed the tryouts. Is that right?"

"You're new in Oak Grove?" The weight in Evie's chest lightened at the girl's nod. "What position did you play on your old team?"

"Pitcher."

This is too lucky to be true, Evie thought before addressing the girl once more. "Are you any good?"

"I pitched in the state championships last year. But we didn't win."

"Hot dog!" Evie clapped her hands, then bent down to snatch a baseball from the ground. Tossing it to the girl, she said to Adam, "Let's see what she can do."

In seconds Evie's team had taken position in the outfield. The boys had played together since childhood, with few additions or deletions. They were a great team. All they needed was a break.

Evie stood at home plate and lined up to bat. With

a smile, she nodded to the girl on the pitcher's mound.

The windup.

Steady eyes, Evie thought. *Looks good.*

The throw. Fast and straight on.

Evie swung, expecting to hear her bat connect with the ball. Instead, she stumbled forward when her bat connected with her left shoulder. Turning, she stared in amazement at the ball resting in Adam's glove.

She'd whiffed! She hadn't whiffed since high school.

Shading her eyes, Evie squinted toward the pitcher's mound. "What's your name?" she shouted.

"Antonia. But everyone calls me 'Toni.' Toni Scalotta."

Evie's hand dropped back to her side and hung, a dead weight. "Scalotta," she muttered. "That figures."

JOE HAD DRIVEN TONI to the baseball diamonds, but, at her request, he stayed away from where she was playing. His daughter wanted to do this on her own, and she knew too well how teenage boys reacted to the sight of Iceman Scalotta.

Instead, Joe walked around the section of the field where the smaller children practiced. He found their antics as they learned the basics of baseball endearing.

Standing on the outskirts of one diamond, Joe

watched in amazement as the boys and girls in the field played a game he'd never seen before. It looked to be some kind of tackle baseball, with every child on the field racing for the ball, even going so far as to take it away from a teammate by force. Then, when the winner tried to throw the ball back to the infield, he or she discovered there was no one left to throw the ball to. They had all left their posts to chase after the runaway hit, and now the runner headed for home, stubby legs pumping like an old-fashioned steam engine.

Joe had to bite down on his cheek to keep from laughing. A tug on his pant leg had him looking down into the bright blue eyes of a redheaded tyke.

"Hi," Joe ventured. "Are you lost?"

"Nope. I'm Danny."

"Uh-huh. Did you want something?"

"Yeah. A T-ball coach. My team's the only one without a coach. If we can't get one, we can't play."

"Why don't you ask your dad?"

"Can't. He's dead."

Joe frowned. *Poor kid. Cute little thing, too.* Still, Joe had to discourage the child right away. He knew nothing about little boys and even less about coaching T-ball. As he stared out at the team he'd been watching, he noticed another redheaded kid in the outfield.

"That your brother?" Joe pointed to the milling crowd of players.

"I've got a big brother. Adam. He's on the Big League team. Over there." Danny shot a thumb over his shoulder toward the field where Joe had last seen Toni. "Hey, mister, what about bein' my coach?"

The kid wasn't going to be sidetracked. "Did you ask your mom? I'm sure if you explained your problem, she'd help you out. Moms are like that."

"Can't. She's already coachin' my big brother's team."

"Oh." Joe frowned. Now what? The kid kept staring at him, big blue eyes full of hope. Joe tried one more time. "I'm sorry, Danny. But I don't know anything about T-ball."

"That's okay. Neither do we." Danny fixed Joe with a smile that was all the sweeter because of the two empty spaces in his bottom row of teeth. "I'll get my mom. She's in charge of the coaches, too. You can talk to her."

Before Joe could stop him, the redheaded imp raced off. Joe had been bamboozled by a pint-size sharpie. He couldn't remember saying yes, but somehow he felt as though he had. Well, he'd just have to find a way to extricate himself from the situation once he talked to Coach Mom.

"Here she is, mister." Danny's voice piped above the shouts of the other children.

Joe turned and froze. "You."

"I think we've had this conversation before," Evelyn Vaughn said. "Why is it I can't seem to take a step without running into you or your offspring, Mr. Scalotta?"

In the midst of admiring the legs of the lovely Mrs. Vaughn—he'd never had a teacher who looked that good in shorts; heck, he'd never had a teacher who *wore* shorts—Joe frowned and glanced up. "You've met my daughter?"

She raised her eyebrows at his perusal but didn't comment.

"She seems to have ended up on my team."

"How did that happen?"

"I was short a player, so the next kid who signed up was mine. I'm sure the other coaches think it's a riot I got a girl." She grinned, and there was a bit of wolf around the edges. "Are they gonna be surprised."

"You teach, coach Big League *and* manage all the coaches?"

The smile hovering on her lips froze. "Do you have a problem with that?"

The way she asked the question, chin up, a little defensive, made Joe think of his ex-wife. Karen had always met any hint of conflict head-on, sometimes before any conflict appeared, just so she could be on top of the situation. And she had been forever on the go, taking any job or volunteer position in order to climb higher up the ladder. Why should Evelyn Vaughn be any different?

"I don't have a problem with your multitude of jobs. Do your children? Seems to me a mom should be with her kids."

Someone on a nearby diamond shouted, "Hey, Evie! How's it going?"

She waved and nodded. They all seemed to know

her in this town, and why wouldn't they? She looked to be involved in just about everything.

Evie turned back to Joe with a scowl. "My kids are none of your business. So you can keep your outdated, chauvinistic attitude to yourself."

She was right, and Joe realized it. He couldn't help how he'd been raised or what he believed. He was a fifties man living in a new-millennium world. What he needed to do was keep his thoughts to himself. Most of the time they just got him into trouble.

Evie took a deep breath, as if for patience, and when she spoke her voice held a professional distance that matched the expression on her face. "Danny tells me you'd like to coach T-ball."

"Well, I didn't exactly say so."

"That's what I figured." A sharp sigh blew her bangs upward. She went down on one knee next to her son and gazed into his eyes. "Mr. Scalotta is too busy, and he probably knows nothing about baseball. We'll find you another coach."

"But I want *him*." Danny stabbed a finger in Joe's direction.

"We don't always get what we want. That's not news."

The little boy's shoulders slumped. "I guess. But why can't I get what I want just once?"

Evie rolled her eyes, then ran a hand over the top of her son's head. "I'll find someone to coach your team. Just give me a little time. I'll find you the best coach. Someone who really knows the game and understands seven-year-old kids."

Joe gritted his teeth at the slight. He wasn't a total moron. He did have some knowledge of baseball. Just because he'd played football didn't mean he was ignorant of every other sport. What he didn't know about T-ball he could pick up from a manual. He could read, after all. And he'd spent years playing games with grown men—huge, mean men. After that, how tough could ten or twelve seven-year-olds be? He could handle the T-ball league with his eyes closed.

Before Joe could think twice about what he was going to do, he stepped forward and put a hand on Danny's shoulder. "Never mind, kid. You've got yourself a coach."

CHAPTER THREE

SUNDAY EVENING and the clock read 8:00. Evie wandered through her house, which was quiet at last, checking the locks as she did every night. The twins lay in bed, having completed their litany of last-minute requests.

"I need a drink."

"One more book."

"I have to go pee."

Adam listened to music in his bedroom, earphones firmly in place so as not to wake the twins, while he finished his homework.

Evie reached the kitchen and debated making a half pot of coffee. Did she really need the caffeine? She stood very still for a moment, and lethargy gripped her. Yes, she did. She had essays to grade for senior health and a final exam to prepare before she could go to bed. Then the twins would be up before the sun. They always were. As she filled the coffeepot with water, Evie stared into the darkness beyond her kitchen window.

Another day over. She'd made it through.

Hard to believe that a week ago the name Joe Scalotta was only one she'd heard on television or read in the paper. Now the man filled her thoughts more often than not. She was attracted to him; she couldn't deny that. She didn't deny it—she just didn't like it. He was exactly the type of man she needed to avoid. Forever playing little-boy games, macho to the core, a total disaster in waiting. Just the thought of the man brought back memories Evie fought every day to keep at bay.

After her husband had been killed in a motorcycle accident when the twins were only a year old, there had been many mornings when just making it through the day sane had been a doubtful prospect. Not that Evie had been crushed with grief—not exactly. By the time Ray had died, she'd felt little beyond contempt for the man she'd once loved deeply.

Ray had remained a little boy at heart until the day of his death. Handsome, fun loving, irresponsible—bottom of the pile in father and husband attributes. He and Evie had been high school sweethearts. Back then, when they were seventeen, Ray had represented a dream come true to the new girl in town who was shy, scared and terribly insecure.

Evie was the product of a policeman father, who taught her sports as soon as he discovered her God-given talent for any game that involved a ball. But while her father had praised such talent and helped her to mold it, the rest of the world saw Evie as something of a freak. Girls did not play as well as the boys in those days, or if they could, they did not admit it. When she moved to Newsome, she felt lost, and alone, and weird.

Until the cutest guy in school fell for her. Evie flowered into a princess, and Ray was her prince. She loved him with all her heart and soul, believing with a childlike hope that she could save Ray from himself. Then the clock struck midnight. Evie became pregnant, married Ray and settled down. For Ray, the playing never stopped.

When Adam was born, Ray was off on a road trip to Chicago with his buddies. It was Super Bowl weekend, and the gambling pools were more impressive in the big-city bars. Though her parents loved her and never turned their backs on her, still their disappointment hovered in the air whenever they came near. So Evie sweated through the sixteen-hour labor alone.

Her husband arrived in time to hold his day-old son.

Evie had so hoped Ray would change once Adam was born. No such luck. For the next nine years, Ray went from one job to the next, spending what money they put aside on fast cars, motorcycles, drinking and gambling.

The coffee burped and dribbled a last drip into the pot. Evie roused herself enough to pour a cup, then carried it to the kitchen table and spread her papers out before her. But once the memories had started, they could not be stopped. Instead of correcting the essays, Evie stared into her coffee and continued to remember.

She had stayed with Ray for her son's sake, but when she overheard him telling Adam to have a sip of whiskey, exhorting him to "Be a man like Daddy," Evie took Adam and went to stay with her parents.

Then the one thing happened that could make Evie give Ray another chance. The rabbit died, and Evie was right back where she'd started at seventeen—only worse. Pregnant, with no options or education, this time with a nine-year-old son, as well.

Ray swore he'd change, and for a little while he had. When the twins were born, he stayed beside her through the delivery and even helped her with some of the night feedings. Then the familiar cycle started over again—gambling, drinking, new cars and motorcycles—until the night when the doorbell rang at three a.m.

Her father stood on Evie's doorstep, and before he opened his mouth, she knew. He held her close while he explained that Ray had been driving his motorcycle under the influence and had decided to play chicken with a pickup truck. His neck broke when he hit the pavement.

Her parents helped Evie with the boys while she earned the teaching degree she'd once given up as lost. One of her father's buddies, who was the athletic director in Oak Grove, offered her a position, and she packed up her children and moved out of town. The boys needed to live in a place that did not look upon them as "sons of that no-account Ray Vaughn."

The twins were too young to remember their dad, but sometimes Evie caught Adam looking at the pic-

ture of Ray he kept on his bedside table. She'd tried
to talk to him about his father, but Adam refused to
discuss the subject. He was a quiet boy, a good boy.
Sometimes, though, she wondered how much he rec-
ollected of his father, and how much like Ray he
really was inside. Such thoughts scared her to death.

JOE STARED AT THE PICTURE of Karen on his daughter's night table. Her pale blond hair had been cut
by a master, who'd made the strands fall about her
flawless face to the best advantage. Karen had been
beautiful, intelligent, seemingly perfect in every
way—until you looked into her eyes. Even in the
picture, Joe saw the coldness that came straight from
his ex-wife's heart.

He should have seen the same coldness when he
looked into Evie Vaughn's eyes. A woman who was
out for her career at the expense of everyone and
everything should reflect that selfishness in her eyes.
Yet Joe thought he saw warmth, and caring, and a
hint of the same attraction that had grabbed him the
moment he realized she was a woman and not a
child.

Toni walked into the room wearing a T-shirt that
sported a sleeping cat. She'd braided her long, blond
hair—a color that Joe always thought of as corn-
husk blond, though he knew his daughter would not
appreciate the comparison—and she appeared
younger than her sixteen years. Joe swallowed the
uncommon lump of emotion in his throat. God, he

loved her, and he had missed so many years of her life.

"'Night, Joe."

"'Night, sweetheart." Joe kissed the top of her head and crossed to the door. "See you in the morning." He turned out the light and left the room.

Tucking in a teenager was pushing it, but Joe couldn't help himself. He had so little time left before she was all grown up. He'd take advantage of every gift she allowed him.

Joe sat in the living room and absently flipped through the television channels with the remote control, not really seeing the programs or caring what they were. He left the television tuned to a rerun of *I Love Lucy* and let his mind wander once more.

He couldn't blame Karen for everything that had gone wrong with their marriage. He'd been attracted by her ambition and drive. Those two traits were as much a part of him as breathing, and he admired them in others. So why had he come to detest Karen for the same traits that had interested him in the first place?

Maybe because he saw in her neglect of Toni a reflection of his own behavior. But one thing he could not forgive Karen for was her never-ending criticism of their daughter. Karen had constantly harped on the girl. Toni never dressed right, walked right, spoke right, ate right or looked right. As a result, Toni now tried too hard to please everyone, rarely considering her own happiness.

Toni's aptitude for baseball appeared to give her

confidence, and though Joe would have liked to keep his daughter as far away from Coach Mom as possible, he couldn't take from Toni this first step toward self-assurance. Since he would be coaching Danny Vaughn's T-ball team, he'd just keep an eye on the boy's mother and make sure she understood how to deal with young girls. He would not let his daughter be ruined further by a woman concerned with perfection to the exclusion of all else.

Joe clicked off the television, listening as the silence settled around him. He hadn't lived in such a quiet place since he'd left home. At night, the sounds of the neighborhood disappeared, one by one, until only an occasional barking dog broke the silence. Oak Grove, Iowa, was peaceful—just the sort of place he and Toni needed. Joe had lived too long on the road with too many people and too much noise. He was tired of it all.

But at least on the road he'd never had a chance to become lonely. Someone was always available for a game of cards, a drink in the bar, an hour of conversation. Now he had only Toni.

He needed to start dating again. There had to be some single women in Oak Grove—stable, dependable women who could help him make a home and understand his daughter.

His dream was outdated, even chauvinistic, but he couldn't help himself. His childhood had been the stuff of a Mark Twain novel: long summer days playing with his brothers, fishing on the Mississippi, camping beneath the stars, followed by cold winter nights studying in the kitchen, endless pillow fights, squabbles and wrestling matches.

Joe smiled. He missed those days. He wanted to experience days like those again—from a father's side of the fence. And he would. He just needed to stay on course, focus on his goal and rush over every obstacle. Kind of like football.

So what if he continued to see Evie Vaughn's face every time he closed his eyes. He could handle that.

No problem.

THE DAY AFTER SCHOOL let out for the summer, Evie held a picnic for the members of her Big League team. The backyard filled with teenage boys, and the twins ran circles around small groups, pestering Adam and his friends.

Evie watched from the kitchen while she made another pitcher of pink lemonade. She loved summer—the warmth, the freedom, the opportunity to shape diverse young people into a team. The self-confidence her players developed while on her team was one of the best gifts of Big League ball.

The doorbell rang, and Evie dried her hands on a dish towel before she went to answer. She stopped at the sight of Joe Scalotta, resplendent in a royal-blue T-shirt and stonewashed jeans, standing on the other side of the screen, his huge hand cupped over Toni's shoulder.

"Hi," Joe said, his voice cool and remote. "When should I pick her up?"

Evie pushed open the screen, smiling at Toni and

motioning her inside. "Everyone's out back," she told the girl. "Why don't you join them."

Toni nodded and went through the living room into the kitchen. The back door slammed as the girl left the house.

Evie fixed her attention on the father. "I'm not exactly sure when we'll be done. If they're having fun and they're not too crazy, they can stay all day. I'll have Adam drive Toni home, if you'd like."

Joe frowned and stepped forward. Evie, who was still holding the screen door partway open, took a hurried step back as he came inside. Biting her lip, she forced herself to stand still. What was it about the man that appealed to her? His size? His looks? His seemingly endless array of colorful T-shirts? Or maybe the cold eyes that made her feel hot all over?

"Adam. That's your son?"

"Yes. He's seventeen—very responsible, I assure you."

"Yeah, aren't they all. I remember seventeen quite well, thank you. I'll pick Toni up myself. Just have her call me when she wants to come home."

"Fine." Evie tamped down her irritation at Joe's implication. He was just protecting his daughter. She'd react the same way if Toni were her child.

Laughter drifted to them on the breeze, and they both focused on the sound.

"Seems they're having a good time already," Joe ventured, returning his gaze to Evie's face.

Evie tried not to shift with discomfort under his perusal. Suddenly she was all too aware of her lack of makeup and short cap of hair, cut close to her head to shear preparation time every morning. She gritted her teeth to keep from looking down at what she wore. If she remembered right, she'd put on her most comfortable pair of cutoff shorts and a loose cotton shirt, favorites because of their age and well-washed softness. Her toes curled against the ceramic tile of the entryway; her shoes resided on the back porch.

An analysis of the reason she gave two hoots how she looked to Joe Scalotta was interrupted by the whirlwind arrival of Benji, who came skidding through the kitchen doorway and slammed to a halt against the back of Evie's legs.

She stumbled forward, and Joe grabbed her by the shoulders. His big hands felt scaldingly hot as they molded the thin material of her shirt against her skin. Catching her breath, she glanced into his eyes. She saw the same heat there, and she hurriedly regained her footing, then pulled away before she did something extremely stupid.

Joe ignored her to smile at her son. "Hey, there, Danny. You ready for T-ball practice next week?"

Benji squinted all the way up the mountain of man, his eyes widening when they reached Joe's face. "Who's he?"

"This is Mr. Scalotta. Toni's dad."

Obviously puzzled, Joe looked from Benji to Evie. "He's the one who asked me to be his coach. Now he doesn't remember me?"

"That was Danny."

"I know." Joe pointed at Benji. "Danny."

"I'm Benji," the boy shouted. "Why does everybody get us mixed up, Mom? You never do."

Evie smiled. Benji and Danny were not above tricking people about their identities. Joe Scalotta would have his hands full coaching the two of them in T-ball. "I don't get you mixed up because I'm your mother and I know everything. Now, go back outside. I'll be there in a minute."

Benji raced off, whatever he'd wanted in the first place forgotten, and Evie turned back to meet Joe's rueful smile.

"Twins," he said.

"Bingo. Want to back out of being their coach now?"

"Not a chance. I'm looking forward to it."

"Why?" Evie couldn't understand what would entice a man like Joe Scalotta to spend his summer with a herd of seven-year-olds.

"I like kids. Always have. But I've never had the opportunity to get involved with them before. And this way I'll be able to keep my eye on things."

Evie got the feeling he was warning her with that cryptic statement—but about what, she had no idea. Before she could ask, he opened the screen door and stepped outside.

Evie watched him go, admiring the way he walked—light on his feet despite his size, as if he knew where he was going, now and for always. It had been far too long since she'd seen such a good-looking man, and she couldn't help but indulge herself for a moment.

Joe turned, and Evie's gaze flew up to his face. He smiled knowingly, and she flushed, feeling like one of her students caught staring at the cutest guy in school. All the more reason to stop this interest before it got the better of her. Ray had been the cutest guy in school, and see where that had led her.

"How do you tell them apart, anyway?"

"Wh-who?" she stammered.

"Benji and Danny. It's a secret that might come in handy to their coach."

Evie shrugged. "Like I told Benji, I'm their mother. I just know."

"Hell. I thought it might be something like that. They're gonna run me ragged." He stalked to his sports car.

"Count on it," Evie called after him.

When the roar of the car's well-tuned engine faded into the distance, Evie rejoined the party. The kids had filled their plates with the multitude of offerings from the potluck picnic. Evie's gaze searched out the twins to make sure they had gotten something to eat without undue disaster. After grabbing her own meal, she planted herself in a lawn chair next to Toni, who had taken a seat at Adam's table. She ignored the frown her son gave her for sitting by him, and addressed the girl.

"Ready to start practice next week?"

Toni paused in the act of cutting her submarine sandwich in half. After carefully laying down her knife and fork, she nodded. "I've been throwing some to Joe here and there, but it'll feel good to get into the swing of the game again."

The girl never seemed to call her father "Dad," but that was none of Evie's business, even though it made her curious. "From what I've seen so far you're a great pitcher. You might even be the best hitter, too."

Toni glanced at the boys, who listened in on the conversation avidly. Her cheeks pinkened and she ducked her head. "I do all right, but I wouldn't say I'm the best."

Evie followed Toni's glance and understood. She'd had the same problem when she'd moved to Newsome eighteen years earlier. It wouldn't do for the new girl to be better than all the boys. Even if she was, she didn't need to flaunt it before the fact was proven.

"Well, we'll see how things go next week." Evie turned her attention back to her plate. Conversation picked up around the table, and her gaze wandered over the backyard. She checked each table to make sure a food fight wasn't in the offing. So far, everyone was behaving, but she knew better than to let her guard down for more than a minute at a time.

Returning her gaze to Toni, Evie frowned. The girl wasn't just shy, she was timid. She had cut her sandwich, but she wasn't eating. Instead, she stared at her plate and snuck glances at Adam from beneath her lashes.

Evie looked at her son. He wasn't shy and he

wasn't timid. He hadn't cut his sandwich, but he was eating it. Like a pig. He wasn't sneaking glances at Toni; he was studiously ignoring her. Same difference.

Evie stifled a sigh. Not only did she have to deal with her own unfortunate attraction to an insufferable man, but apparently she would have to endure her son's first crush at the same time. From the looks of Toni Scalotta, Evie's star pitcher had caught the same fever as Adam.

Evie cast a glance heavenward, hoping for divine intervention.

Puppy love. What next?

CHAPTER FOUR

TONI DID HER BEST not to look at Adam. But she couldn't help it. He was the cutest guy she'd ever seen.

He kept looking at her, too, which only made her nervous, and when Toni was nervous she got quiet. Then people thought she was stuck-up. She wasn't. She was just terrified she'd do something stupid and ruin any chance she had for friends, or boyfriends, in this town. The only time she felt confident was on the playing field. Out on the mound she didn't have a chance to think about how dumb she appeared; she only had time to react.

Adam got up and, without so much as a glance at her, left the table to dump his plate into the garbage can at the foot of the porch. Toni's face heated. She'd turned him off, and she hadn't even said anything. In fact, not saying anything was probably the problem. She'd sat there like a lump. She was so *boring*.

Other girls always seemed to know exactly what to say to guys, how to flip their hair, laugh and wink without winking at all. Toni never could get the hang of that.

Since she was no longer hungry, Toni gathered

the remains of her lunch and went to the garbage can. She wondered if Mrs. Vaughn would hate her if she asked to call Joe now. No one was talking to her. She could tell they didn't want her here. Tears pressed at the back of her eyes, but she forced them away. If she cried in front of the guys, she'd never be one of the team.

Toni turned and bounced off Adam Vaughn's chest. He made a grab for her as she tilted backward. Her heart leaped into her mouth when his hands closed about her upper arms, steadied her, then clung. She cocked her head to look into his face, and he grinned. Her stomach twisted, and she couldn't seem to breathe. For a long moment they stared at each other as if no one else in the world existed but them—it was the strangest thing.

"Do you want me to tell you about the team?" he asked.

"Team?" The word came out of her mouth before she could stop it, sounding as moronic as it was.

"You know—" he waved his hand at the guys still stuffing their faces at the tables "—the team."

He had a man's voice, and the contrast to her own childish repetition of his words made Toni shiver. He would never like her if he thought she was a baby. She very much wanted Adam to like her. So Toni took a deep breath, swallowed her fear and said, "Why don't we sit over there."

She pointed to an empty table beneath the largest oak tree in the yard, far away from everyone else. He raised one eyebrow, as if he heard her heart beating too loudly and her breath coming in gasps, then he spun about and walked toward the table. Toni followed, praying with every step that she wouldn't trip and fall on her face.

Why couldn't she be more like Mrs. Vaughn? When Toni's coach walked, she did so with grace and confidence. When she spoke, everyone listened. Toni doubted Adam's mom had ever done anything stupid in her life. And with that example in front of him every day of his life, how could Adam ever think Toni anything less than a geek?

She reached the table without screwing up and sat on one side. Adam sat on the other. Her knee bumped his; then their feet clunked together. They both mumbled "Sorry" at the same time. Toni felt her face flush a painful shade of red. She wanted to die. This guy/girl stuff was way out of her league.

"What can I tell you about the team?" he asked.

His voice was normal, just like she hadn't done anything dumb. She glanced at him in surprise, and he smiled. Toni started to relax.

"Uh, well, I was kind of wondering…"

"Yeah?"

"Are the guys going to…uh, you know?"

Adam shrugged. "What?"

Her gaze fell from his face and focused on her hands, which were twisted together on top of the table. "Hate me," she whispered.

"Why would they hate you?"

He sounded so surprised that Toni found the confidence to tell him the truth. "I'm different," she said. "Always have been."

There was a long moment of silence, during which Toni waited for him to get up and leave—to go tell his mom she was a nutcase, tell the guys she was a freak. She'd never fit in, and Joe would know for sure she was worthless, then he'd dump her on someone else and pay that person to take care of her. The way her mom always had.

Toni didn't realize she was holding her breath until Adam reached across the table and put his hand on top of hers. She opened her mouth, and the breath rushed out. Adam's one right hand was bigger than both of Toni's put together, and for some reason that made her feel safe and not so all alone. He squeezed her hands. Warmth rushed through her, and she looked into his face.

"I like different," he said.

Toni was a goner right then and there.

"MAN, OH MAN," Evie muttered as her son touched Toni Scalotta's hands. "Trouble like this I do not need."

The look on Adam's face flashed her back so fast to Ray that she got dizzy. Most of her memories of him were bad, but lately, maybe because Adam was the same age now that Ray had been when she'd fallen for him, she was starting to remember some of the good times. There had been some very good times.

Young love, first love, hormones, passion—nothing was ever that wonderful, or that horrible, again. Funny, but she could still remember when Ray had first touched her hand.

Evie shivered despite the heat of the sun beating down and burning the bridge of her unsunscreened nose. She always managed to slather up the kids and forget about herself.

"Mom, what should we do now?" The twins leaned against her back. With a bright red head on each shoulder, they announced in stereo, "We're so-o-o-o bored."

Evie hunched her shoulders and hooked an arm around each squirming waist. Then she pulled their hot little bodies against her and rubbed her cheek first on the top of one sun-warmed head and then on top of the other. They squealed in mock dismay.

"Hey, there are big guys watching," Benji whispered.

"Sorry." She let them go. "Why do sweaty little boys always smell like sunshine?"

"One of God's little tricks to keep you from killing us," Danny answered, used to the question.

Smiling, Evie glanced around the yard to see what the "big guys" were doing to amuse themselves. The usual—talking, tossing a soft football—and starting a water fight with the garden hose.

Oh, oh.

She stood and started across the yard. But her memories of her dead husband had kept her a bit too long in the past, and the water fight was too far gone to be stopped with a single "Hey!"

The boys had already found extra buckets and cups and had started to douse one another in earnest. The twins left her side at a run, whooping like mad cowboys. Surprisingly, they halted halfway between her and the nexus of the fight, glancing back to see if she was going to put an end to it all.

Evie spread her hands in a "Be my guest" gesture, and they grinned before diving in and wrestling an empty ice-cream bucket out of the third-baseman's hands.

Stepping out of the arc of fluid projectiles, Evie watched the kids with a shake of her head. What could be more fun than a water fight on the first day of summer vacation? Not much.

Benji and Danny got doused more than the rest, but they didn't care. It took a few minutes for Evie to realize someone was missing.

Her gaze turned to the table beneath the oak tree. Her son and Toni were still talking—and holding hands. Time for that to stop.

With a purposeful stride, Evie left the shouting boys behind her and went toward her son. Unfortunately, the moment she saw Adam and Toni so did everyone else.

With shouts that would rival Attila the Hun's, the team tore across the lawn to include the only dry members in the fun. So engrossed were Adam and Toni in each other that they didn't see the sheet of water coming until the tidal wave sloshed over the table and them.

Toni shrieked and jumped to her feet. She turned

to the group, and one of the twins heaved a bucket of water right into her face.

Water dripped off Toni's nose, darkened her blouse, ran down her legs. She opened one eye, then the other, and blinked the droplets from her lashes. The yard was as quiet as Oak Grove on a Sunday night.

Evie held her breath. If Toni acted like a girl with wet hair, she'd never be one of the guys.

Toni approached the hose-wielding third baseman. He watched her, uncertain, the hose hanging from his hands and filling his shoes with water. When she stood directly in front of him, Toni smiled. He smiled back, and she grabbed the hose. In one quick, agile motion she flipped it around and sprayed the group with a stream of water, sending them flying in the other direction. She chased them, laughing, as far as the hose would allow.

Evie grinned. Two points for Toni.

"Mom!"

The twins went running by on either side, nearly knocking her over in their attempt to get away from Adam. He chased them into the fray, wrestled the bucket from Benji, got Toni to fill it, and then sat on his brothers while he dribbled water onto their heads in an impressive demonstration of the Chinese water torture.

She could put a halt to that—Evie sat in a lawn chair and let the sun warm her closed eyelids—but why?

The sound of children's laughter—shrieks, shouts

and giggles—announced summer in full swing. As long as there was noise of a certain kind, everything was fine. When it got quiet or a voice got too shrill, Evie would worry. For now, everyone was happy.

Wham! The coldness of the water nearly stopped her heart—it did take her breath away. A sitting duck in the lawn chair, Evie could do nothing but gasp as the hose drenched her from head to foot.

"Wh-wh-who did that?" she finally managed, gasping for air and blinking the ice from her eyes.

Stupid question. Benji and Danny stood directly in front of her chair, the hose held tandem. When she narrowed her gaze on them, they looked a little scared.

"Give me that." Adam yanked the hose from their hands.

Since the hose was still on, the force of his yank sent a fresh spray across Evie's face. The blast caught her right in the mouth. She choked.

"Hey, you're drowning her," Toni cried, and grabbed the hose, too.

What followed was a display of waterworks seldom seen in southern Iowa. Toni and Adam wrestled with the hose. Water sprayed upward, sideways, all around. The two of them started giggling and collapsed into each other's arms—

"What in hell is going on here?"

Everyone froze as the deep, commanding voice boomed across the yard. All eyes went to the gate, then to Evie. She winced, and turned to meet the icy glare of Joe Scalotta. He did not appear happy to find his soaking-wet daughter locked in the embrace of Evie's equally drenched son. She really couldn't blame him. The two of them looked kind of stuck together in a suction born of water and sunlight.

Evie shoved her wet hair out of her eyes and went to face the music.

JOE HADN'T MEANT to come back and check on Toni. But he hadn't been able to help himself. His little girl amid all those…those…those…*boys.* The thought would not leave his head no matter how hard he tried to get it out.

He'd attempted to amuse himself mowing the lawn. That had taken all of an hour and hadn't been very amusing. Trying to find something worth watching on the television had taken fifteen minutes more. A car ride had occupied two more minutes, then the drive back to the Vaughns' house another five. He'd only planned to meander down the street. If the house wasn't on fire, if there were no police cars blocking access or ambulances waiting in the driveway, he would just make a circle back home.

The street seemed like any other on a weekday summer afternoon—Midwest suburbia. Some driveways were empty, the houses having the deserted air of a two-income family. Other driveways sported a single motor vehicle—usually a minivan—bikes strewn about, colored chalk drawings scuffed and blurred. Screen doors banged; moms called out; children answered, their laughter on the wind. Summer meant freedom.

As he had driven past Evie's house, Joe had been congratulating himself on finding a paradise named Oak Grove—then he'd heard a girl scream.

His blood went cold. His heart lurched into overdrive. He parked half on the curb and half in the street. He didn't bother with the front door, just ran to the backyard, and he'd found—

Chaos.

Joe glared his best Iceman glare at the crowd of drenched teenagers. They appeared suitably abashed, especially the one with his hands all over Toni. He'd bet his Super Bowl ring that was Adam, the responsible seventeen-year-old Vaughn.

"Grrr." The sound came from deep in Joe's throat, and the kids scattered.

Except for the twins, Toni and her octopus. They remained frozen where they were. Evie was already on her way over.

"Adam, take the boys into the basement and dry them off," Evie ordered, keeping her gaze on Joe.

He'd been right. The octopus was Adam. The kid dropped his hands from Toni's shoulders. His face was red, but he met Joe's eyes with a challenge. Joe scowled. Kid had too much guts for his own good.

The twins moaned, but when Evie snapped out a command, moved. Impressive, really, if Joe had been in the mood to be impressed by her parenting skills. After what he'd just seen, he wasn't.

"Toni, you go in the house and use my bathroom."

"No, Toni can get in my car and come home right now."

His daughter gazed at him, then Evie, then the ground, which was steadily becoming mud beneath the hose she held in her hands. She was soaked from her head to her toes, and would resemble a lost, scared little girl—except for one thing.

Her wet blouse revealed she was no longer a little girl.

Joe started growling again.

"Stop that," Evie demanded.

"What?"

"Growling like a bear. This isn't the woods. Toni, turn off the hose and go inside. There's a hair dryer under the sink and some dry clothes in the laundry basket on the kitchen table. Help yourself. And take your time. Your father and I need to talk."

Without glancing Joe's way for approval, disapproval or anything in between, Toni did as Evie told her. To be honest, Toni had been nothing but obedient since Joe had driven away from Karen's condominium. So obedient, in fact, that she scared him, and Joe had been yearning for a single hint of rebellion to prove she was a normal teenager. But right now Joe wanted to roar his annoyance that she listened to a stranger instead of him.

"You look like you're going to have a stroke," Evie observed as soon as the screen door banged behind Toni. "You want to sit down?"

"Grrr," he returned.

"I'll take that as a no, though you really need to relax. A big guy like you, out in the heat, veins bulging in your forehead... One of these days you're just gonna go *splat*. I've seen it happen." She made a tsking sound as she shook her head.

Joe's blood pressure went up a notch. His mother had always done that to him when she'd caught him in an embarrassing situation—cataloguing what he'd done and how he'd looked. But *he* wasn't the one who should be embarrassed here. Coach Mom of the Year was the one who should be embarrassed. The fact that she wasn't—at all—made him see red.

"My blood pressure is fine and none of your business."

"You're right. But if you grit your teeth like that, it's hard to understand you."

"Grr."

Incredibly, she laughed, right in his face, and Joe stood there with his teeth no longer grinding because his mouth hung open. People did not laugh when Iceman Scalotta growled. They choked; they swallowed; they went white; they ran the other way. They *did not* laugh.

"I'm sorry." She rubbed her hand across her mouth as if to make her smile disappear. It did, but her eyes still danced. "That growling—it works for you?"

"Up till now."

"I'm sure it's frightening when you're all padded up and ready to ram the ball down the quarterback's throat. But here—'' she shrugged and waved her hand to indicate the empty yard ''—when you're wearing sandals, and I know you're not going to tackle me...'' She tilted her head. ''You aren't going to tackle me, are you?''

''Hardly. I'd send you into the next dimension.''

''Hmm, maybe.''

''Maybe?''

''My father was a cop. I know some tricks.''

She winked, and Joe's blood pressure continued to rise, though not from anger any longer. She had very nice eyes. They changed color depending on her mood or what she wore. Right now her washed-out purple shirt made them more green than hazel. He'd always been partial to green.

''There aren't enough tricks in the world to stop me, sweetheart.''

Her eyes narrowed. ''Does that 'sweetheart' thing work for you, too?''

''In what way?''

''Do women like it? Or do they knock your teeth down your throat?''

Now it was his turn to smile. ''See any teeth missing?''

''Grr,'' she said.

CHAPTER FIVE

"You're not doing it right," Joe said. "When you growl you have to make the sound come from your gut. Like you really mean it. As if you're going to tear someone's head off if he rubs you the wrong way."

"You have, and I plan to."

He laughed. "You and whose army?"

Joe let his gaze wander from the top of her dark head to the tip of her bare feet. Soaking wet, like now, she might weigh 110 pounds. His eyes were drawn irresistibly up those shining legs. Great legs, he observed—long despite her height, muscles in all the right places. Curves, too. He'd always been fascinated with the way a loose shirt became a tight shirt when you added water to the mix. How on earth had he ever thought she was a high school student, with curves like those?

"The bigger they are, the harder they fall, buster."

The annoyance in her voice made Joe realize what he was doing—ogling his daughter's coach, teacher and counselor as though she were the prime attraction at a wet T-shirt contest. He yanked his eyes back to where they belonged—her face.

A single raised eyebrow made Joe wonder if she knew exactly what he'd been thinking, feeling. Then her words penetrated the sudden and surprising haze of sexual attraction that had clouded his mind.

"The bigger they are…?" he repeated.

Evie crossed her arms over her chest, and Joe's cheeks grew warm. She knew. How mortifying. He felt like the high school kid now.

"A big guy will go down harder than a little guy if you take him out the right way."

"True."

She shifted, dropped her arms and turned around. Joe's traitorous gaze admired how her cutoff jeans had worn thin across the seat. No one cut off old jeans for shorts anymore—and it was a damn shame.

She spun about, and Joe pulled his eyes back to her face, trying to look innocent. Her long-suffering sigh, that of a teacher with an unruly student, showed she wasn't buying his act.

Joe shrugged. "Sorry," he muttered.

"Me, too."

"For what?"

"You've proven your point, Mr. Scalotta. It won't happen again."

"I have? It won't?" He had no idea what she was talking about. His thoughts had been mush since he'd stepped into the backyard.

"I live in a house full of Y chromosomes, and they don't look at me as anything other than head cook and bottle washer."

"Yeah?" He still wasn't following her.

"I'm not used to girls. Having Toni here to-day..." She shrugged. "I didn't realize until you illustrated your point."

"My point being?"

"Toni's a young woman amid a team of boys. And those boys don't look at her the way my house-ful look at me. I never thought something as harm-less as letting them have their first water fight of the summer would be such a mistake. If you hadn't shown up when you did, they might have ogled her as rudely as you ogled me. I'll make sure nothing like this happens again."

Joe let out a sigh of relief. She thought he'd been staring at her to prove a point—and a good point it was. He wished he'd thought of it. Now that he was thinking of it, his blood pressure rose again at the image of those boys looking at his daughter the way he'd looked at Evie.

His face heated. Things appeared a whole lot dif-ferent when you were responsible for a little girl—who wasn't a little girl anymore.

"Maybe baseball isn't the best of ideas," he said. "But she wanted it so bad, I didn't have the heart to say no."

"It'll be fine," Evie soothed. "Toni held her own in the water fight. Acted like one of the guys and not girlie-girl. If she pitches as well as I think she's going to, none of the boys will want to offend her. They want to win."

"Enough to put up with a girl on the team."

"They've got a girl for a coach."

"Good point. Do any of the parents object to that?"

She wrinkled her nose. "To what?"

"Having a woman coach a boys' team."

"It's not a boys' team."

"Anymore."

"Girls have always been welcome. They just don't choose to play at this age."

"So no one objects?"

"They did the first year I coached."

"And?"

"I told them if they could find another coach, or coach themselves, they were welcome to. I got no takers. After the first year, no one objected."

"And why was that?"

"Because I'm a good coach, and we won a lot."

Joe frowned as another thought occurred to him. "Is Toni in for teasing because she's chosen to play on the boys' team?"

"It's not a boys' team!"

He sighed. "You know what I mean."

She nodded, silently conceding his point. "She might get teased. But if she wants something she'll have to stick up for herself. That won't hurt her. And it won't hurt her to have the kids on this team for friends when school starts. I think Adam will keep an eye out for her."

"That's what I'm afraid of," he muttered.

"She could do a lot worse than claiming Adam as a friend."

"Friend? He looked a bit too friendly when I got here."

"I know." Evie glanced toward the house, then back at Joe. Her eyes held the same concern that lived in Joe's heart. "I think we've got a raging case of puppy love fueled by hormones coming our way."

"Great."

"Yeah."

For a long moment they stood in silent commiseration. Finally Joe gave a rueful smile. "I don't want any of those boys near her."

She returned his smile. "Spoken like a true daddy."

Evie seemed so sure of herself, that Joe had a sudden urge to confess—which he held back for all of a minute. "Toni's a mystery to me. I want to do the right thing, but I don't know what the right thing is."

"Does anyone?"

"You sound pretty certain."

"How I sound and how I feel are two different things. I've been around a lot of teenagers and I can *give* advice pretty well. But to be honest, Mr. Scalotta, I don't know what's right any more than the next guy."

"Joe," he said.

This time, instead of refusing to use his first name, she dipped her head in agreement.

Just then the objects of their discussion came out of the house together. Joe scowled. Toni was supposed to be on the ground floor, and that kid in the basement. Yet they'd obviously met up inside. At least Toni had changed from her wet shirt into something dry and presentable of Evie's.

Toni sat on the porch rail and looked up into the kid's face. The late-afternoon sun hit her hair, painting the strands every shade of gold. Joe swallowed a sudden thickness at the back of his throat when he saw the expression on her face as she smiled at Adam Vaughn. If that kid hurt her, Joe was going to… A growl burst from his throat.

"We're back to that again?"

He glanced at Evie and found her gaze on their children. He hoped she was hatching various and devious ways for them to put a stop to this new problem. When she remained quiet and contemplative, Joe decided she couldn't share without being asked.

"What are we going to do about this?" he said.

"Nothing."

"Nothing? That's your professional advice?"

"Yep. My mommy advice is to watch them like hawks." She kept staring at the kids, and her face went all dreamy. "Do you remember what it was like, Joe?"

He was distracted for a minute. It had been so long since anyone had actually called him by his first name in that way. He'd heard Iceman, and Wildman and Scalotta, and Joe instead of Dad. Even his parents called him Joseph. But just Joe? Not lately. He really, really liked how she said it.

"Joe?"

"Hmm?"

She looked at him and not the lovebirds. "Do you recall the first time you fell in love?"

He thought about that one. Love? He recalled the back seat of a Chevy Nova and Janine Petrowski—

Joe glanced at Evie. She watched the kids again, and from the sappy look on her face, he'd lay bets she didn't mean what he'd done with Janine when she talked about love.

After Janine there'd been college. Football. Studying. Parties.

Girls? *Yes.* Love? *No.*

Then there'd been pro football. Another round of parties. Girls. Karen. No love there.

"Not really," he said before she could quiz him further.

"No?"

Evie tore her gaze from the kids, who now sat hip to hip on the porch rail. Too close for Joe's comfort, but Adam wasn't actually touching Toni. Yet.

"Watching those two, I remember like it was yesterday," she said. "The first time you love someone there's never anything like that again. I don't know if it's because you're young and love is so new, and so wonderful and terrible at the same time. Or if what you feel is stronger when you're in the middle of all those confusing changes and there's one person in the world who makes those changes make sense."

Not only was her face dreamy now, but her eyes

were, too. Her mouth had gone all soft and full, as if she'd been kissing someone at a drive-in movie. Did they even have drive-in movies anymore?

Joe shot a glance at Adam and Toni. If they did, those two certainly weren't going there.

"You remember a first love for the rest of your life," Evie continued in a quiet voice. "Even when he becomes a man you don't know, you still remember forever the boy who took your heart that first time."

Joe had no idea what she was talking about with that young love, first-love, forever stuff, but it sounded *really* dangerous. Too hot for kids to handle.

He looked past Evie's dreamy face and caught the same expression on his daughter's.

"Toni!" Her name burst in a panic from his lips. "Time to go." When she hesitated, he ordered, "Right now, young lady."

All the way to the car Joe heard the echo of his father's voice coming out of his mouth—and he decided, maybe that wasn't so bad.

THEIR FIRST REAL GAME came the next week. Evie worried for days that Joe would call and pull Toni from the league. Joe was trying too hard to be a father to a girl who'd never had one. Too much, too late, was not the way to go. But Evie doubted Joe desired her advice on raising his daughter.

She couldn't blame him for wanting to protect his little girl. She wanted to protect her little boy. But sometimes Mother Nature was too strong to stop. From the look on Adam's face as he'd watched Toni leave with her father, now was one of those times.

When should she have "the talk" with him? Damn Ray Vaughn for dying and leaving her with three boys. The point of having boys was that the dad took them to the men's room at the mall, and the dad told them about women, sex and responsibility.

Evie gave a silent snort of derision. There hadn't been a responsible bone in Ray's body. He would have been as worthless at "the talk" as he had been walking the walk of a husband and father.

Adam drove again. Some days Evie wondered if she'd ever get her car keys back. He had on his uniform—team shirt, white baseball pants and the hat he usually pulled low over his brow, now turned bill backward for driving safety. When had he grown up on her?

A low-level argument began between the twins, which Evie chose to ignore. No one was crying or bleeding yet—round one. After the game they would have *a* talk about the continued abuse of rule number four. Evie returned her attention to her eldest son.

Adam glanced her way, then back at the road. "What?"

"Hmm?"

"You keep staring at me."

"Sorry." She stopped.

However, Adam wasn't going to let "Sorry" be

enough. "Staring, staring, staring. Last night, this morning, now. What gives?"

She wasn't about to tell him, before a game and in front of the twins, that she was terrified he was going to fall in love and screw up his life.

Would she have listened if her parents had told her the same thing eighteen years ago? Come to think of it—they had, and she hadn't.

"Mom?"

"It's nothing. You just look so grown-up."

"I am grown-up."

"I know." Her eyes burned. She blinked hard and fast before the burn turned into tears.

Adam had seen her cry a lot of times after Ray died, but not at all since they'd moved to Oak Grove. Evie planned to keep it that way. Their lives were on track now, and she wasn't going back to how things had been. Her son had grown up too fast. Though she'd never asked him to, she still felt guilty whenever he acted like the man of the house. He was just that kind of kid. Responsible.

"There's Joe!" Danny cried.

Evie's heart started to thump in a new sort of rhythm, and she turned her attention to the ball field as Adam pulled into the parking lot. Tonight Joe wore a jade-green T-shirt tucked into white jeans. Very few men could carry off white jeans. Joe Scalotta was one of them.

Before the car even stopped, the release of twin seat belts pinged from the back seat. "Freeze!" she ordered. "Please stay seated until the aircraft comes to a complete stop at the gate."

"Huh?"

"How many times do I have to tell you not to unbuckle until the car has stopped? For all you know, Adam could hit a brick wall, or someone could smash into us from behind."

"It's happened," Adam grumbled. "And then you have chaos."

Evie shot him a glare. He wasn't happy the door that had replaced the one Joe hit was a different color from the rest of the car. His friends had started referring to the car as "Patch," an embarrassment to a seventeen-year-old. For Evie, not so much. She needed a door—pronto—and a red door was the only one in stock.

She turned back to the twins. "Just keep the belts on until the car stops. Don't get out of the car until it stops."

"And don't run in the street unless there's traffic."

"Adam!"

He shrugged. "Sorry."

Evie acknowledged it wasn't easy to have seven-year-old twin brothers. One little brother was a royal pain—but two? Still…sometimes she was amazed at how mean brothers could be. Evie would never understand this complicated relationship that was love-hate all the time.

"Just leave traffic out of it," she admonished.

But Adam didn't hear her, since he was already

out of the car and jogging across the grass to where
Toni waited alongside her very attractive father.

"Grr," Evie mumbled, dragging herself out of the
passenger seat.

"What was that, Mom?" Benji appeared at her
side.

"Nothing. Go chase balls in the outfield, okay?"

"'Kay."

He trotted off in pursuit of Danny, who had already hugged Joe's knees, leaving ten dusty finger-
prints on the pristine-white denim. Evie winced, but
Joe didn't seem to care. He patted Danny on the
head, waved to Benji and didn't even bother to
swipe at the mess on his pants. *Impressive.*

The scowl he sent at Adam's and Toni's backs as
they walked toward the diamond was also impressive. His wide shoulders lifted and lowered with a
deep sigh before he raised a hand to greet Evie. She
nodded, trying not to admire the way the jade-green
cotton molded the muscles of his chest. What was
it about this man in a T-shirt? She was definitely
losing what was left of her mind.

Being attracted to Joe was a very bad idea. How
many times did she need to get hit by the same truck
to know better than to stand in the road?

Joe Scalotta was a womanizer and a…a… She
struggled to think of a single term to encompass all
she'd read about him. A *party animal.* That was
what he was.

Or at least that was what all the papers had said
he was years ago.

Was he a womanizer? Evie chuckled. She'd know about any lingering tendencies if he chose to play the field in Oak Grove. There would be a full report at the Dairy Queen within a day of his first conquest.

Party animal? Evie shook her head. Not in Oak Grove. To find a decent bar he'd have to drive to Cedar City—and make sure it wasn't Sunday, when the whole town went dry.

If Joe Scalotta wanted to be Wildman, he'd come to the wrong side of the Mississippi.

To be honest, he made every appearance of mending his ways. Still, something about the man rubbed Evie wrong. Thus far he *had* been a bit of a chauvinist. She didn't like that, but as an offense it was relatively minor. Most likely, her exasperation with him was due to her own annoying response to his large, toned body and his icy eyes, which seemed to stare right into her brain, and—

"Hey, Coach."

And the deep, somewhat raspy voice, which sent shivers down her spine.

"Coach?" she repeated.

The word came out sounding breathless, a little sexy, as if she were oh, so excited to see him. His light-blue eyes darkened to turquoise when they lit upon her face. Suddenly she *was* breathless, and it wasn't because the bag of bats she'd lugged with both hands from the car to the diamond weighed about twenty pounds. Joe Scalotta, irritating as he was, could take her breath away with a mere look.

"Isn't 'Coach' what they call you?" he asked, single-handedly lifting the heavy bag of bats.

With a shrug, Evie let him. "I guess. If they aren't calling me 'Mrs. Vaughn' or 'Adam, Danny and Benji's mom.' I answer to just about anything."

"Except 'sweetheart.'"

She peered at him from beneath the bill of her baseball hat. "A woman's gotta have limits."

CHAPTER SIX

"SAY, AREN'T YOU Iceman Scalotta?"

Joe sighed, plastered a PR smile on his face and greeted the tenth person who had asked him that in the past hour. What he really wanted was to watch his little girl make her pitching debut. But so far Coach Mom hadn't put Toni into the game.

"Can I have your autograph?"

"Sure." Joe reached for the pen and paper the man held out.

"It's for my boy," the guy said. "Andy. He's one of your biggest fans. Me, too. I didn't believe it when I heard you were actually living in Oak Grove. What for?"

Joe finished scribbling his name. As a kid he'd often practiced giving autographs. Now, after the eight-thousandth time he'd signed his name to paper, football, shirt or poster, he wondered why he'd ever thought it would be fun. He liked talking with people usually, but the signature thing got old fast.

He handed the autograph to the man, flicked his gaze toward the game and shrugged. "Why not here? It's a nice town."

"Sure. Nice but boring. Nothing ever happens in

Oak Grove. What about New York? L.A.? Heck,
even Chicago is better than here."

"Ever visited any of those places?"

"No, but I'd sure love to."

"No, you wouldn't. Too many people. Too many
cars. Smells like…" Joe thought a minute. "Like
burned-up rubber tires and month-old bananas. And
loud, so loud your ears hurt."

"Sounds exciting to me."

Joe grunted. "To each his own, I guess."

"Yeah."

The guy looked puzzled, and Joe couldn't blame
him. You always wanted what you didn't have. He'd
been the same way as a kid. Couldn't wait to get
out of Missouri. Then he'd lived the express version
of "If it's Tuesday, it must be Philadelphia" and
Missouri had started to look pretty darn good—as
good as Oak Grove did right now. He already loved
this place.

"Well, thanks for the autograph," the guy said.
"See ya 'round."

"I'll be here."

Joe returned his attention to the game, just in time
to see his daughter take the mound.

TONI SWALLOWED, but the lump in her throat didn't
move. She hadn't been this nervous since the championship game last year. Why would taking the
mound in the first game of a new season, when her
team was up 3-2 in the bottom of the ninth, make
her so nervous?

She focused on home plate and saw her problem—Adam Vaughn. Toni had never cared what a boy thought of her as a girl—until now. Boys had been her teammates, her buddies, her pals. But this season, something was different. Was the difference in her? Or in the boy behind the mask?

Toni threw a warm-up pitch, hard and wild. Adam let the ball go by, since there was no batter to worry about. But before he went to chase it, he lifted his mask and frowned in her direction.

Toni's fair skin went hot. She wanted to crawl into a hole and stay there. Why on earth had she asked to play ball in this town? Why had she ever started in the first place?

Her mother had gone ballistic when she'd first discovered Toni spent her spare time playing sand-lot baseball. But Toni loved the game, and she was good. Since she was good at very little, according to her mother, Toni had stuck to her guns with baseball, even when her mom had ranted and raved about Toni's tomboy tendencies. Mom had gone so far as to say that Toni was trying to get her father's attention through sports. By winning games, she thought she could win Daddy's love. She also said Toni could never win enough to make that happen. Toni was a girl, and Joe just wasn't interested.

Because her father saw her rarely, and when he did he was so stiff and uncomfortable it was painful to watch, Toni half believed her mother was right—and it had hurt. But she kept playing. Though she might not be able to win her dad's love, she could feel good about herself whenever she won a game.

Adam brought the ball back to the mound, rather than throwing it. Toni held her breath as he approached. He was so cute. Dark hair, dark eyes, tall and lightly muscled. Not big like Joe, but toned.

"You okay?" he asked.

She nodded, not trusting herself to speak. He'd been really nice to her, but she wasn't going to make the mistake of thinking he liked her or anything. He was the most popular guy in town. She could tell from the way kids called "hello" and the way the girls sitting on the home-team bleachers whispered, pointed and scowled in her direction.

"Toni?"

Adam bent at the knees so he could look into her face. She tried a smile, but the attempt no doubt appeared as stiff as it felt. Adam shook his head and put a hand on her shoulder. "Calm down. It's the first game."

She could feel the warmth of his hand through her team jersey and resisted the urge to step closer. The whole town was watching—or at least it seemed so.

"No big deal." He dropped his hand, and she could think straight again.

"You want to tell that to your mom?"

"My mom? What does she have to do with this?"

"She's the coach."

He laughed. "Yeah, so?"

"She'll yell if I screw up."

"She will?"

"Won't she?"

"Did your coach in Chicago yell at you?"

Adam seemed mad. Toni didn't know if he was mad at her, or what. She stared at the ground and squashed a clump of dirt with her spikes. "If I screwed up, yeah. He yelled at everyone." She didn't mention that when her coach yelled at her, she'd wanted to cry. She hadn't, but she'd wanted to. "My coach liked to win."

Adam made an exasperated sound. "I've never seen my mom yell yet. At a player, anyway—"

Toni glanced up in time to catch his wink.

"The twins are another story. She does like to win. Who doesn't? But she likes to teach kids even more." Adam held out the ball.

"Really?" Toni asked.

The ball dropped into her glove. "Really."

They smiled at each other, and suddenly Toni felt just fine.

TONI PITCHED WELL and got the save. Joe was a nervous wreck by the time the game was done.

When Toni walked a batter, some bozo shouted, "Take out the girlie-girl." Joe had been on his way to rearrange the guy's world, when he caught Evie's glare.

He hesitated, and she turned to the bozo. "Put a sock in it, Randy. You know the rules."

"…Watch nice or go home!"

"…Be an adult or at least pretend!"

"…Set an example or get out of town!"

The admonitions came from different sections of the bleachers, both home and away. Randy did put a sock in it, and the rest of the inning passed without incident.

Evie seemed to have control over more than her team. Joe had to admit he was impressed, and a bit embarrassed that his first instinct was toward violence. How would his behavior have looked to Toni?

He wasn't used to worrying about how he behaved all the time, but he'd better start. He had his first T-ball game in less than twenty-four hours.

Toni ran up and threw her arms around his waist. "I did it, Joe!"

The joy on her face made his heart turn over. The spontaneous hug caused him to think that perhaps they were starting to break through the stiffness that had always existed between them. He wanted very badly to be the kind of dad she needed, if he only knew how.

"You sure did. I haven't seen anyone pitch that well in years."

She grinned and danced out of his arms. Joe dropped his hands, which suddenly felt empty, and watched as Adam approached. Toni's face changed, and Joe had the urge to grab Adam by the throat and tell him what would happen if he so much as put a finger on any part of Toni's anatomy.

"Is it okay if I go have ice cream with the guys? Adam will drive me home."

He wanted to shout, *No, you're too young!* Instead, he nodded. "Be home by eleven."

Joe's eyes met Adam's over Toni's head, and he gave the kid his Iceman stare. Adam Vaughn, like his mother, didn't even flinch.

JOE HATED TO ADMIT IT, but he was nervous about a peewee T-ball game. He'd arrived half an hour early, just in case one of the kids needed him. He'd ended up sitting alone on the bench and thinking.

He'd had several practices with the kids, and they'd improved immensely from the chaos that had reigned the first time he'd seen them. But at the end of every practice, Joe was exhausted. They ran, they jumped, they fell. They talked and talked. The questions made his head spin.

"Coach Joe, why are you so big?"

"Coach Joe, why is your hair white?"

"Coach Joe, my daddy says you're famous. What's 'famous'?"

"Coach Joe, my mommy says you're a stud muffin. Is that better than blueberry?"

The last had come from a boy whose mother made no secret she was divorced and in search of contestant number two. Joe wanted to date, and he wanted to get married again, but frankly, that woman scared him to death. She was pretty enough—if you liked tight jeans, high heels at the ballpark and big hair. But she had the look of a hungry panther on the prowl. Joe had no desire to be the monkey feast in her sights.

No, what he wanted was a nice, normal, wifely woman. Whatever that was.

The sound of a slamming car door brought Joe's attention back to his little slice of Iowa. He glanced at the parking lot and was treated to a view of Evie Vaughn. She definitely did not meet his requirements, but she sure was nice to look at.

What was it about her that appealed to him? She was petite—a type he'd never been attracted to. A guy of his size had no business with a woman he could break if he wasn't very careful. She was abrasive at times—maybe only with him—but still abrasive. Then there was her overabundance of jobs. And her son, who had the hots for his baby.

Joe sighed. As he watched Evie walk, confident, light on her feet, as if ready for anything—and with those twins, she probably was—he found himself wondering if she would taste as good as she looked.

Yep, he was definitely losing his mind.

The twins barreled past, hooting and hollering. She didn't even flinch when they careered into her. Joe had to smile. The more he saw Evie the more he thought she was good at the mom thing. And he liked the twins. They kind of grew on you—like a fungus that wouldn't let go.

They hit him at the knees, one attached to each leg. "Hey, Coach Joe!"

"Hey, Benji. Hey, Danny." He had no idea which was which. He usually addressed them both at the same time until he could figure out who was wearing the red shirt or the blue cap.

Joe took in the identical faces framed by identical caps, identical uniforms covering identically sized bodies, and he rubbed his eyes. When he lowered his hands, the double vision remained the same.

He didn't want them to know he had no idea who was who. That would be asking for trouble he didn't need. "Go out and warm up," he ordered, and they released him to run onto the field. He greeted Evie. Perhaps he could catch a clue from their mother.

She shielded her eyes from the sun at his back and peered into his face. "Ready for the first game?"

"Sure." He didn't sound sure, even to his own ears, and when she laughed, he knew he hadn't fooled her, either.

"Calm down." She dropped her hand. "This is T-ball. The only fans in the stands will be the parents, and they just want their kids to have fun and learn a little."

"They don't want to win?"

"In T-ball?" She stared at him as if he'd said Martians were going to play football against the Minnesota Vikings. "We don't worry about winning at that age."

Joe sighed with relief. Though he'd been competitive all his life and winning had been his business, the more he worked with little kids, the more ridiculous the old ideas of winning and losing and being perfect seemed.

"Good," he said.

"That's okay with you?" Her voice reflected surprise at his attitude, which annoyed him.

"Are you here as a parent, or my boss?"

She tilted her head, studying him. "Both. Though I'm not really your boss. It's not like you get paid or anything."

"But you can fire me."

She grinned. "There is that."

He pointed to the twins. "They like to play."

"They like to do what their brother does."

He slid a glance in her direction. "And where is their brother?"

"At the batting cage, practicing."

"He's that serious about baseball?"

"Weren't you that serious about football?"

"I guess I was. You think he has a chance to go pro?"

"How many kids go pro?"

"Not very many."

"Right. Especially from a town like Oak Grove. Hard to get noticed unless you win championships, and that doesn't happen here very often."

"Until now?"

"That's what I'm aiming for."

"Serious aim you have."

"I always do."

"I don't want Toni terrorized for Little League."

"It's Big League, and do I look like a woman to strike terror into the hearts of children?"

He eyed her for a long moment, considering. Finally he admitted the truth. "I don't know."

Her lips tightened. "I guess you'll find out."

"Hmm."

Evie had said they didn't worry about winning in T-ball. But T-ball and Big League were two different things. Joe recalled how Toni had looked every time her mother criticized her. He didn't want her upset because this woman had an agenda. Still, yesterday when someone had yelled at Toni, Evie had put her foot down. He'd wait and see what happened when Toni lost a game. If Evie didn't behave like a lady, Toni's pitching days were history.

"So which one is which?" He pointed at the twins again.

Her lips twitched. "You don't know?"

"I can usually figure it out by the middle of a practice, then I keep them straight by who's wearing what. But now…" He shrugged helplessly.

"You realize they'll switch on you, just for fun?"

"They do that a lot?"

"Not to me."

"I guess it doesn't really matter."

"No?"

"So they switch and one plays outfield and the other plays infield. If they're happy, I'm happy."

"That's the kind of attitude I like to hear in a coach."

"I live to please," he said sarcastically.

She raised her eyebrow. "That's the kind of attitude I like to hear in a man."

Evie sauntered off before he could say anything more. Joe just enjoyed the view.

EVIE SAT AT THE TOP of the bleachers and watched in dismay as the stands around the T-ball diamonds filled with spectators.

What was going on? Even if every kid brought parents, siblings, grandparents, aunts and uncles, that didn't explain all these people.

Joe looked up at her for the fifth time and lifted his hands in supplication. Another person asked him for an autograph, and he turned away to comply.

Evie admitted the truth she'd suspected for the past twenty minutes. All these people had come to see Joe.

Something had to be done, and she was the one who would have to do it. Evie jumped down from the bleachers and strode toward the field.

The middle school kid who had drawn this game to umpire stared into the stands with a white, still face. Evie put her hand on his shoulder, and he jumped.

"Relax," she said. "It's just a game like any other game." He didn't appear convinced. "Go on," Evie urged. "Start. They're here to watch Scalotta anyway. They won't pay attention to you."

He swallowed, and the movement made his Adam's apple seem even more prominent than it was. Poor kid.

"Play ball," he shouted, and his voice cracked in the middle.

Evie observed for a while, sighing with relief as the game went on without incident. The kids were enjoying the increased attention rather than being intimidated by it. Luckily, this had happened at the T-ball game and not the AA League. First graders liked to be watched. Middle school kids did not—

"Isn't this marvelous?"

Evie winced. She knew that voice.

"Mrs. Larson." Evie greeted the elderly patron. "What brings you to Little League?"

Decked out in her usual attire—dress, hose, heels, pearls, hat and purse—Mrs. Larson looked as though she'd arrived from a garden party. She just might have, since they still had those in Oak Grove.

"I'm here to see this, dear." She swept out a perfectly manicured hand, indicating the game and the crowd. "Isn't it wonderful?"

"Wonderful?" Evie echoed.

"Oh, my!" Mrs. Larson pointed to the parking lot. "Why, this is a dream come true."

Evie followed Mrs. Larson's finger. A crew from Channel 8 News hurried toward them.

"A dream? It's shaping up like a nightmare."

"What are you mumbling about? This is splendid. Look at all the spectators. Look at that concession stand."

Evie did—and moaned. The parents who were running it were—well, they were running. The line was long and getting longer. If this kept up they'd have to close down, or go and get more stuff to sell.

The level of noise surrounding the game was amazing. Evie turned toward the field. Joe no longer seemed to notice. Why would he? He was used to doing his job in front of television cameras, beneath field lights and under the scrutiny of thousands. This was nothing to him.

What had she done in letting Iceman Scalotta coach T-ball? Would this chaos repeat itself at each and every game? If so, how could she stop it?

"I'll have to fire him," she blurted.

"You'll do no such thing, missy." Only Mrs. Larson could get away with calling grown women "missy"—and she knew it. "That boy is the best thing to happen around here in aeons. The school board, and Don Barry, have plans for him."

Don—her father's oldest and dearest friend—was the athletic director who had hired Evie to teach at Oak Grove. Also the vice principal, he had the final say on who was employed. He wouldn't screw up her life for a sound bite, would he? The school board, of which Mrs. Larson was also the president, was another story.

"What about the board?" Evie asked, though she had a very bad feeling she wasn't going to like the answer. "What would they want with Joe Scalotta?"

"If he can bring this many folk to a Little League game, just imagine what he could do for our varsity program."

"Varsity baseball?"

"What else, dear?"

What else, indeed. At Oak Grove, baseball was all she wrote.

"He's a football player!" Evie's shout drew disapproving glares from several people engrossed in the game—or rather, in watching Jock Hollywood.

"What difference does that make?" Mrs. Larson frowned. "Just look."

The camera crew set up shop right next to Joe and began filming the game from his point of view. The reporter stuck a microphone next to his mouth and taped his words of wisdom to the kids. Scalotta didn't even flinch; he just kept right on coaching. At least he didn't stop the game and give a live, prime-time interview.

"Just because he was a football hero doesn't mean he knows diddly about baseball," Evie pointed out, quite calmly, too, considering her roiling stomach and the state of her mind.

"If he doesn't know 'diddly,' as you say, then why have you allowed him to coach your sons?"

Evie glanced at Mrs. Larson. Just as she'd thought, the sweet-voiced question did not match the deliberation in those eyes.

Evie didn't think Mrs. Larson would be happy to hear "He was the only man for the job." *Only* being the operative word. Evie hadn't searched elsewhere for a better candidate because there weren't any other candidates, let alone better ones. Therefore, because Evie had let Joe coach her kids, he had just become Coach Extraordinaire in Oak Grove.

And Evie was hung with her own rope.

She spent the rest of the game helping at the concession stand, while trying to glimpse what was happening on the field. The news that one of her Big

League coaches had fallen off his roof and broken his leg made Evie's night complete—completely disastrous. How was she going to find another coach at this late date?

"Only one disaster at a time, if you please," she muttered as she tried to keep her mind on the worries at hand. Namely, that they had run out of hot dogs in half an hour, and soda in forty-five minutes. There was no candy left by the fourth inning, and there were people whining all over the place.

When the game wound down, Joe's team had lost. Evie would have taken childish and unprofessional pleasure in that, except no one seemed to care about the loss. Everyone gathered around him, slapping his back and shaking his hand as if he'd just won a gold medal.

So she returned to her own disappointment. She'd been promised that varsity coaching job if she won the championship. She'd been willing to work hard to get it. Now Joe would likely be handed her prize on a platter just for being a great big manly man. *Grr.*

Mrs. Larson approached Joe and introduced herself. Evie was close enough to hear what followed, though she pretended to be checking the bench for leftover caps and gloves.

"Mr. Scalotta, I'm the president of the Oak Grove School Board, and we're convening a special meeting tomorrow night that we'd like you to attend."

Joe appeared puzzled, but he nodded. What else could he do? He had a child in the system and no idea of the kind of politics that went on in a small town. He probably thought the school board was like some welcoming committee.

Well, Evie wasn't going to roll over and play dead. Not yet, anyway.

CHAPTER SEVEN

JOE HAD NO CLUE why the little old lady wanted him at the school board meeting, but he also knew better than to argue with a woman like her. When she said jump, Joe bet, most of Oak Grove didn't even ask how high.

He tried to get Mrs. Larson to tell him what was going on, but she merely smiled and said, "We want to talk to you, sonny. Make you welcome and all that." By the time he stopped chuckling over someone of her size calling someone of his size "sonny," she was gone. The woman moved amazingly quick for an octogenarian.

With all the people waiting to talk to him, it took Joe another half hour to get to his car. He hadn't thought there were this many people in Oak Grove. Now that he did, he realized there weren't. Some of his new best friends had mentioned driving in from neighboring towns.

Joe hoped this circus atmosphere was a one-night occurrence. Why would people watch him coach T-ball once a week? How boring was that?

Evie had disappeared in a flash, just like Mrs. Larson. The few times he'd glanced her way during the game, she'd looked shell-shocked. He figured he should give her a call and reassure her that he didn't think this fiasco would repeat itself.

Joe drove home meaning to do just that. But when he arrived, and Toni wasn't in yet, he got caught up in pacing the floor.

She showed up before eleven—by five minutes, but still before. Joe, who had been staring out the window down the long, empty street, wishing and waiting for headlights to appear, dove for a chair and the remote control when twin beams turned onto his road.

By the time he heard the car door slam, Joe was sufficiently engrossed in the "Nick at Night" episode of *Happy Days* to answer any quiz on this particular adventure—mainly because he'd seen it ten times already.

The fifties—now those were the days, or so he'd heard from his parents. He himself had grown up in the seventies. By then a lot of the innocence had gone.

Growing up in the nineties and the first years of the new millennium? Joe shivered. Toni had a tough road ahead. He only hoped he'd be able to help her negotiate the trials without making things worse. The terrors out in the big bad world were enough to cause a grown man to cry for his mother. Joe planned on doing so regularly. His mom had raised four boys and no girls, but she was all he had available for expert advice. Joe was a firm believer in the adage When the Going Gets Tough, Call Mommy.

The front door opened—then shut with unnecessary force. What was it about kids and doors? They had to slam every one.

"Hi, Joe."

He glanced up, trying to act as though he'd fallen asleep in the chair. Toni leaned in the doorway, that new dreamy smile on her face.

"Did you have fun?" Joe narrowed his gaze and checked her for telltale rumples or hickeys, keeping his sigh of relief silent when he found nothing. He'd moved to Iowa to eliminate some of the everyday dangers of the world, but even in Iowa they had teenage boys.

"Yes. Fun."

She sighed like a teenage girl who'd just gone out with Elvis. Make that Paul McCartney. No, not him, either. Who the heck was the dreamboat of the decade? Probably Adam Vaughn. Joe resisted the urge to growl.

"What kind of ice cream did you have?"

"Hmm?"

"Ice cream. You were going for ice cream."

Suddenly she focused on him and caught him focusing on her. "You checking up on me, Joe?"

He blinked at the unexpected ice in her voice. Where had that come from? He'd heard teenaged girls could switch moods in a heartbeat, but he'd yet to see such behavior from Toni. Still, he'd only had her for a few weeks.

"Checking up on you?" he repeated.

"Asking me what kind of ice cream I had, like I didn't go to the DQ or something."

"Where else would you go?"

She peered at the television. "Inspiration Point?"

He followed her gaze and saw the Fonz escorting a duo of giggling, taller women to just that location. "They have one of those here?"

"I doubt there's a Point, or even a Hill, but I'm sure they have a make-out place."

"And if they do?"

She returned her gaze to Joe and anger flashed in her eyes. "What are you asking me? If I'll go there? Or if I'll tell you where it is?"

"Why would I want to know where the equivalent of Inspiration Point is?"

"According to the papers, you're quite the ladies' man."

Joe winced. "You read about me in the papers?"

She shrugged but didn't answer him.

"I did a lot of things I'm not proud of," he acknowledged. "Before I met your mother and after."

Toni stiffened. "Like having me?"

"No! You're the best thing that ever happened to me. One of the few things I *am* proud of."

She didn't look convinced. Why would she be? She barely knew him.

"I just want you to be happy here, baby. With me."

"I'm not a baby anymore. I haven't been for a long time."

"I know, and I'm sorry I missed it."

"Missed what?"

"Your being a baby."

"Well…you did." Belligerence colored her voice.

Joe sighed. He felt as though he was walking on thin spring ice and could break through into cold deep water at any time.

"I can never get back those days no matter how badly I want to, no matter how sorry I am for screwing up. But I can be with you now. And if you'll let me, I want to be your dad."

"You *are* my dad."

"Just because your last name is Scalotta and my name's on your birth certificate doesn't give me the right to be your dad. I have to earn that privilege, and I'm willing to do whatever it takes."

If he could only figure out what that was.

Toni didn't say anything—didn't dispute or agree. Instead, she turned around and walked upstairs without even a good-night. Joe let her go. They both had to get used to each other before they engaged in deep conversations about the past.

Or maybe Joe was just too chicken to hear what he had done that was so bad she could not bring herself to love him. Because maybe it was so bad she would *never* be able to love him. And cowardly though it was, he'd rather not know that his dream might not come true.

The next day Toni was even more quiet than usual, and Joe didn't pester her. She would have to come to him on her own.

When Joe was ready to leave for the school board meeting that night, he found her sitting in the living room with a book open in her lap and the television blaring a music video. Her hair still wet from a shower, she wore her sleeping-cat pajama shirt, and curled bare legs beneath the knee-length hem.

"How can you read and watch TV at the same time?" Joe asked.

She shrugged. "I always have. You should see me *study* and watch TV."

Joe frowned. Didn't sound productive to him, but that would be a discussion best saved for fall, when school started. "I'm going to the board meeting. It probably won't take more than an hour."

"Okay. Adam's coming over."

Joe already had his hand on the front doorknob. After that announcement, he walked back into the living room. "For what?"

"Huh?" She looked up from her book, her eyes unfocused, no doubt still thinking of the story—or Vaughn.

"What's he coming over for?"

"To watch television. His mom's going to the same meeting as you."

That threw Joe for a minute. Why was Evie attending this "welcome to the neighborhood" thing? Maybe she was on the welcoming committee. "And the twins?"

Toni rolled her eyes. "Are not my problem. But Adam said they were at a bowling party tonight, or he'd be stuck watching them."

Joe grunted. Toni was right. The twins weren't his problem—at the moment. Toni was.

"I assume you'll put on pants before he gets here."

"Why?"

"Toni," he warned.

She laughed. "Yes. I'll put on pants, and a shirt, even."

When Joe hesitated, she waved toward the door. "Have a nice time. See you later."

"I'm not sure I like the idea of him being here while you're alone."

"Jeez, Joe. We're gonna watch a movie. Besides, you'll be back in an hour. What could happen?"

Joe knew very well what could happen, but since she didn't seem to, he didn't want to give her any ideas. "All right. See you." He started out once more, then poked his head around the door. "Soon," he reminded her. She just raised her eyebrows and stared at him, unsmiling.

Joe's uneasiness followed him all the way to the meeting. It only increased when he walked in on a room full of people who took one look at him and immediately started whispering.

SCALOTTA DIDN'T APPEAR too pleased at the size of the welcoming committee. *Fancy that.*

He stood in the doorway. Actually, he filled the doorway, and for a minute Evie just sat back and enjoyed the view. She'd never seen him in anything but T-shirts. Tonight he wore a powder-blue dress shirt, the cuffs rolled up to just below his elbows, revealing muscular forearms. Evie nearly groaned. The man had a way of playing to her weaknesses.

The shade of that shirt brought out the intense blue of his eyes. As he scanned the room, she shivered. Very few men—heck, very few humans—had eyes that shade of blue. He *was* impressive—the stuff outright fantasies were made of.

Unfortunately, she'd been having quite a few fantasies lately—and Joe was always in them. Like the one last night, where she'd imagined him without a shirt, out in the sun, on a beautiful summer day. He'd been painting her house—something she badly needed done but couldn't afford. His muscles, all of them, had glistened, and not with the pretty-boy oil bodybuilders used but with a combination of sunshine and well-earned sweat.

Joe was not a boy. Thank God. She really did enjoy looking at men who were built like him—tall and firm, and large in all the right places. Too bad he was off-limits to all but her secret fantasies.

Since she was an underpaid, overworked, overtired, school-teaching mother of three, Evie continued to fantasize. She was entitled.

How much hair did he have on his chest? How much did she like? Just a little, so she could see all that glistening skin. Presto chango—just what she wanted.

Washboard stomach? You betcha.

Pants tight over the rear but loose enough at the

waist to gape and allow a teasing hide-and-seek glimpse of a golden line of hair leading down to—

"Evie?"

She opened her eyes to find the subject of her fantasy leaning over her. With the harsh light of the fluorescent bulbs behind him, his hair looked more silver than blond and his eyes had gone dark.

"Oh, yeah." The two words escaped before she could prevent them. The tone of voice—husky, sexy, inviting—was not one she'd ever heard herself use.

Joe blinked as if the lights had suddenly blinded him, or as if he'd also heard a stranger's voice coming out of Evie's mouth.

"Pardon me?"

Evie blushed. She couldn't help it. Even though Joe had no idea she'd just been having mind-sex with him, she still wanted to crawl in a hole and pull the hole in after her. Just because she hadn't had sex in…oh…six years did not mean she had the right to conjure visions in the midst of a school board meeting—no matter how appealing they were.

Evie sat up so fast that her tailbone bumped against the metal foldout chair, and she hissed with pain.

"You okay?" Joe asked, holding out his hand.

She ignored the hand, even though the palm was wide, the skin tanned and the fingers long—just the kind of hand she liked. The man who owned it probably knew just what to do with it to make her every fantasy come true.

Her entire body went hot, and she pulled on the scooped neckline of her ivy-green dress, hoping a little air would help. It did not.

"Evie?"

Joe appeared worried now, and she couldn't blame him. She was acting like a lunatic.

"I'm fine," she hastily assured him, more to get him to back off than because she was fine.

The way he loomed above her made Evie's flushed skin tingle. The way he smelled... She caught herself breathing deeply of his scent and mind-cursed both him for smelling that way and herself for being aroused by it. Joe Scalotta smelled better than any man had a right to—like summer heat and winter breezes, picnics and ice skating, lemonade and hot tea.

How could he be so contradictory, yet so enticing? She didn't know, but he was. Heaven help her.

Evie scooted onto the empty chair at her side, then stood. Her attempt to get away from him didn't work. That huge hand reached out and took her arm—gently—but that didn't stop the shudder of awareness that rippled through her. The contrast of his hard hand and his gentle touch made her mind spin. She just stared at him like a zombie.

Thankfully, Joe didn't notice. Or maybe he was too polite to mention it. Iceman Scalotta polite? No. He just hadn't noticed.

Then his thumb stroked—once, twice, up, then down—her inner arm, above her elbow where no one ever touched, and her shudder became a shiver.

She looked up, up, up into his eyes and recognized a confusion that mirrored her own, seconds before something hotter, more intense, more dangerous, sprang to life—

"Ladies and gentlemen, if you could take your seats we'll begin." Mrs. Larson's voice boomed over the microphone, making both Evie and Joe jump away from each other as if they'd been caught necking in the back seat of a car.

Evie's face flamed at the image. Remembering having necked in a parked car with Ray, she struggled for control.

She wasn't going to let an attractive face and a great body, no matter how appealing, entice her into ruining life for a second time. She was stronger than that. Wasn't she? No longer the naive young girl who'd adored a man beyond reason, she'd learned from that mistake and would not make it again.

She had three boys to think of. Their futures depended on her. That was why she had come here tonight—for her sons. Now, if she could only figure out what she must do to stop the tide before it became a tidal wave and washed over everything she'd worked so hard to achieve.

"We've gathered here tonight," Mrs. Larson continued, "to welcome a newcomer to our town. Most of you have heard that Joe Scalotta and his daughter have moved to Oak Grove—" Mrs. Larson beamed at Joe as if he'd just won the Nobel Prize for medicine.

The entire room stared at him.

Evie, too. His confused frown made him look like a little boy who'd just been awoken from a deep nap and wasn't sure exactly where he was.

"After last evening's spectacular example of what Mr. Scalotta's presence can mean to this community and its sports program, the school board—on the recommendation of Don Barry, the athletic director—has unanimously decided to offer Mr. Scalotta the coveted position of varsity baseball coach at Oak Grove High."

Thunderous applause broke out. Joe's frown became a full-blown scowl, and he shook his head, even though people were already slapping him on the back and congratulating him.

Taking advantage of everyone's preoccupation, Evie slipped to the front of the room. Her heart beat a cadence of panic. She glanced at Don, but he would not meet her eyes. Guilty as charged.

Her father's best friend had offered *her* job to Joe without even giving Evie a chance to protest. Don Barry hadn't asked her opinion, or even apologized for taking her dream and stamping on it. From the way they were all ignoring her, they expected her to be a good little soldier and accept what they'd decided.

Not in this lifetime.

Evie's panic turned to fury. Before she could think of an adequate game plan, she spoke above the congratulations of the crowd. "That job was promised to me."

The murmurs stopped as everyone turned to stare at her, obviously amazed she had the guts to contradict the grand dame of Oak Grove or the man who had brought Evie to town in the first place.

She discounted them all and pressed on. "I don't think it's fair or in the children's best interest to give the job to a man we barely know just because his name's been in the papers and his face all over the television."

Mrs. Larson's mouth scrunched up like a day-old lemon, but she managed to speak, anyway. "He's a professional athlete, Evelyn."

Oh, oh. Mrs. Larson had called her "Evelyn." *Bad sign.* The old lady was spitting mad—though she would never so much as raise her voice. She never had to. No one argued with Lillian Larson. Until today.

"He *was* a professional athlete. And even then he was a football player."

"I hardly see the relevance of football to this discussion."

Evie wanted to shriek in frustration, but impatience with Mrs. Larson's lack of understanding would not endear Evie further. To a woman like Mrs. Larson, a ball was a ball. You threw it, you caught it, that was that. She did not see that football and baseball were two different—well, two different ball games.

Evie gave up on Mrs. Larson and addressed Don. "If you want to offer him the football team, that's

fine. That would make sense. But baseball—'' Evie
shook her head ''—he isn't qualified.''

Don's ruddy face darkened. ''Don't tell me my
job.''

Oops. Evie realized her mistake too late. Don
might be her dad's oldest friend, but he was also
one of those macho men you had to tread very carefully around. Instead, she'd stepped right on his toes.

''I hired you as a favor to your dad, and I can't
say I'm sorry, because you're an excellent teacher
and a great coach. But we're talking about the high-
est profile job in this town. We don't want a little
gal like you taking those big kids to the state championship.''

His comment about hiring her as a favor stung. It
was no doubt true, and at the time she'd needed the
job too badly to care. Now she was just furious.
''What difference does it make who takes the team
to state? Do you want the best coach? Or do you
want the best sound bite?''

''Could I say a word here?'' Joe was suddenly
right behind her.

''No,'' Evie snapped without even turning
around. She couldn't fight Joe, Don and Mrs. Larson
all at the same time. ''Why do you want to ruin the
best chance those kids have to get scholarships by
hiring the wrong coach?''

''Hey!'' Joe protested. ''I'm a great coach.''

Evie spun about and nearly bumped her nose on
Joe's chest. She refused to step back, even though
he was so close she had to crick her neck to glare

into his face. "You *were* a great football player. You have never *been* a coach."

He leaned down. "Have you ever coached an all-male varsity sport?"

She went up on her toes so they were nose to chin. "What does *that* have to do with anything—"

"Ahem."

Evie did an about-face, to find Mrs. Larson's lemon lips had thinned into a single line. Don wasn't looking at her again, which meant Mrs. Larson had the floor. Evie expected to be sent to her room without supper—for the next several years. Which is exactly what would happen if she lost this job. She would not be eating supper for however long it took to save enough money to send the boys to college. Her stomach growled in protest, and she winced.

"I'm sorry—" Mrs. Larson began.

"Wait!" The word constituted Evie's second interruption of the evening. Had she just dug her own grave? Even if she had, she could not sit back and watch these two bury her dream. She would fight until the bitter end for her children's future.

She tried to speak rationally—like a teacher with a student who just didn't get it. "I was promised that job. How can you justify taking it away from me for no other reason than sexual discrimination?"

"Oh, oh," Joe murmured at her back. His breath skated down her neck, and Evie shivered.

Would she ever learn the trick of treading lightly around touchy issues? It didn't look like it. The realization of what she'd just said, and the fury on

Don's and Mrs. Larson's faces as soon as the words left Evie's mouth, made her shiver for another reason.

In Oak Grove you handled your own problems. You did not whine to the police; you definitely did not file a lawsuit. Any conflicts were solved by talking face-to-face, and if that didn't work you sent an emissary—like your great-aunt Hester, who had gone to school with the uncle of your neighbor's cousin. Lawyers were for wills, the occasional divorce and real-estate transactions. That was all.

"Your father would be ashamed of you," Don said.

Evie doubted that. Her father had only been ashamed of her once. But because he'd been her father, he'd stood behind her anyway. He'd stand behind her now, too. That knowledge gave her courage. She met Don's eyes. He looked away first, and she knew he would stay out of the fight. Macho he might be, but no one messed with—

"Are you threatening me?" Mrs. Larson's voice trembled.

So did Evie's hands, which she quickly clasped behind her back. "No, ma'am."

"Good." Mrs. Larson eyed her for a long moment. "If I recall, the decision about this job was contingent upon your team's going to the state championship."

"Which isn't until August. I haven't had a chance to prove myself."

Mrs. Larson was shaking her head before Evie

finished her sentence. She had to do something. *Anything*. If Mrs. Larson uttered the final word, there would be no going back.

Panic made Evie desperate. "You want the best person for the job, don't you?"

Mrs. Larson frowned. She couldn't admit, in front of the school board and assembled parents, that all she wanted was a celebrity coach. Everyone might *know* that, but she couldn't *say* it; it would mean publication in the school board minutes on page four of the *Oak Grove Sentinel* next Tuesday or Thursday morning, and invite a scandal

"Of course we want the best *man,* Evelyn."

Evie ignored the sarcasm and the "Evelyn." "And you just said you were going to give me the job if I took my team to the championship."

"Correct."

"Bob Cummings broke his leg yesterday. I need a coach for his team."

"That is not my problem, dear."

"No, it isn't. But I have a solution to both our problems." Evie paused.

Mrs. Larson glanced at the crowd. What she saw there made her eyes narrow, but she returned her gaze to Evie and bowed her head with a regal little nod of acquiescence.

Evie drew a deep breath and hurried on. "I propose that Mr. Scalotta take Bob's place. If his team finishes higher in the standings at the end of the season, the job is his. However, if my team finishes higher, the job is mine. Deal?"

Mrs. Larson shook her head again; Don scowled and did the same. Evie's heart did a free fall toward her toes. The old lady opened her mouth, but it was Joe's voice they all heard.

"Deal," he said.

The room went wild.

CHAPTER EIGHT

"...Most exciting school board meeting I've been to in a dog's age."

"...This is going to be one rip-roarin' summer."

"...Can't wait to see what those two come up with for round two."

The comments, jokes and good-natured laughter swirled around Joe. Since he had agreed to Evie's proposition, the two of them had been surrounded by people, and they had been unable to talk to each other. From the set of Evie's mouth, she wasn't pleased with him, even though he *had* agreed to her crazy notion.

Why had he? Because she'd stung his pride, yanked his machismo, thrown down the proverbial gauntlet. Since childhood Joe had been competitive. In fact, his mother said he'd come out of the womb expecting to win.

Joe himself thought that having three older brothers who always told their "little" brother he couldn't play might have made him more susceptible to challenge than most guys. Naturally, he had to prove that he could. It was a character flaw, but at least Joe knew it.

To have someone announce in a room full of

peers that Joe Scalotta wasn't up to a job… Well, childish though it was, he just couldn't let that go by. Even if he'd never wanted Evie's job in the first place.

Why did she want the job so badly anyway, especially when it would take her away from her children even more? Was it any of his business? Probably not. But now that the twins were under Joe's feet half the time and Adam looked to be a new boarder at his house, what went on in the land of Vaughn had suddenly become far too interesting to Joe Scalotta.

He was brought back to the room by an avid slap on his shoulder. Joe looked down into the face of a shriveled old man, too frail to have slammed him that hard. But even as he thought it, the old guy grabbed his hand and pumped up and down with a grip that would rival that of a world heavyweight champion.

"Name's Norville Hoyt. Good going, son. I haven't had this much fun since they stopped letting me watch that Jeffrey Springer fella on the television. Said I get too excited and my blood pressure—"

He let go of Joe's hand and flicked a gnarled finger upward as he whistled through his teeth. "I just love a good battle. Especially between a little gal and big guy. Can't wait to see how this comes out in the paper."

"Paper?"

"You betcha." He pointed at a young man with

a notepad and pen, who still scribbled madly, at the table near the window. "That there is the school board reporter. Not a very important beat, don'tcha know, so they give it to a high school kid. But he got an earful tonight. Wouldn't be surprised if he sends the thing to the television station. After all the interest last night, this here meeting will be news."

Joe groaned. More publicity. *Grr.*

Hoyt slapped him on the arm. "This is going to be a great summer. I just love them baseball games, but now, with you two goin' at it—" He whistled again, the sound shrill and loud above the noise. "It's goin' to be a doozy. I bet the crowds are huge." Stepping closer, Hoyt nudged Joe in the gut—hard. "She's a pretty little thing, ain't she?"

Joe rubbed his belly. "Who?"

"Coach Vaughn."

Joe followed Hoyt's gaze to where Evie stood surrounded by several parents. The dress she'd worn to the meeting was plain and simple, but perfect for her, and Joe caught himself admiring her shapely shoulders and smooth skin, which the thin straps of her dress revealed.

Hoyt's whistle this time was of the wolf variety and drew Evie's attention from the group toward them. She frowned at Joe, and he shrugged and pointed at Hoyt. Her frown turned into a genuine smile of affection, and she excused herself from her circle to join them.

Evie kissed Hoyt's wrinkled cheek, and the tough

old guy blushed. "Good show, girlie. I'm impressed."

"I aim to please."

"Well, I'm leaving before Merlene comes lookin' for me. You know how she gets when I'm late. I'll see you at practice, Coach." He walked off with a spring in his step that belied the years on his face.

"Practice?" Joe asked.

"He's my assistant."

"Hoyt? He must be eighty."

"Eighty-three. He played with DiMaggio."

"No way."

"Yes, way. He knows more than I do. But while the mind is willing, the body just can't keep up anymore."

"He's got a grip like a sumo wrestler."

"That he does." She looked over Joe's shoulder. "I guess they're waiting to lock up."

Joe followed her gaze. The custodian stood in the doorway, jingling his keys. Everyone else had disappeared. "I'll walk you to your car."

"No need. This is Oak Grove. The most dangerous thing wandering the streets at night is a stray cat."

"I think we need to talk."

"Oh." She colored. "Of course."

He followed her from the room, down the long hallway lined with lockers and out the door that emptied into the parking lot. Only his car remained, with no sign of Evie's.

"Your car?"

"I walked."

"Walked?"

"Yes, walked. It *is* summer."

"That must be two miles."

She laughed. "Don't sound so surprised, he-man. Walking is good for the lungs, and even better for the mind when you rarely get to be alone. Besides, Adam took the car to your house."

Joe tensed. How could he have forgotten his baby was home alone—or rather *not* alone? Joe resisted the urge to jump in his vehicle and tear out of the lot to rescue his little girl. When he looked down at Evie, she was smiling.

"What?"

"You might be Iceman, but when you think about Toni—everything you feel is all over your face."

He shrugged and turned away, embarrassed.

"It's one of your appealing qualities." She sounded both amazed and amused.

He turned back to her with a raise of his brow. "I bet you figured I didn't have any."

"You're right." She walked across the parking lot.

He caught up with her in two strides, his long legs eating up the ground much more quickly than hers. "Any others come to mind?"

"Not that I can dredge up offhand." Her tone was sarcastic, but the way she ducked her head, shy and embarrassed, made Joe think she liked other things—guy-girl things, man-woman things—and the secret attraction that he'd tried to deny since the first time he realized she was a woman and not a child sprang to life.

They reached his car, and she slowed. "Do you want a ride home?" he asked.

"No, thanks. I've seen how you drive."

"Really, I can drop you off."

"Really. No, thanks."

"Fine." Since he wanted to touch her shoulders where the moon glistened silver on gold, he tucked his hands into the pockets of his khaki pants and glanced around, at a loss what to say now. What was it about this woman that made his glib words and usual moves seem inappropriate and crude? When he slid a look back at her, she was gone, already at the playground equipment that sat between the schools.

"Hey, wait up!" he called.

She'd reached the swing set, and plunked herself down on one of the swings. A quick push with her feet and she swayed back and forth. Joe watched her for a few minutes, then trudged across the grass.

"You suddenly felt like swinging?" he asked when he got to her.

She smiled. "I suddenly felt like sitting. This is the only place, unless you wouldn't mind me sitting on the hood of your car."

Joe winced, and she snorted.

"That's what I thought. So let's talk. Have a seat."

"On that?" He glanced suspiciously at the modest strap of canvas hooked between two chains. "I don't think so."

"Suit yourself." She pushed off again, and the swing swung higher. "Talk."

What had he planned to talk about? Oh, yeah—the bet he'd just been snookered into making.

"Why do you want the varsity coaching job so bad?"

She'd been leaning back in the swing, staring at the stars. At his question her head jerked upright and her eyes narrowed. "None of your business."

She looked embarrassed, and Joe wondered for a minute if she had money trouble. But what good would a coaching job next year do her if she needed money now? Besides, according to the local grapevine, her husband had died in an accident, which meant insurance money of some sort, not to mention her full-time job.

No, the reason had to be her competitive nature. Since Joe was competitive, too, he understood, and although he had sworn off competitive women, he had to say this one intrigued him. Arguing with her made him feel more alive than he'd felt since leaving the playing field.

But while he was attracted to her, she seemed to despise him, and he was curious why.

Joe had never been one to beat around the bush, so he asked, "What have you got against me?"

"Me?" She appeared genuinely surprised at the question. "Nothing."

She continued to swing. Joe was becoming nauseated, so he stepped forward, caught the chains and stopped the swing mid-flight.

"Hey, what're you doing?" She jumped off, bumping her chin against his chest. The sharp intake of her breath echoed in the stillness. The way she held herself, with an aura of awareness that almost hummed from her body to his, made Joe think that perhaps she didn't despise him so much, after all.

He should step back, he knew, far enough so he could see her face but not so far that she could run off again.

Yeah, he *should.* But for some reason he couldn't move. The warmth of her body, even in the heat of the summer night, called to a chill within him—a chill that had been there for a very long time.

She smelled so good—he'd noticed that about her the very first day. But on that day she'd smelled of Ivory soap; tonight she smelled like wild-cherry pie. The full moon shone on her hair like a spotlight, making the dark cap glimmer. If he wanted, he could lower his cheek and rub his mouth along the top of her head, feel the softness of her hair against his lips. If he wanted... What was he thinking, *if* he wanted. He wanted—bad.

When had his hands come up to cup her moon-kissed shoulders? Didn't matter. His hands were there, caressing her arms, learning the contours of her skin with his palms.

"Joe?" she whispered, and her breath blew along the exposed flesh at the open collar of his shirt.

His body hardened and his hands tightened. He

stepped back that single step, and when she raised her mouth, no doubt to tell him to go straight to blazes—he kissed her, right there in the playground.

THEY SAY IN THE SECONDS before you die, your entire life flashes before you. Evie didn't know about that, and hoped she would not find out soon, but she did discover that when you're sexually deprived, every fantasy you've ever had about a certain annoying, intriguing man flashes through your mind the first time he kisses you.

She'd lost her train of thought when his big hands touched her bare shoulders. Those hands skimmed her arms, as if he wanted to memorize the texture of her skin with his palms. His mouth tasted hers, softly at first, with a gentleness to those firm lips that made her heart stutter and dip. There was something about a rough, gruff, gentle man that did wicked things to a woman's insides.

If she didn't hold on, she'd fall. If she didn't touch him, she'd go mad. So she slipped her hands around his waist, her fingers encountering rock-hard muscle wherever they brushed. His shirt had a silky sheen and rubbed between her fingers and his flesh with a sexy slide.

He moaned against her mouth, and his hands went from gentle on her arms to demanding upon her back. Pulling her closer, he deepened the kiss, his tongue lining the seam of her mouth, sending a sharp trill of dangerous desire down her spine.

Her lips opened. His questing tongue slid along

her teeth, met, mated and retreated from her own. He enticed her into his mouth, where they played an arousing game of hide-and-seek.

The man knew what to do with that mouth of his. She could not recall ever being so excited by a single kiss. He had not moved his hands from her back, though his clever fingers soothed the knots from her shoulders in such a skillful, enticing way that she moaned with pleasure from that, as well as from the heat of his lips and the glide of his tongue.

Wherever this desperate need and yearning hunger had come from, it was too strong to deny. It had been so long since she'd felt anything beyond duty and responsibility and pressure to be the best mommy in town.

Evie stiffened. *Mommy.* What was she thinking? What was she doing?

She tore her mouth from his, and he took the opportunity to nibble her jaw, then nuzzle her neck. She nearly melted right back against his lips.

"Stop," she muttered. Her voice sounded unconvincing, even to her ears, but he pulled back.

Then he lifted his head and his icy eyes stared into hers. "Stop?" His voice, hoarse and sexy, made her insides twist. The man sounded as if he'd just spent three days in bed—without sleeping one of them. "Why?"

Evie pushed against his shoulders. He let her go, and she slipped out of his reach. The sultry night turned cold.

She glanced around furtively and breathed a sigh

of relief to find they were still alone. She could just imagine what would happen if news of this got around.

Evie winced as a sportscaster's voice filled her mind: *Big League manager caught playing footsie with Iceman Scalotta on playground just minutes after challenging Iceman to a duel of teams. Will the decision be made on the diamond or in the bedroom?*

"Evie?" Joe's voice was no longer hoarse and sexy, but confused and annoyed.

She looked back at him. He stood on one side of the swing, leaving her on the other. His mouth still shone wet and his shirt tangled half in and half out of his pants. He was so appealing that she wanted to shove the swing aside and haul his mouth back on hers.

Where would that lead?

The shiver that passed over Evie made the hair on her arms stand up. Her breasts tightened; her nipples hardened, rubbing against the cotton sundress in a movement that was both pain and pleasure, yet unbelievably arousing.

Joe took a step forward, and Evie put out a hand, palm facing him. "No. You stay over there."

"Why?"

"Just do it, hotshot. I can't think when you hover over me."

That made him smile in a satisfied, male way, which made Evie want to smack him. But to smack him she'd have to touch him, and right now touching would be a very bad idea.

"I'm going home," she said.

"I'll drive you."

"No!"

She wanted nothing less than to be caught in a small, enclosed space with Scalotta. That would also be very bad.

"I swear I'll drive slow and easy."

"I don't care if you drive slower than a tricycle. I'm not going anywhere with you tonight."

"I suppose you want me to apologize for kissing you. I won't do that."

"And why not?"

"Because I'm not sorry. I want to do it again. Right now."

He yanked the swing to the side, but before he could step toward her, she ran.

She wasn't proud of it, but she had little choice. She'd just learned something. There were things much more dangerous than stray cats out and about in Oak Grove at night.

CHAPTER NINE

JOE THOUGHT ABOUT THE BET and the kiss all the way home. Mostly the kiss. He hadn't kissed, or been kissed, that thoroughly for a very long time.

Though Evie was petite, she was not frail. She might only come up to his chest, but the muscles he'd traced with his fingertips had been firm, real, worked for on a field and not at a health club.

The breasts that had tickled his chest were real, too. Joe snorted. As though Evie would have had a boob job. She'd bloody his nose for the thought alone. And he'd deserve it.

To be honest, she always seemed taller—with her confidence, her opinions, and that mouth that told him where to go and gave him directions how to get there. But when he'd had her in his arms, he'd felt how tiny she was, and he'd wanted to hold her close and protect her from all the big, bad bogeymen of the world.

She'd laugh in his face if he told her that. If there was a woman on earth who did not need him to take care of her, that woman was Evie Vaughn.

Why should that bother him? Because he needed to be needed? Karen had never needed him, or wanted him—not after that first year. Her rejection had hurt. More than he had ever admitted to himself or anyone else.

Evie was the same way. She needed no one, least of all Joe Scalotta. She'd shown him that when she'd coolly stopped their embrace mid-kiss.

Joe had been lost in the wonder and heat of her. She'd tasted so sweet, felt so soft, smelled so good. When she'd yanked herself away, his hands had itched to yank her right back. When she'd run off into the night, leaving him alone beneath the moon, his gut had clenched so hard that he ached. Was it from denied passion or the eternal loneliness that threatened him every night after Toni fell asleep?

The sight of the Vaughn station wagon still parked in the driveway made the memories of a magical kiss leave Joe's body like air freed from a balloon. He was even less happy when a glance at the front windows revealed a darkened living room. At least the silver shadows of the television screen chased across the ceiling. If they hadn't, he would have run inside—rather than walking very fast.

Joe slammed the door, hoping that if there was any necking going on it would stop before he walked in. He didn't know what he'd do if he caught Adam with his hands and mouth where they did not belong. Especially since Joe's hands and mouth had just been where they didn't belong on Adam's mother.

Joe winced. That sounded bad, even to him. But what had happened between Evie and him had not been bad—it had been one of the best things to happen to him in years. He could still feel the remnants of sexual arousal deep within.

Why her? Why now?

Stepping into the doorway of the living room, Joe pushed aside philosophical questions to deal with the problem at hand. He scanned the occupants. They sat on the same couch, but not on the same side. They did not look guilty. But that didn't mean they weren't.

"Hello, Mr. Scalotta." Adam stood.

Joe nodded, proud when he kept the growl in his throat from coming out of his mouth.

"Hey, Joe." Toni wore shorts that covered less of her than her nightgown had, and a tank top without a bra. The growl broke free, but before he could follow up with words, Toni spoke, and Joe's train of thought disappeared.

"You and Coach Vaughn are getting to be the main source of entertainment in this town."

"You heard? How?" The grapevine in Oak Grove worked faster than CNN.

"News." She pointed at the television. "You just missed it."

"News?" He eyed his watch, which read 9:10. He'd been on that playground longer than he'd thought, but not long enough for the evening news to come on. On the East Coast they had news at eleven, so here it should be at ten. Shouldn't it? "They interrupted for a bulletin?"

"You weren't *that* important, though you were

the lead story. The news is at nine here. Farmers don't stay up until ten.''

"Don't they have any murders or robberies or kidnappings to report?''

Adam laughed, then swallowed the sound when Joe's gaze swung toward him. ''Nothing like that in Oak Grove. The last thing missing was Cory Radway's mountain bike.''

''Jeez, Joe, what were you thinking to make a bet like that with Adam's mom?'' Toni asked.

Joe shrugged and flicked on the light. The teens blinked in the glare, and Adam inched nearer to Toni. Joe came into the room, debated squeezing between the two, and decided such a move would just be too obvious. So he sat in his recliner, close enough to grab Adam if he needed to.

''Seemed the thing to do at the time,'' he said. ''Don't worry, honey. I doubt my team will get too far ahead.''

Toni started laughing. ''She's gonna smear you, Joe. We all are. It'll be embarrassing.''

Joe was speechless. His daughter was taking the other side. Then he realized—his daughter *was* the other side. What had he done, and how was he going to get out of this mess?

The phone rang, blaring in the momentary silence. All three of them jumped.

Toni answered, then held the phone out to Joe. ''It's for you. Steve Jameson.'' She smirked. ''He saw the news.''

Joe sighed and reached for the phone, then tried

to pay attention to what his boss, the athletic director of Oak Grove Community College, was telling him, as his daughter and *that boy* went outside to say good-night on the porch.

"Joe, what's this I hear about you getting involved in a little excitement tonight?"

"Uh, I don't know." Joe got up and moved to the front window. "What did you hear?"

Through amazing feats of contortion that stretched his back muscles in ways they hadn't been stretched for years, Joe discovered he could see the front porch quite well. And he didn't even have to twitch the curtains as his mom always had. A perfect little opening existed.

"Joe?"

He put his ear back to the phone and ended up tapping the glass with the earpiece. The sound seemed to echo throughout the house, and no doubt throughout the neighborhood. Wincing, Joe pulled back from his 007 position.

"Yeah," he said. "I'm here. What was that?"

"I said, it's a pretty smart move on your part to get in with the local media. And this bet with the teacher is pure brilliance. It's a human interest angle everyone will eat up like candy. Even though I had to fight to hire you, the way things are going, I'll be proved the smarter guy in the end."

Joe had been trying to peer through the curtains again, but as Steve's words registered, he straightened and devoted his attention to the conversation. "What do you mean you had to fight to hire me?"

Steve cleared his throat, uncomfortable. "Well, I guess it isn't a secret that most folks here wanted a teacher for this job and not a professional athlete."

"It was a secret to me. I do have a degree, you'll recall."

"Now, Joe—"

The voice was condescending, and Joe's teeth clenched.

"—everyone knows how athletes get degrees."

Joe counted to ten. Just because he was big, and he'd played football, everyone assumed he was dumber than the nearest rock. He had finished college, and he'd *earned* his degree.

"I am qualified to coach. I have a degree in physical education, and I trained for just this job."

"You did?"

Joe's lips tightened. The guy hadn't even read his résumé? He had done pretty well in college, considering he'd been on the road half the time, traveling to and from games, and practicing another quarter of the time. People always assumed college athletes were morons, but the truth was that a lot of them just couldn't manage the schedule.

"Never mind, Joe. I was right. You're a media dream boy. You'll bring the fans out in droves. If you can do it for a T-ball game, you can do it for football. That's what we need. People. Ticket sales. Money for the program."

"You hired me to be your dog-and-pony show?" Joe had spent most of his adult life as an exhibit of some kind. As much as he loved football, sometimes he'd felt like a circus animal more than a man. It stung to find out that the job he'd thought he'd gotten on the merits of his talent and education had been given to him so he could be another main attraction.

"Nothing like that!" Steve assured him—too fast to be telling the truth. "You're the coach. We've got an up-and-coming team. I hired you because I thought you were the best one for the job."

"I am." Joe hesitated. He could quit right now. He didn't *need* the money. But he'd signed the contract, and he'd never reneged on an agreement in his life. How would such behavior look to Toni? As though he were caving in when the going got tough, that was how.

Besides, the way news traveled around here, his contract disagreement with Oak Grove Community College would be on the Channel 8 breakfast edition the next day. He doubted he and his daughter would then be as welcome in town as they had been.

Deep down Joe really, really wanted to use the degree he'd worked so hard for all those years ago. To back out would not only look bad, but would probably keep him from getting another job for quite a while. He and Toni would have to move. He didn't want to do that to her. She seemed to like it here.

That thought made Joe lean forward and twist again—just in time to see Adam jog down the walk toward his car. Well, the kid couldn't very well have ravaged her on the doorstep in that short space, but

Joe was still annoyed he'd allowed himself to be distracted from his parental responsibilities.

Steve continued to talk, fast and furiously. "Truly, Joe, we want you here. You'll be great. The fact that you have a degree is only icing on the cake. I apologize. I should have told you that you're our last chance to save the football program at OGCC, but I was afraid you'd back out if you knew how important it was."

"Why would I have backed out?"

"Uh, well…" Steve stopped talking, and the line buzzed with an uncomfortable silence.

"Just say it, Steve. I'm a big guy."

"Your rep, Joe. All that Wildman stuff in the papers. Your divorce. Your daughter raised by nannies. People frown on that around here."

Joe winced. "I frowned on it myself."

"I realize it's none of my business. No one's business. But your image isn't that of a responsible public figure. Will you stick if things get tough?"

Joe sighed. He should have considered all those years ago what effect the press would have on his future. But he'd been too busy being Iceman—the Wildman—Scalotta. Now he wanted to change. He *had* changed, but no one believed him. So he would have to make people believe him by being what he had always wanted to be—a man just like his father.

"I hear you, Steve. But times have changed. I plan to put down roots here and be a pillar in this community. When things get tough, I'm going to be your man."

"Great." Steve's voice was too cheerful, down-right hearty, annoyingly fake. He didn't believe Joe, either. And he didn't care…as long as Joe did his job—which was bringing people back to football at OGCC. Well, he'd do that job by being the best darn coach they'd ever had, by making the team all that it could be. That didn't necessarily mean winning, either—something he was learning by coaching the little ones in T-ball. But he wasn't going to share his philosophy with old Steve.

The outside door opened, then shut. Toni appeared in the entryway of the living room with a dreamy look on her face that made Joe's teeth grind.

"Thanks for calling, Steve. I'll be in touch." With his eyes on his daughter, Joe hung up on Steve's continued assurances that Joe Scalotta was the best thing to hit Oak Grove since cable television.

His main worry was Toni. Not OGCC, not football, not baseball, not even his own stupid mistakes. Just Toni. Joe was going to do everything in his power to guarantee Toni did not make the same mistakes he had.

Which meant Joe wasn't going to make any more mistakes, either. What had happened between him and Coach Mom tonight would not be repeated. He'd screwed up by following the pull of his body and ignoring what was sensible, responsible and right.

He had come to Oak Grove to start a new life: raise Toni, get married, create a family. He was not going to get involved with a woman who was everything he did not want in a wife.

No matter how good she tasted. No matter how easily she fit in his arms. No matter how much he wanted her back there.

Because if he did that he'd be just the kind of guy everyone thought he was. The kind of guy he'd always been.

The kind of guy he'd determined never to be again.

EVIE LAY IN HER solitary bed and thought solitary thoughts. The twins were gone, and Adam had long since come home, shouted good-night and shut his door. She might *want* to call him in and quiz him on his relationship with Toni, but she wouldn't. She couldn't. If she didn't trust him the first time trust was called for, he'd never trust *her* again.

Whatever you teach them during the first ten years lays the groundwork for the rest of their lives. That was the motto of Evie's father, and he was a very wise man, not to mention an excellent small-town cop. Of course, Dad had never been able to explain those kids who had horrible childhoods but turned out fine and dandy, or the kids who became serial killers while their parents frowned and mumbled, "He was such a nice boy."

For the most part, Evie believed what her father had preached, which only made her more nervous where Adam was concerned. Because Adam had been eleven when Ray died, and Ray had been one big disaster—as a man, a husband, and particularly as a father. Still, if Adam were going to follow in Ray's idiot footsteps, Evie figured she'd have seen some indication of it before now.

Sighing, she turned over and stared at the ceiling. She could still hear Adam moving around in his room, but the sounds were comforting. She was not completely alone in the house, yet the near quiet was bliss.

Instead of lying here, not sleeping, she should probably be doing some of the things she could not do when the twins were around: like reading a book that would rot her mind instead of improve it— though she rarely had time to read improving books, either—or paint her toenails, or take a bubble bath.

But in her present state she would not be able to read; she'd only stare at the book and think of ice-blue eyes heavy with desire. She'd paint her ankle, not her toenails, while she thought of moonlit nights. In the bathtub she would imagine big hands sliding over wet skin, lips following the trail, bodies naked, writhing, warm, wet and—

"Doggone it!" Evie sat up and put her head between her knees.

Didn't help. Her brain still swam with lust. How was she going to face Joe at the ballpark? How was she going to sleep with visions of him in her head? How was she going to live without another kiss like that?

"Get over it, Evie. It was only a kiss," she muttered.

But it hadn't been *only a kiss*. For her, anyway. She did not go around kissing strange men. That made her laugh out loud, a sound she quickly stifled against the bedclothes before Adam heard and thought she'd lost her mind for good. She didn't go around kissing strange men because there were no strange men in Oak Grove. Okay, she didn't go around kissing anyone—except family, and that didn't count.

The only reason she could still feel Joe's mouth on hers was that she hadn't kissed a man in…Evie raised her head and tried to remember.

It seemed like forever and a day. No wonder she'd wanted to put her hand under that silky shirt, spread her palms over his very nice chest, put her lips to the tanned hollow of his throat and yank him down on the cool sand beneath the swing set.

Evie groaned and let her head fall back between her knees. As the twins would say, she was in deep doo-doo.

What was she going to do about it? Let nature take its course? Very bad idea, no matter how appealing.

Ignore him? Scalotta? Impossible.

Avoid him? Childish and impractical. Not only was she his de facto boss in the Little League department, but he was the twins' coach. And their teenagers looked to be gearing up for a summer of the age-old favorite game "attached at the hip." She wasn't even going to think about the bet they'd made and the consequences thereof.

"Well, you know what you're *not* going to do, Evelyn Ann," she said in her best mommy voice. "What are you *going* to do?"

The quiet was broken when the phone rang, shrill and stunning. She gasped, heart thundering, and grabbed the receiver before it could ring a second time. Visions of the twins in the emergency room had her levering her feet over the edge of the bed, toes searching for her shoes. The voice on the other end of the line made her freeze.

"Evie?"

Having Joe's voice whisper in her ear so soon after thinking of him in so intimate a manner, in the dark, in her bed, caused Evie's breath to hitch in shock.

"I hope I didn't wake you."

How could his voice sound so sexy? Was it because she couldn't see him, so she imagined him, instead? Was he sitting in his own bed—stark naked and aroused? She was aroused, but at least she was clothed—in a very old, faded, asexual button-down shirt.

"Evie, you there?"

She was dizzy, hot, and she couldn't breathe. Maybe because she was holding her breath. Letting the air out in a rush, then filling her lungs once more made the dizziness recede, at least a little.

"Yes, I'm here. Is something wrong?"

It was his turn to be silent, but she could still hear him breathing. In and out, slow and easy. Her skin tingled as she thought of his mouth near the phone, the phone near her ear. She could almost feel his breath, warm upon her neck. A caress like the wind stirring her hair.

"I wanted to apologize for tonight."

Evie blinked as her fantasy dissolved, and she groped for the meaning in his words. "Apologize?"

"For kissing you."

"You said you weren't going to apologize."

The words he'd uttered only hours before drifted through her mind; *Because I want to do it again. Right now.*

"I was wrong to kiss you. It won't happen again."

"All right." She knew she sounded as confused as she felt.

"I don't want you to get the wrong idea."

Annoyance beat a rhythm along her spine as she started to catch on to his problem. "And what would the wrong idea be?"

"That there could be anything serious or permanent between us."

Bingo. Just like a guy—kiss a woman and then panic because she might think you meant to marry her. Well, Evie wasn't going to let him off that easy.

"And there couldn't be anything permanent between us because…?"

"Well, we might have a kind of chemistry."

"Chemistry? You think so?" She put enough surprise into her voice to make him hesitate. Luckily, he couldn't see her smirk.

"Uh, yeah. Physical chemistry, but we wouldn't

be a good match. I figured I should put a stop to any thoughts in that direction.''

Her amusement turned to amazement, then blistered into outright anger. The nerve of the man! He really did believe she was already planning the reception.

"Hey, Wildman, I know your type. It was a kiss. Nothing more, nothing less. Don't flatter yourself into thinking it was special. You're good, I'll give you that. But I've had better." That ought to hurt. Men like him did not like to hear they weren't the best thing in pants.

"You don't need to get mad. I just don't want any hard feelings. I'm ready for a serious relationship. I'd like to start dating again, but—"

"Not me."

"You have to agree it would be a bad idea with all that's happened. The bet, and the news, and the kids."

"I agree. Bad idea."

"I meant to tell you—I don't want your job."

For a moment Evie just sat there, trying to keep up with the way his mind worked. The reminder of what had happened earlier that night, as frustrating as their kiss had been and as annoying as this conversation was, made her speak more sharply than usual.

"If you don't want my job, why did you agree to the bet?"

"I saw which way the wind was blowing. They wouldn't have given you the job, either. Mrs. Larson looked like she'd swallowed a bug. I thought you could use some help."

Evie hadn't asked for help since she'd applied for a job at Oak Grove. Which had gotten her indebted to a chauvinistic jerk. Twice over. "I don't need your help."

"And I don't want your job. If you want it so bad, I'll give it back to you when this is done."

She hadn't thought she could get any angrier. She'd been wrong. "*Give* it to me?" Her voice sounded high and thready. "Give it to *me?* Don't do me any favors. I'm going to win this bet, Scalotta. You are toast."

"That's what Toni said."

"Believe her. Good night."

"Hey, wait a minute."

She hung up on him. He was right about one thing—dating would be a very bad idea. Especially since right now she wanted to do him bodily harm. Still, he didn't have to say it right out, like she wasn't worthy or something. She didn't want to date him, either.

And she'd prove it. The next guy who asked her out, she'd say yes instead of no, for a change. She didn't need Joe Scalotta for kisses, dates or anything else.

CHAPTER TEN

TODAY WAS THE DAY Joe began his new life. He'd decided that this morning while drinking coffee on his porch as he watched the sun rise and spread day across his lawn. During those years when he'd lost control of things—playing football, traveling, partying, running to Chicago whenever he could to see Toni—he'd often soothed himself with the thought of drinking coffee at sunrise on his very own porch in some out-of-the-way town. For a change, the reality proved every bit as good as the fantasy.

Somewhere in the perfect hollow of Oak Grove was a woman for him. He just had to find her.

But first he had to stop thinking too much—about Evie.

He'd spent several sleepless nights caught between remembering the magic of their kiss and lecturing himself to forget her altogether. Evie hadn't seemed impressed or affected by their embrace. In fact, he'd made an idiot out of himself by calling her, and had angered her in the process.

"Good going, Joe," he muttered now as he drove to another game. "If it's Thursday, it must be T-ball. Monday and Wednesday are Big League."

When he arrived, several of his kids were practicing under the watchful eye of one of the moms. Joe recognized the red heads of the Vaughn twins, but a quick survey of the small, before-game crowd did not reveal Evie. He hoped her annoyance with him didn't extend to skipping the twins' games.

"Hey, Danny, Benji," he greeted them as the two ran up and hugged his knees. "Where's your mom?"

He winced when two pairs of bright blue eyes contemplated him with too much knowledge. "Why?"

Joe shrugged. He only asked because he didn't want her avoiding the game on his account. Not for any other reason. *Really.*

"You're here and she's not. Just curious."

"She had to drop Adam off at the high school diamonds. Him and Toni were going to practice, then she's coming back."

Joe frowned. Toni hadn't mentioned that.

"Hey, Coach Joe." One of the twins tugged his hand. "You're growlin' again. Mom says you do that 'cause you don't know how to come—come—"

"Communicate, moron," the other one offered.

Unfortunately, "moron" gave Joe no indication which twin was which.

"Shut up, Benji."

Aha! The one holding Joe's hand was Danny. Joe reached down and turned Danny's hat backward with a playful tug. That would help keep their identities straight for a while.

"That's what your mom said, huh?" For some

reason the fact that Evie had discussed him with the twins made Joe smile. Bad sign—especially since what she'd discussed with them hadn't been complimentary. He needed to stop caring about what she did, what she said, where she was.

The crowd for the game itself wasn't as large as the previous week's, but it was bigger than usual—or so he later heard. Joe turned his attention to the game. He enjoyed the job. Kids at this age were so joyous. They didn't care if they screwed up. They just wanted to have fun, and in teaching them, Joe discovered he just wanted to have fun, too. He'd never had the chance before. He'd played many years of ball—but he'd never really *played*. Until now.

And the best part of T-ball league? While occupied with the six- and seven-year-olds, he couldn't think about Evie, or Toni, or Adam, or anything but those twelve kids.

His team lost the game, and he didn't care. Neither did they. They beamed at him, slapped his hand, hugged his knees. It was so cool.

"Great job, guys. I'm proud of each and every one of you. You did your best and you had fun. That's what we're here for."

As they headed off to their parents like ants spilling from an anthill, Joe grinned. He would really like to have a bunch of kids of his own someday, but until then, he'd make due with these rentals—

"Coach?"

A woman's voice brought him out of his private

dream. He looked into a new face, a very pretty face. "Yes?"

"I just wanted to thank you for taking the team. My daughter, Kendra—" she pointed at a pigtailed little girl covered in dust "—is having a very good time."

"I'm glad." Joe grabbed his glove from the bench and surreptitiously glanced at Kendra's mom's left hand. No ring. Hmm...

"I have to tell you, I was concerned when I heard you'd taken the team."

"Join the club."

She smiled, and dazzled Joe. He'd always liked women—all kinds of women. They were, well, *women*—soft and sweet, and they smelled really good. When you spent most of your time with hard, loud, rough men who did not smell good at all, women became even more special.

"I was afraid you would be one of those win, win, win coaches who screamed all the time and expected perfection."

"From seven-year-olds?"

"You'd be surprised how many people do."

"Not me."

"Glad to hear that. Tell me, have you ever coached girls?"

"I have a daughter, Mrs...."

"Hanson. But it's not 'Mrs.' anymore—and you can call me 'Julie.'"

Joe nodded, stifling a smile.

"I know you have a daughter. May I call you 'Joe'?"

"Feel free."

She smiled that smile again. Joe really liked her smile—great teeth and excellent lips, though a bit too much makeup for a ball game. That made Joe frown.

He was comparing her with Evie, who didn't wear makeup at all and managed to look just fine. The thought of Evie made him glance about—only to discover her deep in what appeared to be a stimulating conversation with...a guy! The annoyance that flashed through Joe was strong and unwarranted. The man was probably another coach or some kid's dad, and Joe had no right to be jealous, or even wonder who she was talking to.

"Joe?"

"Yes." He turned back to Julie. "Sorry."

"Anyway, I was pleased to hear you had a girl of your own. A lot of coaches yell, and as you must know from your daughter—yelling at girls is a very bad idea."

"It is?" This was news to him.

Julie's eyes narrowed. "I thought you had a daughter."

"I do. But I just got custody."

"Oh?" She stood up straighter, and Joe couldn't help but admire the view. Julie had a very nice figure, though not as nice as— *Grr.* Why couldn't he quit comparing the two women? "You're divorced?" Julie asked.

"Yeah." Joe left it at that. He had no desire to spend his first conversation with an attractive, Oak Grove single woman talking about his fiasco of a past and the death of his already ex-wife.

"So you don't understand girls."

"Not at all," he confessed.

She laughed and put her hand on his arm, leaving it there too long.

For some reason, Joe glanced at Evie again, and caught her scowling at him while still talking to that guy. He yanked his gaze back to Julie.

"So, Julie, if you yell at girls, what happens?"

"They cry."

"So do boys."

"No!"

"Yes, just not in front of anyone. Unless they're little, like the guys here."

"Do you cry, Joe?"

"No one's dared to yell at me lately."

Her fingers flexed on his biceps. "I can see why."

Well, if that wasn't an opening, he'd never heard one. Joe took the plunge. "How about we continue this conversation over dinner tomorrow night?"

"I thought you'd never ask."

"Where should we go? I'm new in town."

"You certainly are." She sighed, as if in relief. "There's a halfway decent Italian restaurant on Main Street. Family owned. Been there forever. It's really the only game in town."

"Bertolusi's?" Joe asked, having seen the sign.

"That's the one. What time?"

"Pick you up at seven?"

While they went over the particulars of where she lived and how to get there, Joe looked toward Evie yet again—just as the guy leaned over and kissed her cheek.

"Excuse me?" Julie asked, peering at him strangely.

"I didn't say anything."

"You growled."

"Really?" He watched as Evie and her new friend walked toward the parking lot together. "I didn't realize."

"IF YOU USE TODD as your cleanup pitcher, I really think you'll be glad. I've been teaching him since he was itty-bitty, and if I do say so myself, I was quite the player in my day."

She deserved this, Evie knew. But that didn't make listening any easier. This was what she got for accepting the first date that came her way. But how on earth was she going to make the memory of Joe Scalotta's kiss a thing of the past when all she did while Chad Roland droned on and on about his son was fantasize about kissing Joe again beneath an Iowa moon?

Bertolusi's was rarely crowded, even on a weekend. Tonight was no exception. Four couples, including Evie and Chad, graced the dining room.

The restaurant resembled an old-time drugstore, complete with soda counter. Perhaps because that was what it had been twenty years ago. The owners had converted the antique counter into a bar and hung plastic grapes and vines across the front. This gave the illusion of Italy on a shoestring. But the decor became irrelevant once you tasted the great food.

"Evie?"

She glanced at Chad and realized he'd actually stopped talking long enough to hear her opinion. He wouldn't like it, but that wasn't going to stop her from giving it.

"I agree that Todd is a good pitcher, but he does better as a starter. He does not pitch well under pressure, which usually comes at the end of a game."

"And that Scalotta chick does?"

Evie had been picking at her fettuccine Alfredo. The food was excellent as always, but the company had ruined her appetite. She gave up trying to eat and put the fork down very carefully next to her plate, lest she reach across the table and stab Chad in the hand.

"Her name is Toni. She's a young woman and not a chick. And, yes, she does pitch well under pressure."

Chad was too oblivious to catch the undercurrent in Evie's voice. He just went on—and on.

"She didn't do too hot last time she was out there. Your team lost."

"She didn't let things upset her and she kept going. I'm trying to build young men and women of character, not neurotic brats who only know how to win."

He continued on as if he hadn't even heard her. He probably hadn't. "If you'd give Todd a chance, you'd see he can do the job."

"I've given him a chance, and it didn't work out."

"So all you care about is winning? I should have known that, considering the bet you made in front of God and everyone."

Luckily she'd put the sharp object down, because now she was really mad. "You know me, and you know how I coach. I don't put wins ahead of kids. Todd does not play well at the end of a game, and it upsets him when he loses."

"So what? He needs to get used to pressure. It's a fact of life."

"Not at sixteen. He's got enough pressure worrying if everyone likes him, or if the zit on his chin will be gone before Saturday night. He doesn't need to worry about acting out your fantasy in Big League. Baseball isn't that important in the scheme of life."

"Really?" He leaned back in his chair and stared at her. "I never thought I'd hear that from you. I figured you'd do whatever it takes to make your team number one."

"You figured wrong."

But Chad's words made Evie think. She'd been so mad about the school board offering Joe her job that she'd made a bet dependent upon winning. Not that she would have to exert pressure on her team to win. They were good—because she coached them well and knew each kid's strengths and weaknesses. She was a good teacher. She *was* the best person for the varsity coaching job. Evie truly believed that, or she wouldn't have asked for it, nor would she have decided to fight for it. But to get the job, she had to win.

So was she setting a bad example by this bet? Probably. Should she call the whole thing off?

Evie sighed. If she did, Joe would get the job. He said he didn't want it, but then why had he made the bet? She didn't trust him—and why should she?

Still, she hadn't seen any indication he was a bad influence. *Yet.* But his past did not bode well. Sure, he might settle down long enough to get Toni acclimated, but then what? Maybe Evie should talk to Joe, if she could manage to be in the same room with him and not belt him—or kiss him.

"Well, isn't this interesting." Chad peered over Evie's shoulder toward the door with a smirk on his lips. "If it isn't the Wildman himself. And look who he's hooked up with. Unruly Julie."

Evie didn't dare turn around and ogle, though all the others in the place did just that. If Joe was dating Julie Hanson, that meant trouble. Julie had always been a problem.

Every town had its wild child, and Oak Grove had Julie. In a town this small, everyone knew everything she did almost before she did it. The one thing Julie wanted more than anything else, and she made no secret about it, was to get out of Oak Grove forever. She must have latched on to Joe hoping for a ride.

In Evie and Joe's annoying phone conversation, Joe had said quite plainly that he wanted a serious relationship. If that relationship was Julie, then Joe didn't mind leaving Oak Grove in the future—the near future, if Julie had her way.

Joe's choice of date made Evie rethink her position on their bet. She *would* be the best person for the job. She wasn't going anywhere, probably for the rest of her life, and that was just fine with her. She loved Oak Grove. Everything she'd ever needed or wanted was right here.

As Joe and Julie passed her table, Evie looked up, right into ice-blue eyes. Joe seemed surprised to see her. She had to admit, though, it *was* strange they both had a date at Bertolusi's on the same night.

Joe nodded politely, but Julie kept on going. She and Evie were acquaintances, no more, since Julie was about ten years younger than Evie. Trust Joe to find a date barely past the age of majority.

Chad snickered as Joe and Julie took their seats. Evie pulled her gaze from Joe, who looked far too good in a suit and tie, back to her date.

"So what do you think?" He nodded toward the other couple.

Evie shrugged. "Not my business."

"No? I kind of figured you and Scalotta had something going."

Evie's hand jerked, and she nearly spilled the water she'd been about to drink. "Why would you figure that?"

Chad's smile widened. "Everyone saw you two nose to nose at the board meeting. The sparks flew. To be honest, I was surprised when you agreed to go out with me."

So was I, but it won't happen again, Evie promised herself.

"There's nothing between Joe and me but that bet."

"Hmm. Then how did his kid get to be your number-one pitcher?"

"Because of her talent, not her father's charm—such that it is. Is that what this is all about, Chad?" She waved her hand to indicate the restaurant, the table, them.

He shrugged but he didn't speak, which told her the truth. Her first date, and it was because someone's daddy wanted to weasel his baby boy a better position on her team. Well, she'd always had to learn the hard way. Why should this be any different?

"Thanks for the dinner, Chad, but I'll walk home. Think about what I said, and let Todd find his own path."

Evie stood, picked up her purse and calmly exited the restaurant. As the door swung shut behind her, she vowed this would be the last date for her.

JOE WASN'T PAYING attention to Julie; he was watching Evie leave her date high and dry. He'd be a liar if he said he didn't enjoy that.

When he'd come in and seen her there, the rush of joy had been followed quickly by a surge of jealousy toward the pretty boy who had brought her—the same guy who had kissed her cheek at the ballpark. Joe would never kiss any woman's cheek, for crying out loud. Maybe women enjoyed it, but that was just too bad.

The guy looked like her type. A blond, sunbronzed, suit-and-tie boy—not too tall or too bulky; he wouldn't tower over Evie the way Joe did. He would never yank on his tie and wish he could rip the thing off before he strangled. That guy probably slept in a tie—and liked it.

"Hey, Joe?"

He brought his attention back to Julie with an apologetic smile. "Yeah, I'm here. Should we order some wine?"

"Ooh, could we get champagne? We can celebrate."

What they had to celebrate, Joe didn't know, but he hated to disappoint a lady. He shrugged and handed her the wine list, which she pored over like a kid taken to a candy buffet. At least that kept her quiet for a while. She hadn't stopped talking since they'd gotten into his car.

She was too young for him. Joe could see that now. At the ballpark, beneath the night lights, which flattered no one, he'd thought her at least thirty. Since she had a six-year-old daughter, that seemed right. But now he could see she was twenty-five, if that, which made her more than ten years younger than him. He just wasn't going to go there.

Though he'd admired Julie's shiny red dress when he picked her up—how could he not when the fact that it was a size too small showcased her ample charms to the utmost?—now she reminded him of Marilyn Monroe when she'd sung "Happy Birthday" to JFK. He'd read somewhere that Marilyn had to be sewn into her dress, and this had contributed to her breathy, sexy rendition. Joe could imagine Julie needing the same treatment to get into her red number. She'd definitely need to be cut out of it. Joe didn't plan to be the guy holding the scissors.

After seeing Evie in her buttercup-yellow sundress and sandals, bare legs and feet peeking from beneath the hem as she swished out the door, the sight of Julie made his eyes sore.

Tonight Evie had worn a little makeup, too, just enough for her summer tan to glow. A little blush, a bit of lipstick. And she'd done something to her eyes that had made him go hot all over. Joe wiped his forehead with his napkin. Or maybe it was just too warm for a suit and tie.

"How about Dom Perignon?" Julie asked. "I've always wanted to try some."

"Fine." Joe signaled the waiter and placed the order. Champagne was champagne to him. All things equal, he'd rather have a Budweiser.

"So tell me about the bright lights and the big cities," Julie said as she guzzled Dom. At this rate she'd be loopy before the main course. Joe nudged the bread basket her way, but she just kept staring at him over the rim of her glass, waiting for an answer.

"Not much to tell. You don't see a lot of a town when you're on the road."

"No? I always thought you guys got star treatment. The best bars, the best restaurants, limos, champagne."

Joe resisted the urge to roll his eyes. She was so young. "Not exactly. You zoom in a few days before a game. Practice so you know the field. Eat at the hotel. Rest as much as you can in another strange bed. And try to focus your mind on your job."

Her smile became a pout. "That doesn't sound like the party-loving Wildman I've heard about."

"I admit I did my share of partying in my youth."

She lifted the bottle in a toast before pouring herself another glass. "So I hear. You're going to have slim pickings around here. This town is hick-ville."

"I find it charming."

She laughed, too loud, and the few patrons in the restaurant glanced their way. "Charming? As in 'Prince'? That's my plan, Wildman. You're my Prince Charming."

Joe frowned. He didn't like talk of plans. Of course, *he* had one, but that didn't count. His was wholesome and American. He had a feeling Julie's was anything but.

He downed his champagne and refilled his glass,

more to keep Julie from drinking than because he liked the stuff. Seventy-five dollars a bottle. *Jeez.*

Their salads arrived, and Joe dug in. Julie picked at hers. He wished she'd eat, but he suspected eating wasn't an option in that dress.

"So what are your plans, Julie? Your hopes and your dreams?"

"They're all the same. Get outta this dump."

Joe glanced around, hoping the waiter wasn't nearby. "This is a nice restaurant."

"It's the best in town, which isn't saying much. But I meant get outta town. When you go, I plan to go with you."

Joe choked on a cherry tomato, took a gulp of champagne and choked some more. When he finally got his breath back he shook his head. "Julie, I'm not going anywhere. I've come to Oak Grove to stay. I plan to settle down, have a family."

Her bull's-eye red mouth fell open. "No way."

"Yes, way."

She ran a fingertip down the back of his hand where it rested on the table. He felt nothing.

"I could change your mind. Just think of how impressed everyone would be if you showed up with a young, gorgeous wife. You'd look like the stud I'm sure you are."

Actually, he'd look like the idiot he was. Joe sighed. "I think we've misunderstood each other's motives. I want a woman to spend the rest of my life with. And I plan to spend it here, in Oak Grove.

I want more kids. A dog, even. The American dream.''

Julie shuddered. "You mean 'nightmare.' Let me clue you in, Joe. You won't find a woman who wants to share that dream within fifty miles of here. We all want out." She tipped back the last of her champagne. "Preferably yesterday."

CHAPTER ELEVEN

JOE KEPT TRYING. He'd never been a quitter. But after several weeks, and many more dates, he had to admit Julie was right. Every single woman *in* Oak Grove only wanted *out*.

Dating became a chore, like a job he despised. Since Joe hadn't had a job he hated this much since he was fourteen and spent the summer baling hay—a dirty, sweaty, backbreaking, soul-smashing job—he didn't know how to handle the helpless despair that came over him when he discovered his dream was everyone else's nightmare. The unaccustomed feeling of failure kept him awake nights, which only made his aching loneliness worse.

He was busy enough. He had T-ball games and practice, and Big League games and practice. The little kids had no idea who he was—or, rather, had been. They just liked him, and Joe liked them. The big kids had taken a few days to warm up. They'd gotten his autograph, tiptoed around, asked him about star teammates, then got back to business. Even the kids on Toni's team now seemed to see him as just another dad. Joe was glad.

To be honest, he probably scheduled more practices than necessary just to have something to do.

But it was summer; his kids were bored, too, and they didn't seem to mind.

What Joe minded was the continuing interest in his team, Evie's team and the silly bet they'd made. Attendance at T-ball increased, his Big League games were standing-room only and Evie's weren't much better. Every week or so a camera crew showed up and filmed a game, or the kid reporter who had written the first story on the school board meeting wrote another article, keeping the bet the talk of the town. Joe had to figure Mrs. Larson spent her spare time piling kindling on the already smol-dering fire between Evie and him.

He even got a letter from the president of OGCC, thanking him for being such a team player, which made Joe feel like a fraud. He had no one to blame but himself, his overblown sense of competition—and his secret desire to rescue damsels in distress, even when they spit in his eye. The fact that he had no one to talk to about how he felt made Joe lonelier than ever.

Toni spent as much time with her team as Joe spent with his. Then there was Adam, hogging all her attention—not to mention the days and evenings she spent in the Vaughn household. Heck, she was over there right now. Joe was supposed to meet her at the game. Even when Joe managed to catch Toni home for an hour or two, all he heard was "Coach this" and "Coach that" or "Mrs. Vaughn says..." blah, blah, blah.

It took Joe awhile before he admitted he was jealous of Evie's relationship with his little girl—a self-ish reaction. Obviously, Toni needed a woman in her life right now. But along with dreams of a family and a white-picket fence, Joe had harbored dreams of a special friendship with his daughter.

"So much for every dream I've ever had," Joe muttered as he pulled into the parking lot of Oak Grove's only grocery store.

The one thing he'd discovered joy in was cooking. Go figure. Someone had to do it, and the shopping, and the cleaning. He could hire a housekeeper, but why, when he really didn't mind the work? Besides, he didn't want anyone hovering about and interfering with the small amount of time he did get with Toni.

That she seemed to enjoy what he prepared and was proud that he wasn't all thumbs in the kitchen made Joe continue to hone his newly discovered homemaking skills. In fact, whenever Toni caught him at something domestic, she smiled as though he was doing something clever and cute. He lived for those smiles.

Joe especially liked the grocery store. All that stuff to pick from, so many choices, so many possibilities. He puttered through the place at least twice a week.

"Hey, Joe!" called the produce manager. "Need anything special today?"

"Got any portobello mushrooms, Frank?"

"You Italians, you always want the best for the sauce, eh?"

"Only the best makes the best," Joe agreed amiably. Frank had become the closest thing Joe had to a friend around here. The others all seemed to have their circle of friends from childhood and no one seemed eager to add Joe to the mix. Probably because they figured he'd be gone soon enough. He doubted his reputation helped, either.

Joe contemplated the mushrooms, then the tomatoes. He had his hands full of zucchini, when someone smashed into his cart.

"Oops, sorry. Oh, Joe."

He looked up to find Evie staring at him in shock. He smiled, truly pleased to see her, which was a bad thing, he knew, but right now he felt so lonely that he needed one little ray of sunshine—even if it was the forbidden woman of his dreams.

"You shop?" she asked, her face and voice filled with amazement.

"Sure. I find it..." He searched for a word to describe his enjoyment of the process.

"Irritating? Horrifying? Time-consuming? Pointless?"

It was Joe's turn to look amazed. "I was going to say soothing. Enjoyable. A barrel of fun."

"Ha! You're joking right?"

"No. I *really* like it."

"What is there to like? You spend a ton of money, then you come home and everyone says, 'There's no food around here.' Or, 'You bought the wrong thing.' Or they complain there's not enough of one thing, or not the right things to make anything. Then in less than a week you have to do it all over again. I loathe grocery shopping. I never figured you'd be doing it.''

''If not me, then who?''

She frowned. ''Don't you eat out a lot?''

He could tell by her expression that she recalled the last time they'd seen each other when not at a ball game. Bertolusi's. The scene of his first, but not his last, disastrous date. Since he didn't want to discuss that, Joe ignored the implication.

''Eating out all the time wouldn't be good for Toni, even though she eats at your house more than mine.''

''The more the merrier. Toni helps me out.''

''She does?''

''Sure. The twins love her. She keeps them out of my hair. And Adam's.''

''I'm glad you're enjoying her.'' Joe immediately wished he could take back the comment; he sounded cranky. But what was said was said. He shrugged and placed the zucchini he most admired in his cart.

Evie tilted her head. ''I suppose you'd like her back once in a while. I apologize for monopolizing her. She's a great kid.''

''So you don't want to keep her away from your baby boy anymore?''

''I doubt anything I say or do would change that. They seem pretty stuck on each other.'' She looked about as happy about it as Joe was. ''Right now, I prefer the devil I know over the devil I don't. Besides, if they're in my living room, I can keep tabs on where they are and what they're up to.''

''Devious.''

''A mother's middle name.''

They smiled at each other—companionably, like friends. Joe enjoyed it.

Evie glanced into his cart and her face reflected confusion. ''You cook?''

''Once again, someone has to.''

''I figured you for a TV dinner kind of guy.'' She held up her hand. ''I know—not good for Toni. But where did you learn to cook?''

''From a book.''

''You can do that?''

''What? Read?''

There must have been enough lingering anger in his voice to reach her, because she appeared embarrassed. ''I didn't mean that.''

''I know. It's just…''

''Everyone thinks you're stupid because you're a football player?'' He nodded. ''Frustrating, isn't it?''

''What would you know about it?''

''Just because I'm a girl, everyone wants to put me in a slot I don't want to be in.''

''Like?''

''Teach home ec rather than phys ed. Or coach the girls' softball team, not the boys' baseball team. What's the difference?''

''Girls aren't boys.''

"Really? I wish I'd known that before I raised three sons."

"Touché," Joe said.

"Joe Scalotta speaks French? Stop the presses."

"Please, don't. I've had enough press for one life-time."

"Me, too." She indicated with a toss of her head that they should continue on. "If I have one more microphone shoved in my face, I'm going to scream into it."

Joe smiled at the image as he grabbed a loaf of Italian bread. Evie grabbed three loaves of generic wheat bread.

"Our teams are tied," he observed.

She shot him a glance. "So I hear," she said dryly.

Not surprisingly, that was all anyone talked about—at the drugstore, in the barbershop, on the news. He wished someone would grow a duck-shaped potato or something and get him off the lead at nine.

"Mrs. Larson looks ten years younger," Evie went on. "This is a coup such as she never dreamed of. I played right into her hands, losing my temper like that and making the bet."

"So did I. They weren't going to go for it until I opened my big mouth."

"So back out."

"I thought you didn't want me to 'give' you the job?"

"Quitting isn't the same as giving."

"I can't quit."

"Sure you can."

He sighed. "Not anymore. My boss at OGCC thinks all this publicity will be good for the school. I didn't know it when I came here, but if I can't turn the football program around, there won't be one. I want that job. I trained for it. I've wanted to be a teacher and a coach since I was a kid."

"Me, too."

Joe glanced at Evie. She stared at him with a serious, contemplative expression on her face—almost as if she'd never seen him before this moment.

"I'll be good at that job," he told her.

She nodded. "And I'll be a good varsity coach. Much better than you."

Her attitude made Joe's teeth grind. He didn't want her job. But the way she kept on insisting he couldn't handle it made him see red. "Do you really think it's in your children's best interests for you to take another job?"

She had been holding a can of ravioli. When she threw it into the cart with more speed than necessary, he flinched. "It's none of your business what's in my children's best interests, *Wildman*."

With that she pushed her cart down the aisle as if she were driving a bumper car and disappeared around the corner. A smash and a curse had him shaking his head.

Temper, temper. She certainly had one. Why did he suddenly find that so appealing?

EVIE DROVE DIRECTLY from the grocery store to the house, and while Adam and the twins dragged the bags inside, Evie and Toni threw the perishables into the fridge and freezer, then left the canned goods on the counter to be attended to later.

She only lost one gallon of milk when Benji and Danny decided to make an assembly line and toss things from one to the other between the car and the kitchen door. It was absolutely amazing how far a gallon of milk could splatter when it hit the pavement. NASA should do a study on the physics involved.

Getting mad was counterproductive, given the amount of time she had left to transport them all to the game. So she docked each twin a dollar and a quarter, and corralled all four kids into the car.

Why did her life always run on fast-forward?

The twins squabbled in the back, even though Toni sat between them. With an admirable calm, considering the teenager couldn't be used to such commotion and arguing, Toni ignored them both, even when they climbed all over her.

"Guys?" Evie settled into the passenger seat, and Adam started the car. "What ever happened to rule number four?"

"He's not my em-eny," said Danny, throwing an arm around Benji's neck and yanking him as close as the seat belt and Toni's body would allow. "He's my brother."

Evie's eyes met Toni's, and they smiled at

Danny's persistent mangling of *enemy*. They really were cute—sometimes even when they were awake.

Evie hadn't lied to Joe when she'd said she was fond of Toni. The girl fit into the Vaughn household as if she belonged there. Evie was used to having most of the kids in the neighborhood at her house in the summer. She was one of the few parents on the block at home all day, and it didn't bother her to have kids there, as long as they behaved. But the extras were usually boys.

Having a girl around, especially one who so obviously needed a woman's attention, gave Evie a warm feeling that she hadn't had since the last time one of the boys had sat on her lap and cuddled. However, Joe's sad face when he talked about Toni not being around had struck a chord in Evie. He loved his daughter—and in Evie's book, the depth of that love in such a rough, gruff man made up for a lot of annoyances.

She focused on the twins, who were now giving each other noogies. "If he's not your enemy, then why are you fighting?"

"We aren't fighting." Benji sat up, which at least put him back on his own side of Toni. He appeared genuinely puzzled at her question. "Besides, Mom, we've been trying to keep to the rules, but you haven't even noticed how we've been drying our Hot Wheels off instead of throwing them into the sink. What good is trying if you don't even notice?"

Evie *had* noticed, mainly because the two of them had used her last pair of un-run pantyhose to do their drying. She deserved it for hanging those hose to dry in the bathroom, then putting the twins into the tub.

"Give it up, Mom," Adam said. "You lose."

Evie sighed and faced forward. Sometimes she felt as if there were a great big *L* on her forehead. *Loser.* She couldn't seem to win. Her life spun out of control. Never enough time to do what had to be done. Never enough money to do what she dreamed of doing. Never enough Mommy to go around.

Then Scalotta had the guts to say she might not be doing what was best for her kids. How could that man haunt her dreams, when most of the time she wanted nothing more than to kick him in the shins? Or make him disappear—*Poof!*—never to bother her again.

The way he'd been dating nearly every unattached woman in Oak Grove above the age of consent and below Social Security was the talk of the town, right below "the bet." Though his relationship with Unruly Julie hadn't lasted more than a single date, still, Evie harbored a secret fear that one of his honeys would convince him that anywhere was better than here, and he would indeed be gone—*Poof!*—and Toni, too. Evie wasn't ready to lose the girl yet, even if it meant putting up with Scalotta at twenty paces.

They pulled into the parking lot, to find Joe sitting alone at the top of the home-team bleachers. He looked so lonely there, the setting summer sun blazing on his hunched shoulders and shading his silver-blond hair white.

Evie glanced at Toni and caught her frown. Something was going on with those two—and it was really none of Evie's business. But the tension between them troubled her.

The twins tumbled out of the car, shrieking, ''Joe!''—then raced straight for him. No matter how many times she admonished them to call him ''Mr. Scalotta,'' they still called him ''Joe.'' He didn't seem to mind. In fact, he really got along well with them, having a lot more patience with their antics and chatter than Evie did.

They swarmed up the bleachers and sat, one on either side. His smile was warm, and Evie heard his laugh rumble across the heated air, then dance down her spine. What was it about this man that set her teeth on edge and shifted her body into overdrive?

Toni and Adam pulled the equipment out of the back. ''We've got it all, Mom,'' Adam said. ''Go on.''

She smiled her thanks and meandered toward the field, watching Joe with her two sons. They talked to him the way they talked to everyone they met. But they also leaned into him, put their hands on his arm or his knee, completely trusting of this huge man who had so recently been a stranger.

Joe's face lit up as if he'd discovered a secret, and he reached over and playfully turned Benji's baseball cap around. His eyes met hers over the boy's head, and there passed between them one of those moments she often remembered in the darkest part of the night. Though she'd made mistakes of epic proportion in her life, she wanted, right now, to make another. She wanted to kiss Joe Scalotta again. She wanted to kiss him, and she didn't want to stop there.

With the double-vision granted to all mothers in childbirth, Evie held Joe's gaze and was still able to observe the twins grin, giggle; then Benji pulled his hat forward, and Danny slid his backward. They bounded down the bleachers and raced after Adam and Toni.

Evie stopped at the foot of the stands. "You do realize they're onto you."

Confusion dropped over Joe's features like a storm cloud over a sunny afternoon. "Who?"

"The twins. It's their favorite game."

"You've lost me."

"I told you they'd switch on you. They think it's a riot when you call them by the wrong name."

He grinned, the expression lighting his eyes, and she had to smile back, even though she was still annoyed with him for questioning her parenting, and for being so darn attractive. He couldn't help it, but that didn't mean she had to like it.

"But I've figured out how to tell them apart."

"Uh-huh." Her voice reflected her skepticism.

"No, really. I talk to them until one of them lets slip who's who. Then I turn back their caps, or turn up their sleeves."

"And as soon as you look away, they switch."

"What?"

She laughed at the shock on his face. "They just did it with their hats. They might be seven, but they're not stupid."

Joe shook his head and gave a wry chuckle. "I thought I was so clever."

"Cleverer minds than yours have been foiled by those two. They have an uncanny ability to know when someone can tell them apart on sight."

"And how many people possess this mystical ability?"

"Me and Adam."

"What about their teachers?"

"They're in separate classes. It's better for them not to be together all the time. So each poor teacher knows which one is in his or her class from day one."

"And have they switched on their teachers?"

Evie smiled. "Only once."

He nodded. "I see. You caught them."

"Yep."

"And then?"

"It wasn't pretty."

"So what should I do?"

"Keep going as you have been. But as soon as you make your mark, assume they've switched. After you've identified them a few times correctly, they'll think you've acquired the gift and quit yanking your chain."

"Sounds like a plan."

"I'm great with plans."

His gaze sharpened on her face, as if she'd said something fascinating, though Evie couldn't think what that might be. Before she could ask, Adam called to her, and Evie became caught in the whirl of pregame warm-ups.

The increase in the size of the crowds for these games had so far been an annoyance more than a problem. Little League, in all forms and sizes, carried a written rule of good sportsmanship—for the coaches, players and parents.

No one was allowed to taunt an umpire or a player. The umpires, being older players themselves, made mistakes. They were learning, just like the players, and to argue a call was not permitted. Not only did it encourage everyone to argue everything, but arguing with authority figures set a bad example for players. If something needed to be discussed, the coach and the umpire spoke quietly, away from the scene of the action.

It was the coach's responsibility to keep the team and the crowd in line. Evie always nipped trouble in the bud, just as her father had taught her, and had therefore never had a serious crowd problem before. But there was an exception to every rule.

The culprits materialized as a gaggle of sixteen-year-old girls who had their sights on Adam. Since he never noticed anything that wasn't wearing a baseball uniform, they had taken extreme measures, fashioning themselves into the Adam Vaughn personal cheerleading section.

The entire thing, though embarrassing to Adam,

was not cause for ejection from the game. Tonight, however, their cheers for Adam turned to catcalls for Toni, when Evie's closing pitcher walked in a run. The fact that Adam had taken notice of a girl in a uniform had turned his crowd of admirers into antagonists.

"...Pull her out!"

"...We want a pitcher, not a belly itcher!"

"...Pitcher can't pitch."

"...She throws like a girl."

"...But she can't be a girl. Look at her."

Shrill laughter followed each taunt. Evie glanced at Toni, who had flushed red and seemed to shrink in upon herself. Her next pitch hit the batter in the back, and the away crowd hissed.

Evie stood up. Time to get rid of the problem.

The girls saw her coming and blanched.

Evie didn't plan to make an issue; she just planned to make them go. "You know the rules, girls. Home."

Several started to shuffle away, but one—there was always one—took a belligerent stance and stepped forward. "It's a free country, Mrs. Vaughn."

Evie lowered her voice so only Laura could hear her. She knew better than to embarrass a teenager in public, no matter how much it might be deserved. "You're mistaken, Laura. You're standing in my little country, and it certainly isn't free. Not if free means taking potshots at someone who's doing her best in a tough spot. Now, you can leave, quietly, since you've embarrassed yourself enough. Or I can call your daddy and tell him what you've been up to.''

Since Laura's daddy was also a coach, and a stickler for the rules, Laura resorted to dagger glares and slunk off after of her friends.

The game continued while Evie did her job, though no one watched the ball in play; they all watched Evie. Upon her return to the bench, Hoyt informed her that Toni had thrown a wild pitch, but Adam had tagged out the lead runner when the kid tried to steal home.

''You'd better get that little girl and bring her on in,'' Hoyt advised.

Evie shook her head. ''I don't think so.''

''She's gonna blow a five-run lead!''

''Then she blows it.''

''You know, sometimes I wonder if you want to win that dang bet or not.''

''I only want to win if I win doing things my way.''

''Sinatra? I don't hear him.''

Evie sighed. Sometimes Hoyt got on her nerves as much as the twins did. Though his hearing wasn't the best, his eyes were as sharp as a fifteen-year-old's. He could tell if a pitcher pulled up too soon, or if a batter swung too late. Evie depended upon Hoyt to watch when she could not.

''Never mind Sinatra,'' Evie said, as Toni walked her second batter.

''You gonna go get her, or should I?''

"I guess I'd better talk to her."

"Talk? You wanna win this game or not?"

"Not—if it means I take out a kid who'd be better off in. You know, Hoyt, I think today just might be Toni's man-or-mouse day."

"Huh? Whatcha talkin' about?"

"You know—what are you, a man or a mouse? Woman or wimp? I think she's a woman. You wanna make a bet on that?"

He considered her for a long moment. "No, ma'am," he finally said.

Evie called time and walked toward the mound, waving Adam off when he would have followed. Before she even spoke, Toni handed her the ball.

"Sorry," she mumbled.

"Do you want out?" Evie asked.

Toni glanced up, surprised. "Don't you want me out?"

"No. But it's up to you. If what just happened has thrown you too much to keep going, I'll let Todd finish. He's been whining about it enough." *Like father like son,* Evie added silently.

Toni gave a small smile, which encouraged Evie. "I'll tell you what my father always told me. Kids are mean. It's sad, but it's true. And I don't know why."

"Adam's not mean."

"No. But then, Adam's never been much of a kid."

"I want to win," Toni whispered.

"That's fine, if that's what *you* want."

Toni's glance from beneath her baseball cap made Evie frown. Seemed she'd hit a nerve.

"Coach!" The umpire warned Evie her time was up. She would need to explore that winning-losing nerve at a more opportune moment.

Evie tossed the ball in the air, then held it in front of Toni's nose like a prize. "In or out? Your choice."

Toni took the ball. "I've never been much of a kid, either."

Evie resisted the urge to kiss her. Just barely. She gave a thumbs-up to Hoyt, who returned the gesture with a sweet smile of confusion. Before Evie gained her seat, the guttural shout of "Strike!" erupted from the umpire.

Evie smiled. She absolutely loved it when she was right.

CHAPTER TWELVE

JOE WAS FIT to be tied. How dare Evie convince Toni to stay when she was obviously done in? After those rotten little brats had hurt his baby's feelings, he'd wanted to go and haul her out on his own. He'd restrained himself. With difficulty.

The rest of the game he spent in anguish for Toni, but she seemed to come through fine—earning the save, slaps on the back from her teammates and an annoying, too-familiar whirl in her catcher's arms that made Joe grind his teeth.

While the kids were occupied with their celebration dance, Joe stalked over to Evie. Her slight smile of welcome became an openmouthed expression of confusion when he asked for a private chat.

"Why didn't you take her out?" he demanded as soon as they stepped away from prying ears.

"Excuse me?"

"She was obviously upset, and you convinced her to stay in the game. Why?"

"I didn't realize you possessed super-hearing powers."

Her sarcastic tone brought him up short. "What's that supposed to mean?"

"You heard what I said to her? All the way from the stands to the pitcher's mound?"

"Of course not."

"Then how can you be so sure I convinced her to stay?"

"She's your best pitcher. Why wouldn't you?"

He'd seen Evie blush, but he'd never seen her flush with anger. She looked ready to slug him. Joe cast a glance at her hands and found them balled into fists. What had he said?

Though she was visibly furious, she didn't shout at him. Come to think of it, he'd never seen her shout, either, and with the twins around that was pretty talented. Instead, when she spoke her voice was so low that Joe had to lean close to hear her.

"Regardless of what you believe, I'm a mom first and a teacher second."

"You've lost me."

"Obviously, I never *had* you. Ask Toni what I said, then you can convict me."

She turned on her heel, but almost immediately whirled back. "You aren't doing her any good fighting her battles for her and hovering about making sure she never falls down."

"How would you know?"

"I have a father, too. A big, bad cop of a father, who did the same thing to me."

"You're calling me overprotective?"

"Aren't you? Let her grow up. Stop babying her."

"But I never got to." All the anger went out of

Joe in a rush of sadness for what he'd lost and could never get back.

Her face softened. "That's your problem, Joe. Not Toni's."

She walked away and left him alone with his thoughts.

A HALF HOUR LATER Evie's anger had waned and the guilt had set in. She didn't want anyone telling her how to raise her boys; she had no business telling Joe how to raise Toni.

The way he'd said *But I never got to* had nearly made her cry. All parents harbored guilt about things they'd done—be they right or wrong. Parental guilt was as common a malady as hangnails, and as much of a hazard to child raising as drugs. People did a lot of stupid things to make up for the stupid things they'd done.

The twins had gone to the DQ with the neighbors, and Evie was left with Adam and Toni. Joe had tromped off in a snit almost immediately after she'd walked away from him. Evie decided to take Toni home for a change, and then have another, calmer, chat with Toni's dad.

Toni and Adam climbed in the back of the car. Every few minutes Evie peeked in the mirror. She couldn't help herself. Thus far she hadn't come upon the two of them making out. Was the relationship only friendship? And if so, should she be happy or concerned?

Adam was seventeen years old and he'd never

had a girlfriend. A date? *Yes.* A second date? *Rarely.*
A third? Not that she could recall. Once she'd gotten
over the shock, Evie had taken the courting of Toni
as a good sign. Adam was behaving like a normal
kid, instead of a responsible semi-adult.

Had Adam been permanently scarred by his parents' mistakes? There was that parental guilt again.
And what should she do if that was the case? Evie
had no idea how to explain "guy" feelings, since
she'd never had any. She'd studied the biology, even
the psychology, but those classes wouldn't do her
one bit of good with her son. What was he feeling?
How could she help him? Should she ask? Or keep
her big mouth shut?

Upon reaching the Scalotta house, Evie shelved
those questions for the time being. Lights blazed inside and outside. Joe's car sat in the driveway. She
pulled in behind and shut off the engine.

"Toni, I want to talk to your dad."

Toni's wide eyes appeared in the mirror. "Did I
mess up, Coach?"

Adam snorted. "You won the game, Toni. Relax." He put his arm around her neck, pulling her
close and rubbing her head with his knuckles—just
as if she were one of the guys. Evie frowned. His
technique left a lot to be desired.

But Toni giggled and squirmed and looked at
Adam as if he were the most amazing man next to
Mark McGwire. Evie just shook her head and got
out of the car.

"I'll let you in." Toni led the way. Adam sat

down on the porch and waved for them to go ahead without him. He avoided Joe whenever possible, and Evie couldn't say she blamed him. No sense running after trouble, especially with a man the size of Joe Scalotta.

Evie and Toni stepped inside, but the front of the house lay strangely silent and completely empty. "He doesn't have another car, does he?" Evie asked, concerned that Joe wasn't there at all. She didn't think she'd have the guts to come back another day.

"No. He's probably in the kitchen. He fools around in there a lot." Toni grinned over her shoulder as she led the way toward the back of the house. "I don't understand it, but he's a pretty good cook."

The place was spotless, though without three boys and a truckload of their friends, hers could be, too. *Yeah, right.* "Your cleaning lady is good," she observed.

Toni stopped in the narrow hallway and turned. "Dad does it." She shook her head. "He says he *likes* it! And you know what else?" Evie shrugged. "He asked me to show him how to sew."

"Sew?"

"Buttons. Ripped pants. That kind of stuff."

"Hmm. I figured him for a 'throw it out and get a new one' kind of guy."

"Me, too." Toni tilted her head and pursed her lips, considering. "I guess I don't really know him as well as I thought." She glanced into the kitchen, then stepped back out of sight. "He's in there," she whispered, before scooting down the hallway, leaving Evie alone in the semidarkness.

Now, why had the girl acted as though they were on some secret spy mission? If Evie didn't know better, she'd figure Toni didn't want Joe to realize anyone was in the house. But why would that be?

Evie walked into the brightly lit kitchen and saw Joe. But not the Joe she thought she knew. No, this was a Joe she wanted to know a whole lot better.

He had his back to her. A good thing, because she probably drooled. The kitchen was steamy with mist and ripe with the scent of fresh tomatoes, real garlic and sautéed onions. And it was hot. Perhaps that was why he cooked without a shirt.

Evie had admired him in a myriad of colored T-shirts, but without a shirt—oh, boy. He had the smooth, olive skin of his Italian ancestors pulled taut over an exceptional physique. She'd considered his muscles well defined in royal-blue cotton. They looked much better in nothing at all.

But the thing that really did it to her was the bare feet peeking out from beneath black cotton pants. He'd planted them wide on the floor and curled his toes against the ceramic tile, as if trying to draw the coolness into his body from the ground up.

The scene was a sensual delight, something out of a painting she might hang over her kitchen table—someday when she didn't have to be concerned about water spots from low-flying cups.

Evie couldn't move or speak; she could barely breathe. What was it about this man that called to a

person within her she had never known existed until
he stepped into her life? Seeing Joe like this made
her think of dark red wine, Italian crystal, black ol-
ives and blistering sunshine on the water.

As if in answer to her fantasy, Joe reached over
and brought to his lips a goblet of bloodred wine.
The stem of the glass looked ludicrously small in
his huge hand, but he held it as if born to do so.
When he tilted his head back and drank, a tiny gasp
of arousal escaped her throat before she could stop
it.

He spun toward her, swallowed the wine with a
gulp and stared. She stared, too, since his front was
nearly as good as his back. Though the hair on his
head was silver-blond, the hair on his chest was
golden. Not too much, not too little, and a perfect
complement to the shade of his skin. Broad shoulders, narrow waist, stomach rippling with muscles.
He even had the top button of his pants undone, as
if he'd thrown them on in a hurry after making love
on the kitchen table.

Evie blushed, and the spell broke. She could
speak and stutter. Lucky her. "I'm s-sorry. I—I
brought Toni home and she let me in. I didn't mean
to disturb your…"

What? He was cooking. So why did she feel as
if she'd walked in on an erotic bit of foreplay?
Maybe because his body made her bothered. His lips
looked as though she could taste the wine if she
kissed them— Oh-oh, she was so out of her league
here.

"You got any more of that?" She poked her finger in the direction of his wine. The top of her mouth seemed glued to her tongue. Adam could drive home.

Joe glanced at his hand, and his face creased, as if he was surprised to see the glass there. Shrugging, he reached into the cupboard for another glass. Evie was unable to tear her eyes from the sight of his arm stretching upward, pulling all the muscles of his back into a different, yet equally fascinating, pattern.

He poured garnet-red wine into a glass and crossed the room. The way he approached made her think of a tiger she'd seen once at the zoo, pacing his cage, lean hips swaying, eyes on his prey, so close to her, yet so far, far away.

Joe held out the glass, and his eyes met hers. He hadn't spoken, and his silence only added to the tension between them. When she accepted the glass their fingers brushed, and she started so badly at the jolt his touch caused that she feared she would drop the beautiful crystal goblet.

That fear, combined with the heat in his eyes and the steam in the room, made sweat break out on Evie's forehead. She didn't have any glasses half so fine, and it surprised her a man would take the time to buy wineglasses, let alone use them while drinking alone.

She put the glass to her lips. His gaze held hers. The wine tasted different from anything she'd ever had, and she licked her lips so as not to lose a drop.

His gaze went to her mouth, and she shivered despite the heat.

He stepped closer, crowding her in the doorway, looming over her, his chest so near that she could touch him, if she wanted. She definitely wanted. Evie moved forward.

The *hiss* of water on a hot stove made Joe curse and whirl about, then hurry across the room to attend the pot that had boiled over. Evie remained where she was, her body still thrumming with all that could have, would have, been.

He turned back, picked up his wine and had a sip, watching her with eyes the color of ice in a face hot with hunger. Why didn't he say something and end this odd spell created by the heat and the approaching night? For that matter, why didn't he put on a shirt?

"Don't you have any air-conditioning?"

He lifted a brow. "In an old house like this? Sacrilege."

"How do you sleep at night?"

"Naked, beneath a fan."

Evie groaned; she'd had to ask. Next topic?

She raised her glass. "What is this?"

"Merlot. Ever had it before?"

"My wine preference tends to jugs and boxes."

He winced. A connoisseur.

"Nice glasses," she observed, making polite small talk until her body quit humming. She might have to exhaust several more inane topics before that happened.

"Thank you. It seems a shame to put something this rich into a jelly glass."

She shrugged. "Wouldn't it taste the same?"

"Bite your tongue."

She wanted to bite *his* tongue. Evie gulped more wine before she said something stupid. This small-talk idea was not working at all, but she had to keep trying.

"You weren't kidding when you said you liked to cook."

"Why would I kid?"

"Where did you learn about wine?"

"My father. Italian, you know. He used to make wine. Learned from his father, who came over right before the war."

"Which war?"

"WWII. Mussolini sent a lot of folk scrambling out of the country."

"Can't say that I blame them."

The wine was going to her head. Though she'd gone grocery shopping, she hadn't eaten. She wasn't used to wine without a splash of white soda as a complement, and the scent of this stuff alone was enough to make her tipsy. Combined with Joe Scalotta in a steambath, it set her nerves on edge, caused her skin to tingle. She'd come to… What?

"So what brings you here?" He took the question right out of her mind.

"I thought we'd better talk some more about Toni."

"I have to apologize."

She shook her head. "That's not why I came."

"Still, I jumped to a conclusion. An insulting conclusion."

"Yes, it was."

He sighed, picked up his wineglass and the bottle, then walked over to the kitchen table. He poured himself another glass and tilted the bottle in her direction with a question in his eyes.

"No, thanks," she said. If she had a refill, she'd do more than fantasize about that kitchen table. She had to remember two teenagers were hanging about somewhere outside the house. And one of the rules of parenting was that as soon as you even contemplated doing anything you didn't want them to know about—they would show up. Though with Joe still walking around half-naked, she was having a harder and harder time thinking of anything but him.

He leaned his exceptional rear end against her fantasy table and stared into his glass as he swirled the ruby liquid around and around. "You said I was overprotective."

"I apologize. It's none of my business."

"I wish you'd make it your business. You know about kids. That's your job, right? I'm trying, but I don't seem to be succeeding. Toni doesn't know me. I don't think she wants to. Hell, she still calls me 'Joe.'"

"I noticed that."

He shot a glance at her, and in his eyes was a despair that beckoned to her soft heart. Before she could offer any kind of sympathy, he looked away and returned to his wine-swirling exercise. "She stopped calling me 'Dad' a long time ago. It's like she doesn't want to need me." His shoulders slumped, and he took a sip of the wine he'd been staring at. "Or to love me."

"I'm sure she loves you. But you might be right about not wanting to need you. She lost her mother only recently."

"Her mother saw her less than I did."

"Toni mentioned that."

His head went up. "She did? Does she talk to you a lot?" He sounded hopeful and resentful at the same time.

"She talks, but not about anything serious. Baseball, the twins, school."

"But she told you her mother left her to be raised by nannies?"

"Yes, she did."

"So how could Toni be afraid of needing someone if Karen was never around, anyway?"

"Just because Karen wasn't around doesn't mean Toni didn't need her, then lose her. Karen was still her mother."

He sighed. "And no matter what I do, I can never be her mother."

"No one can."

Joe shifted his hip on the table so he faced her. "Not even you?"

Evie narrowed her gaze on Joe's face. He wasn't looking at her again. "Is that what you think? That

I'm trying to be her mother? I'm just trying to be her coach and maybe her friend. She seems to need one.''

''I know.'' He eyed her, and she saw the truth a second before he admitted it. ''I'm jealous. It's embarrassing, but I am. I want her to be my little girl.''

''She isn't a little girl.''

''I wish she were.''

''Wish away. She's a young woman. Overprotecting her will only make her rebel.''

''Did you?''

Evie finished her wine in one huge gulp, hoping the jolt would give her the courage to remember her youth—when she was only a little older than Toni and a whole lot dumber.

''My dad was a cop, and he knew all the bad things that could happen to kids, even in small-town Iowa. Because of that he hovered. When I was seventeen we moved to Newsome because he became the police chief. I was scared and shy and lonely. Ray—my husband—was the cutest guy in school.''

Joe groaned. ''That sounds too familiar.''

''Don't I know it. But Ray was different from Adam.'' *God, please let that be true,* she said to herself in a quick, familiar little prayer. ''He was irresponsible, a party guy. He liked fast cars, cheap beer and easy money.''

''And you?''

''Of course.''

''So, what happened?''

"My dad always kept tabs on me wherever I went. Checked out my friends. He made my decisions and got me out of any jam that came my way."

"And what about your mother?"

"Dad was the boss. He was so protective, she pretty much let me be. She was of the old school, where you didn't talk about unpleasant or embarrassing things—in public or in private. She didn't make decisions, either. That was Dad's job." Evie just shook her head, still amazed that her parents were married and happy. But times had changed, and were still changing.

"I understand. That's how things were at my house, too."

Evie smiled, recalling some of his outdated, chauvinistic ideas. They had infuriated her, but seeing Joe in the kitchen and at the grocery store, and hearing about his attempts to do the best for his daughter, made Evie think that perhaps Joe wasn't as "Ward Cleaver" as he professed to be.

"When we moved to Newsome, my dad was busy with his new job. I wanted to be an adult, but I didn't know what that meant. I had no idea how to make a choice. So I made a bad one with Ray. Pregnancy was not a jam Daddy could get me out of."

"He could have gotten you out of the pregnancy."

Again she shook her head, disavowing such an option now as she had then. "But he couldn't get

LORI HANDELAND 191

me out of love with Ray. Ray was the only one who could do that.''

''And did he?''

''Oh, yeah. He might have been handsome, and fun, and charming, but he was a great, big, selfish jerk. I figured that out before Adam was born. But it was too late. I tried my best, but Ray never did grow up.''

''What about you?''

''I grew up at eighteen.''

''So what do we do about your son and my daughter?''

''Maybe we should talk to the two of them. Tell them about the mistakes we've made.''

''Think it'll help?''

''Can't hurt.''

''You sure about that?''

''It might hurt us, but them...?'' She shrugged. ''I think they need to know how one bad choice can mess up an entire future.''

He was quiet for a long moment, swirling, swirling, swirling that wine again. ''If you could go back, knowing all that you know now, would you do things differently? If you did, you wouldn't have Adam.''

She'd thought about that many times, and she'd made her peace with her past as best as she could. ''My kids are worth a lot of pain and agony, which is lucky, since pain and agony for me seems to be their main goal in life most days. I try to believe everything works out for the best. Or, at least, that there's a reason for everything, even if we can't see it."

His eyes widened. "You believe that?"

"I have to. Otherwise life's just too darn hard."

CHAPTER THIRTEEN

"WHAT DO YOU THINK your mom wanted to talk about with Joe?" Toni asked.

Adam shrugged and started walking toward the back of the house. "Who knows with them."

True enough. Still, Toni was kind of worried, despite Mrs. Vaughn's assurances that she had done nothing wrong. Though Toni had been living with Joe long enough to stop feeling guilty about every little thing, she still expected Adam's mom to find fault with her somehow, just as her mother always had. No matter how hard Toni tried to do the right thing, nothing had ever been right enough for her mom.

But with Mrs. Vaughn, nothing was ever *wrong* enough. Heck, Toni figured if she walked in ten runs and lost a game, her coach would just pat her on the back and say, "You did your best."

Since Adam had told Toni what was at stake for his mom in this bet with Joe—then made Toni swear not to say a word, since Mrs. Vaughn would have a cow if anyone knew she needed the money—Toni didn't understand how her coach could be so relaxed, or how she could continue to tell the team at every practice and every game that "their best" was all she was after. Toni wished she could relax about life-altering episodes the way Mrs. Vaughn did.

Toni wasn't relaxed; she was confused. Her mom always said winning was what was important. If you weren't a winner, you were a loser. And Joe—well, winning had been his business. But in this town, with this coach, sometimes Toni forgot about winning altogether.

To be honest, Joe didn't seem to care much, either. In fact, since they'd moved to Oak Grove, he was pretty laid-back. She wondered if he always had been and the tension she'd sensed in him when he'd visited her had actually been between Joe and her mom and not because of his disappointment in having only a daughter and not a son.

He made no move to hire someone to watch her, or even to hire someone to do all the house stuff her mom always called "the sadistic, oppressive assignments of the male aristocracy," whatever that meant. It hadn't been complimentary; that much Toni knew. And when her mom had hired nannies and housekeepers with the same mumbling and grumbling, Toni soon understood where taking care of her rated in the scheme of life. So she tried to be as little of a problem as she could, so as not to be sent packing if she screwed up—as most of the nannies and housekeepers eventually were.

But Joe seemed to like doing those "oppressive" chores. And he seemed to like her—everything about her. Even when she got snippy he looked like *he'd* done something wrong, not her. Toni just didn't understand life, or men, at all.

There were a lot of confusing thoughts racing through Toni's mind these days, with Adam Vaughn at the top of the list. She kept waiting for him to find fault with something she did—like worrying that no one liked her and agonizing over every tiny mistake. Then he would stop being her...whatever it was that he was.

Friend? Boyfriend? Toni hoped the latter, but was terrified it was the former. She lay awake nights imagining that Adam pitied her for being new and lonely, hearing his laughter when he told his friends that his mother had made him be the new geek girl's friend so Toni would stay on the team.

One thing Toni knew for certain: sweet sixteen and never been kissed was embarrassing. She wanted Adam to be the boy who kissed her first, yet she had no idea how to get him to do that.

Thus far he'd done nothing but hold her hand, which was so sweet she wanted to cry, but she also wanted to cry because he didn't seem interested in anything more than that. And she was terrified to kiss him for fear he did see her as just another one of the guys. If he wanted her to be his girlfriend, wouldn't he have tried something by now?

The uncertainty was driving her crazy. She couldn't ask Adam, because if he knew how much she loved him and he didn't feel the same, she'd lose the little bit of him she had. She couldn't ask Joe—*ha,* that would be the day she'd ask Wildman for advice on love. And the only woman she'd ever trusted was Adam's mother. Jeez, was this a mess or what?

It suddenly occurred to Toni that Adam had not really answered her question about his mom and Joe. To tell the truth, he never talked much about Joe at all, or *to* him, if he could help it.

Had he noticed the way Joe looked at his mom? Toni certainly had. It was embarrassing. Joe'd never looked at *her* mom that way. Not once. Maybe that had been the problem.

Toni put aside thoughts of her mother and father as young lovers as just too weird, and concentrated on her problem: Adam Vaughn.

He sat on the back-porch swing. The gentle sway of the seat only revealed how quiet he was, his face more pensive than usual, and this on a boy who seemed deep in thought most of the time. His seriousness was one of the things that drew Toni to him. Adam made her think of lost boys, brooding poets and tragic heroes from romantic novels. She wanted to hold him, to heal him, to save him. But from what?

"Adam?"

He glanced up. She hovered at the top step, unsure if she should join him on that narrow swing or sit along the railing to her right. He smiled and stopped the swing so she could get on. She did, and he let the swing go once more. They swayed, the movement peaceful in the fading light. Toni resisted the urge to lay her head on his shoulder and cuddle against his side.

"Those girls tonight…" Toni let her voice trail off.

"What about them?"

"What do you think your mom said?"

He grinned. "I'm sure she let them have it."

"Why?"

"My mom doesn't like mean kids, and they were being little snots, she'd say. One thing Mom's always taught us is empathy."

"Empathy?" Adam used a lot of big words in regular conversation. Toni figured that came with having a teacher for a mother. But Adam never made her feel dumb if she didn't know what he meant. He just explained without missing a beat.

"Walk a mile in the other guy's shoes. Do unto others. Even the twin rats try to be nice to everyone except each other."

Adam laid his arm across the back of the seat. Toni tensed. Was that an invitation? Or merely a stretch?

She inched closer. Their hips bumped. His hand cupped her shoulder and he hugged her. Her heart triple-flipped and a warm feeling spread through her stomach. With a sigh, Toni let her head fall onto Adam's shoulder.

His cheek rested on her hair. She didn't think she'd ever been so happy, or so scared, in her life.

"Those girls seem to hate me, and I've never even met them."

"They're mean. Forget them. If they try that again, I'll make sure they regret it."

"Why?"

He raised his head, and she tilted hers to see his face. Sometimes, like now, he looked so handsome that her eyes hurt.

"Don't you know?"

She was unable to speak, afraid she'd blubber or stutter. So she shook her head.

"You're my girl, Toni. I'm not going to let anyone make you sad. Is that okay with you?"

She nodded.

He laughed. "Can I kiss you?"

In answer, she raised her lips. Adam Vaughn had been well worth waiting for.

TWIN SHADOWS WAVERED on the porch, drawing Evie's attention to the window set within the door. Adam and Toni swung on the swing, their backs to the house, as they watched the sun go down. Her son put his arm around Toni, and she laid her head on his shoulder.

Evie didn't realize she herself had moved, but suddenly she stood at the back door, her nose nearly pressed to the glass. Her son and Joe's daughter lifted their heads, gazed into each other's eyes and kissed.

Evie's eyes burned with tears. She keenly remembered her first kiss. The technique had not mattered—only the feelings. They'd been so strong, so new, so incredible. No kiss had been that good since. Though one—recently—had come pretty close.

Joe's breath whooshed past her ear, hot and sharp. "What in hell does he think he's doing?"

"What do you think?"

He growled and reached for the doorknob.

Evie grabbed his wrist and held on tight. "Don't," she said.

The way he leaned across her body brought his face close to hers. "Don't what?" he whispered, and their breaths mingled.

They were closer than their kids. All that she'd been imagining returned in a rush of feelings that were new, yet familiar. She couldn't seem to stop staring into his eyes.

"Don't interrupt them. It's their first kiss. Can't you feel the magic?"

"Yeah. But is it us, or is it them?"

Good question. Evie shifted, and her breast brushed his arm. Joe straightened, and his bare chest slid along her shoulder. His gaze lowered to her mouth, skimmed back up her face. A spark of heat melted his ice-blue eyes.

Then he was kissing her, and she was kissing him. He tasted better than the wine, the tingle of his lips on hers more arousing than champagne.

The scent of the room—Merlot, basil and steam— would forever mean Joe in her heated night dreams. Her palms slid across his beautiful, bare skin, slick and wet, arousing not only because of his breadth and strength but because of his aching vulnerability to her touch. Muscles vibrated beneath her fingers, as if responding to her call, begging for more and for more. She soothed them, smoothed them, wooed them to flex and release against her hands.

His mouth left hers to trail along her jaw. She ran her thumbs beneath the waistband of his pants, and the muscles of his stomach leaped in response. He moaned into the hollow of her neck, then suckled upon her thundering pulse.

How had she ended up pressed to the length of his body? Had she moved into his embrace, or had he drawn her there? She touched him all over, with fluttering fingers that couldn't seem to touch fast or often enough. His large hand snaked around her waist, palm to the curve of her hip, fingertips along the line of her spine; her breath hitched, then released.

This was getting out of control, but from the moment she'd seen him standing at the stove in nothing but jeans, the desire to feel his body against hers had pounded in her belly to the beat of her heart.

As if in answer to her unspoken thought, his thumbs stroked her stomach, slipped beneath the waistband of her shorts, stroked lower, along the elastic of her panties. He swallowed her moan with his mouth, used his tongue in ways she'd only read about.

This was insanity, and it had to stop.

She pulled her mouth from his and stepped back so their bodies no longer pressed together like glue and paper. Her hands were still plastered to his chest. His fingers still circled her waist. The harshness of their breathing filled the room.

Evie stared at him. Joe stared at her. He didn't seem to know what to say, either.

The porch door rattled, and they jumped apart as if they'd been caught in a despicable act.

Well, they had almost been caught, but the act had been nowhere near despicable.

"Mom, I'm going to take Toni to the DQ, then I'll swing back for you."

"I'll come now."

Joe coughed. Evie blushed, then shot him a lethal look. If he hadn't been too far away, she'd have kicked him in the shins.

"Why don't you stay for dinner," he invited. "Then I'll take you home."

Very bad idea, she thought. "I'm not hungry," she said.

Her stomach rumbled loudly in the silence that followed her words. Joe raised his eyebrow, then crossed his arms across his scrumptious chest.

Evie glanced at Adam, to find her son scowling at Joe like an outraged father. Toni hovered in the background with a hopeful expression on her face as her gaze darted from Adam, to Joe, to Evie, to Adam again.

"We'll get some ice cream and go home to meet the rat boys," said Adam.

Evie flushed. She'd forgotten the twins were being dropped off at nine. She'd forgotten a lot of things while Joe's mouth was on hers.

"Fine." Evie waved her hand at them both. "Go." *Desert the sinking ship.*

They did so without a backward glance, leaving Evie alone with her doom.

THE KIDS WERE GONE, and they were alone. Joe wasn't sure how he felt about either one.

Joe's body still throbbed. Thank goodness his pants were of the loose variety or he'd be embarrassed. As it was, Adam Vaughn's glare showed the kid was not so dumb. He knew Joe had the hots for his mom, and he liked it even less than Joe liked the kid kissing his baby.

"You think they saw us?"

Joe glanced at Evie, who still leaned on the counter as though she would fall if she stepped away. He stifled a grin, knowing she would not be happy to recognize his pride in having kissed her senseless. Heck, he'd been as gone as she was. Why was it that no one made him feel the way she did?

"I don't think they saw."

"But they could guess."

He shrugged. "We're adults."

"Yes, we are. So we should be able to resist this…this…" She threw up her hands in frustration. "What *is* this?"

Joe picked up his shirt from where he'd draped it over a chair earlier and shrugged his arms into the garment, leaving the front hanging free. The heat in the kitchen was too high for him to button up. He opened the back door, and an evening breeze swept the room, eliciting a sigh of relief from them both.

"I have no idea." He pulled plates from the cupboard. When he turned, she stood right next to him. As she put her hands on the plates, their fingertips touched, and his body ignited all over again.

What *was* this between them? Lust? He'd lusted before—a lot. He'd never felt like this—ever. He wanted to kiss her again, right now. Drop the china, pick her up and take her on the kitchen table with the door wide-open. He wasn't going to, but knowing that didn't make him want to any less.

She tugged on the plates, and he let them go, then turned to the stove while she set the table. The scene was so domestic that he paused in the act of scooping pasta into a serving bowl and just stood there thinking. *This* was what he'd come to Oak Grove to find, but he had never thought to find it with Evie Vaughn.

What had she whispered about magic? He recalled a conversation they'd had about love. Her face had been all dreamy. Joe had an uncomfortable feeling his face had been pretty dreamy when the kids walked in. Had he fallen in love with Evie?

No way. He barely knew her. She annoyed him. She was too competitive, too driven, too domineering, ever to be happy sharing the kind of life he dreamed of.

Then Joe thought of all the other women he'd dated. Not one of them had made him feel a bit like Evie made him feel all the time. He'd kissed every one, and that had been enough. He'd never wanted to do anything more than take them to their house, then run back to his.

He wanted to take Evie to bed, then stay there forever.

To be honest, though they argued, he enjoyed it. She was smart and funny, and she gave as good as she got. He liked her, and though he'd prefer to lock Adam in a closet and throw away the key, Joe had to admit her kids were great. She knew how to be a mom, and Toni adored her.

He turned with the food in his hands, and relished the view of Evie leaning over the table to position silverware at each place. Her shirt had pulled up, revealing an enticing bit of skin at her waist. She looked good enough to eat, and he was very hungry.

She straightened. "All set." Glancing over her shoulder, she caught him staring, and her welcoming smile became a confused frown. "What?"

"Nothing." Joe crossed the room and set the bowls on the table. He had a lot of thinking to do, and he wasn't going to share his fantasy with her— at least, not yet.

AN UNSPOKEN TRUCE went into effect during dinner, for which Evie was thankful. She was light-headed, whether from the heat, the wine, the smell of food after eight hours of abstinence or the kiss, she didn't know. What she did know was that she didn't have the energy to spar with Joe any more.

The meal was exquisite. "Do you cook like this every night?" she asked.

"Not like this. But I cook."

"Every night?"

"I like to eat every night." He shrugged, and the movement caused his shirt to open.

He didn't notice, but Evie did. She drank some water and stared anywhere but at his chest. She'd always been a sucker for a great chest.

"Don't you ever eat leftovers?" she inquired.

"Never liked them much."

"So you throw out the extra?" Evie couldn't keep the incredulity from her voice.

"What do you do with them?"

"Leftovers are one thing I don't have to worry about. Three boys at the table resemble a three-hosed vacuum cleaner on full throttle. Everything's sucked up by the end of the meal."

"You must have very...ah...pleasant meals."

"Not exactly."

She glanced at Joe in time to see him grin. She wanted to smile, too, but this companionable meal made her nervous. She was too comfortable with him. Though he could be a great, big, chauvinistic jerk when the mood struck him, he could also be funny and interesting and kind of endearingly sweet when he spoke of Toni. She liked looking at him. She liked doing more than looking.

Time to change the subject—both out loud and in her mind.

Joe beat her to it. "You're a good coach, Evie."

She gaped. She hadn't expected him to go there. "I am?"

"Yeah. I'm glad Toni's on your team. She adores you."

"I think she's pretty neat, too. Though girls baffle me, for the most part."

"Join the club."

They smiled at each other again. This was just too darn cozy for comfort. Evie stood and started clearing the table. Her abrupt movement left Joe blinking, but he recovered well enough to help her clean up.

"I appreciate your support," she said. "Most of the men in this town seem to think I need help coaching the boys. As if I haven't been doing it since Adam was the twins' age. I suppose it's our bet. Though I'd think all the macho men would be on your side."

"Macho men, huh?" He found he wasn't offended, probably because her assessment was right. "I've had my share of back-slapping supporters. But no one wants to give me any advice, even though I could use some."

"Really? And I thought you knew everything."

"And I thought we were playing nice tonight."

"Sorry." Evie opened the dishwasher and started loading. "I find it frustrating that everyone thinks you know baseball just because you're a guy. But because I look good in a dress, I need coaching advice from the peanut gallery."

"You do, you realize."

She narrowed her eyes. "Need advice?"

"No, look good in a dress. You should wear one more often."

"Can you see me showing the kids how to slide into home plate while I'm wearing a froufrou skirt?"

Joe laughed. "I'd like to be around if you do."

There was a sudden silence between them. Evie turned on the dishwasher; the hum of the machine filled the air. He was flirting with her. She was flirting back. She liked it.

The clock in the hallway chimed ten—pumpkin time for Mommy. She needed to get home, hose off the twins and put them to bed. No rest for the weary.

"I'd better take you back," Joe said, echoing her thoughts.

She glanced up to find him staring at the kitchen table with a funny expression, almost as if... No, he couldn't be thinking what she'd been thinking.

"Yeah, you'd better," Evie blurted, before she herself could ponder the fantasy any more.

The trip to her house took only five minutes. Heck, driving from one side of Oak Grove to the other took seven, so you could say they lived pretty far apart. Unfortunately, they were not sitting far enough apart in Joe's little red sports car for Evie's comfort.

She could feel his heat. His scent surrounded her, excited her. When his fingers brushed her knee as he shifted the car—who bought stick shifts anymore, anyway?—she jumped, but her knee tingled from the graze of his fingers long after he'd withdrawn his hand.

The car roared into her driveway, and he shut off the engine. A drizzling rain fell, causing mist to rise from the pavement. The windows clouded over as they sat and stared at her house, all lit up, looking like home. Shadows moved beyond the windows, calming her. The kids were safe inside.

"Ten-fifteen and all's well," Joe intoned.

"We made it through another day."

"That's what we pray for."

"Yeah." She took a deep breath. "Well, thanks for dinner and the ride."

"And?"

She shifted her gaze so she could see his face, which was lit by the dashboard lights. He smiled at her. There was no way she was going to thank him for that kiss—though it *had* been better than dinner.

"And…good night."

"No kiss?"

"You had one."

"But don't I deserve another?"

"I think you and I had better stop kissing. It's like spontaneous combustion."

"But what a way to go."

He leaned toward her. She leaned back and her head bumped the window. There was nowhere to run in this car, unless she ran out of the car and into the house. She wasn't that desperate. *Yet.*

Distraction—that was what she needed. "So the plan is for me to talk to Adam and you to talk to

Toni.'' He blinked as if she'd sprouted another head. ''Right?''

He sat back. ''Uh, right. Do you think it'll help?''

''Didn't we already agree it couldn't hurt? Though what I'm going to say to him, I have no idea.''

''I thought you were going to talk about past mistakes, ruined lives—the usual parental talk when a member of the opposite sex has just come into your child's life.''

''I wish I knew how to explain guy feelings.''

''Guy feelings?'' He looked blank.

''You do have them, don't you? Or are all those jokes about guys being led around by their—''

''Whoa!'' He put up his hand. ''Let's stop right there. Guys have feelings.''

''What kind of feelings?''

He pushed long fingers through his hair, a pointless gesture since his short haircut left little to push about. Then he stared out the window. ''I don't know. You're hot—you're cold. Your gut aches. She smells good. She's so soft you have to touch her. Does she taste as good as she smells? You have to find out.''

Evie groaned. ''That's what I thought. All sex. Physical, not mental.''

His head whipped back in her direction, and he crossed his arms over his chest. At least he'd buttoned his shirt, so the distractions for her were kept to a minimum.

''Well, what about girls?''

Evie hesitated for a moment, but fair was fair. He had shared; now it was her turn. "It's a head game. What's he thinking? What's he feeling? Does he like me as much as I like him?"

"Do you think that when we're...you know?"

"Actually, no. Not when we're...you know."

"What *do* you think?"

She blushed at the intensity of his stare. Luckily, the night was too dark for him to see. She glanced at the house. All quiet on that front. "I have no idea," she lied.

He shifted, and the seat creaked. Startled, she turned to find him close, very close. Her heart thundered loud enough that he must hear it in the tight confines of this ridiculous excuse for a car.

Caught in his gaze, she was unable to flee as his hand snaked about her neck and drew her toward him. Nearer and nearer came his mouth, until he hovered less than an inch away.

"Let's find out," he whispered, and his breath caressed her lips.

She discovered that what she thought when Joe kissed her was, quite simply, nothing at all. Worries, fears and concerns about the boys and the team and herself disappeared. All her responsibilities faded. The demands upon her time, the tugs on her heart and the drains upon her soul melted in the heat of the desire only he could bring.

When his mouth was on hers, she was no one's but his.

CHAPTER FOURTEEN

JOE HAD BEEN WRONG about guy feelings—or maybe he'd just never had them before. Embarrassing but true, at the ripe old age of thirty-six, Joe Scalotta discovered a whole new world.

Sure the feelings started with needs, and wants, and desires. He needed to touch her. He wanted to kiss her. He desired to hold her close to his chest and run his fingers through her short, soft hair.

But when she sighed against his lips, cupped his face between her palms and kissed him—deeper, harder, longer—his heart seemed too big for his chest and his stomach did a flip-flop. Was she feeling this, too?

He breathed in her sweet scent—one he would know now in a crowd—and his body tightened in a rush that made him dizzy. He couldn't recall being this aroused since high school. Perhaps because that was the last time he'd made out in a car.

Joe's lips curved into a smile against hers. No, that wasn't the reason. The reason was her; the reason was him. Together, and only together, they made the magic she'd been talking about. The magic he hadn't quite understood until now. Could the magic be love?

She laid her hand on his chest, and he nearly jumped out of his skin. This woman's touch had him poised on an edge sharper than any he'd ever known. She'd spoken of the wonder of first love, the intensity, the newness of the emotions. Is that what was going on here?

Kind of sad he'd never felt this way before. He'd been married, had made a child, and had never wanted to hold a woman so close that he became a part of her—and he didn't mean by having sex. He'd always thought the songs and the poems silly, because he'd never felt the symmetry their words expressed. Until now.

He traced his mouth along her jaw, aroused further by the sound of his name uttered in a hoarse, desperate voice when his tongue found the hollow at her collarbone. He savored the flavor of salt on her skin and the thunder of her pulse against his lips. His heart seemed to beat loudly enough to pound back at him from the fogged windows. Joe pressed a kiss to Evie's temple and opened his eyes with a frown. What *was* that noise?

Twin faces pressed to the window of the car, squashed flat, resembling something from an alien outbreak. Four fists pounded a native drumbeat.

"Hey, Joe! What're you and Mom doin' in there?"

Evie gasped and shoved him away. Turning, she pushed the button on the door and the window slid down.

Danny and Benji hung into the car. "Why's the car all steamed up? Whatcha doin'?"

"Talking."

Her voice was clipped, and she wouldn't look at Joe. He fought the urge to apologize. He hadn't done anything but kiss her a little—make that a lot—but he was far from sorry.

"Nah. You were kissin'. We couldn't see good, but we could see that."

Evie groaned and put her hands over her face. Then she leaned forward and hid her eyes against the dashboard.

"It's okay, Mom," one of them said, looking worried. "We like Joe. You can kiss him if you want."

"Gee, thanks," she mumbled.

"But why do you want to, huh?" said the other—whichever one that was. "You said kissin' spreads germs." He eyed Joe with a serious expression as he imparted his words of wisdom. "I never kiss girls."

"Don't you kiss your mom?"

"Oh, yeah. But I don't do little girls."

Joe choked. Evie tilted her head to the side and glared at him. The twins grinned toothless grins.

"How come everyone's kissin' each other, Mom?"

Evie's head went up like a pointer that had just heard a bird rustle through the grass. "Who's every-one?"

"Adam and Toni were steamin' up the station

wagon when we came home from next door. Now they're steamin' up the living room. Adam told us to—'' He scrunched his face into a perfect parody of a dried-apple doll while he tried to recall his brother's order. ''Go outside and stay outside. Don't leave the yard on parallel of death.''

''That's peril, doofus.''

''Don't call me 'doofus'! Mom, he called me 'doofus.' ''

''Stop!''

They stopped. Impressive.

''Your brother sent you outside in the rain?''

''It wasn't raining then. 'Sides, it's warm out. We like it.''

Suddenly the light in the living room went out, though the television screen still flickered in an eerie dance across the curtains.

All four of them stared, speechless, at the house.

''Oh-oh,'' murmured one of the twins.

Joe reached for the car door, but Evie's hand on his arm made him pause. ''Let me,'' she said.

''I don't think so. This is a job for—''

''Iceman?''

He frowned at the sarcastic twist she gave to the nickname.

''Think about it, Joe. You go blasting in there, shouting, embarrassing her and him, she'll hate you for it.''

''What do you suggest?''

''I'll go in, break it up and send her out. Then we have our talks with them—tonight.''

"What kind of talks, Mom?"

Evie's mouth tightened before she faced the twins. "None of your beeswax." She hit the Close button on the window, and the little boys became shadowy aliens once more. Evie turned back to Joe with a lift of one shoulder and a helpless gesture of her hands.

She was right. He was furious, and he'd say something stupid. "Well, you'd better get in there before they do something *we'll* regret."

His voice was gruff, but she smiled as if she knew what he felt, and patted his arm. Then she got out of the car, but before she shut the door, she leaned back in.

"Thanks for the kiss," she whispered.

As he watched her walk inside, his fury dissipated just a bit.

Someone tapped on the driver's window. Joe glanced to his left. Twin noses squashed against the glass.

"Can we drive your car?"

EVIE RESISTED THE URGE to slam open the front door and start screaming. That situation was the one she'd hoped to avoid by leaving Joe in the car. She'd purposely left the twins out there, too. They wouldn't let Joe out of their sight. For some reason they were attached to the man.

Evie paused with her hand on the doorknob, blew a sharp breath upward to get her bangs out of her eyes, shook off the remnants of Joe's kiss, and went inside to... *Grr.* She didn't even want to think about it.

A flick of the light switch illuminated the living room. Evie sent a quick thank-you heavenward that things weren't as bad as she'd feared. Adam and Toni were sitting on the couch, blinking at her. Close as they could get, true, but though their lips might be red, all their clothes were on. Small favors, she would take.

"Toni, your dad's waiting in the car. You'd better go."

"Sure." She hesitated, as if she'd kiss Adam goodbye. Then glanced at Evie and stood. As she walked past, Evie couldn't seem to stop staring at the girl's face. She glowed; that was the only word for it.

The door shut, and Evie sighed before turning back to Adam. He did not glow. He glowered. *Great.*

She'd just opened her mouth to begin, when the whirlwind came and hit the back of her legs. She was so used to the twins' brand of physical affection that she barely stumbled anymore, even from a sneak attack. Frontal assaults were a piece of cake.

"Start the shower," she ordered, hugging one to each side.

"It's late. We're tired. Shower tomorrow."

"I'm tired. You're filthy. Shower now." Evie pointed down the hall. "Hut, two, three, four."

They marched, mumbling and grumbling all the way.

"We need to talk," she told Adam. "After I get those two to bed."

He didn't answer, and she peered at him, surprised to find a belligerent look on his face. The expression was completely foreign to her.

"Maybe we should talk now," she ventured.

"Don't bother. I know what you're going to say."

"Really? Excellent, because I have no idea."

"You don't have to lecture me on responsibility, Mom. I know all about it."

"You do? Then why did you send your brothers out in the rain?"

"It's eighty degrees out and this is Oak Grove, Iowa—nowhere center of the universe. They were fine."

"Lucky for you."

"I'm sick of them!" he shouted.

Evie's eyes widened. Adam never raised his voice. He rarely got angry, unless the twins poked him one time too many. And he never, ever argued with her. To be honest, his good behavior was unnerving, and sometimes she'd wished for a rebellion—just a tiny one—to show he was growing up all right. Well, she'd gotten her wish. Now, was she a mouse or a mom?

Evie straightened her back and met Adam's eyes. "I can't say that I blame you. The two of them can be a real pain. But you handle them well most of the time. I'm proud of you."

"I don't want to be responsible all the time. I

don't want to be their sitter. I don't want to be their dad.''

Evie winced. Was that what he thought?

"I just want to be me. I want to be a kid for a change.''

"I thought you were.''

"I haven't been a kid since those two were born and Dad died.''

Evie couldn't breathe. Here it was—everything she'd been wondering about, all she'd been afraid of, out in the open. Did she have the courage to hear it?

"So you want to make up for all the years you were responsible by…what? Acting irresponsible, like your father?''

"You hate him, don't you?''

"How can I hate him? He's gone.''

"You never looked at him the way you look at Scalotta. And he's worse than Dad ever was.''

Well, that wasn't true, but she wasn't going to argue worse and better on the idiot-scale.

"Is that what this is about? Joe?''

"Are you going to try for the same mistake twice, Mom? Fall for a guy who's no good for you? He'll hurt you, and you'll cry.''

"Heck, I want to cry now,'' she mumbled.

"I'm serious!''

"I know.'' She sighed. "You are, and I'm sorry. Don't worry about me, Adam. I know what I'm doing.''

"Do you?''

"Don't I always?"

"You'd like us to believe that, wouldn't you?"

"Of course. I gather you haven't fallen for my act?"

He snorted.

She took that as an insult but decided to let it pass. One problem at a time. "You're right. Sometimes I have no clue what I'm doing. I can only try. You *do* deserve time to be a kid, but I don't want you to make my mistake. With Toni."

He shot her a look filled with such derision, that Evie's eyes burned with the advent of tears. "So she can end up hating me, like you hate Dad? So I can ruin her life, like Dad ruined yours?"

Evie forced her next words past the lump in her throat. "Your dad didn't ruin my life."

"No, I did."

Before she could deny it, he got up and left the room. Evie heard his bedroom door close, then lock.

"Well, that went well," Evie murmured, and then she cried.

TONI SAT IN THE CAR with that dreamy look on her face, and Joe had no idea where to begin.

"So, ah...what were you guys doing?"

Her smile turned to a scowl. "Same thing you and Mrs. Vaughn were doing."

"Having dinner?"

"Yeah, right, Joe. Adam and I *saw* you two in the kitchen. You weren't cooking—pasta, anyway."

Joe sighed. *What now?*

"You like her."

The words weren't a question, but Joe answered nonetheless. "Sure. Is that a problem?"

"Not for me. But you'd better think about what you're doing."

"Huh?"

"You said you wanted to stay in Oak Grove, that you wanted to get married again."

"So?"

"Mrs. Vaughn is not someone you want to play with. People like her and respect her. They might think you're cool now, but I'd hate to be you if you hurt her."

"I'm not going to hurt her."

"No? How do you plan to stop that?"

Joe was still trying to figure out how they'd ended up talking about him and not her. He was really no good at this.

"How do you think I'll hurt her?"

"You planning on marrying her?"

Joe scowled. He hadn't thought that far.

"What *are* you planning, Wildman?"

He concentrated on the road while he tried to think of a way to explain what he needed to to his daughter. How could he say that he wanted a fifties kind of wife like his mom, the kind who would stay at home, have kids, when he didn't want that for his little girl? He wanted her to go to college, have a career. Then, if she absolutely had to, she could be a wife and a mommy. Joe shuddered at the thought.

"Well?" she persisted. "I've seen how you look at her. You never looked at Mom like that."

Joe flushed. That was true, much to his embarrassment. "We've already talked about your mom and me."

"You guys made a mistake."

"We weren't responsible. It's embarrassing to admit, especially to you, but we weren't thinking about anyone but ourselves—not each other, and certainly not you. In fact, I think we should discuss responsibility right now."

Joe pulled into their driveway and shut off the car. Silence descended between them. He could hear the *click* of the engine cooling down.

Toni just stared straight ahead. "Adam is very responsible."

"They always are."

"Why don't you like him?" Her voice was quiet and tense.

"I never said I didn't like him."

"You aren't very nice to him, and you always have a snotty comment."

"I'm just scared for you."

"You don't have to be scared. I love him."

Joe groaned. That was what he'd been afraid of. He should have been prepared for it, but hearing her say those words made his heart beat so fast and hard that he pressed a palm to his chest.

She shifted in her seat so she faced him, her back against the car door. "Don't have a heart attack.

Why should love upset you?'' Tilting her head, she studied him. ''Maybe because you've never loved?''

''I love you.''

''You do?''

The complete shock in her voice made him pause. He'd told her when she was little how much he loved her, but once she had started calling him ''Joe'' and the wall had come up between them, he'd stopped. Was the problem between them as simple as that? Did she think he didn't love her? How could he have been so stupid?

Joe was not a man who voiced his feelings easily. Oh, he felt things just fine, but expressing them verbally—he'd rather face a 350-pound offensive lineman out for his blood. Still, women liked to hear in words what went on inside a man's heart and soul. Or so he'd always been told. He'd never bared his heart to anyone, but if there was ever a time for baring, now was it.

''I love you more than anything on this earth, Toni. I always have.''

''You never loved my mother.'' The words weren't a question, they were an accusation. And suddenly Joe understood where the distance between him and his daughter had come from. His lips tightened at the thought of his ex-wife's malice. But Karen was gone, and nothing would be gained by speaking ill of the dead—or by lying.

''You're right. I didn't love her. That was my fault, not hers.''

"If you didn't love her, then how can you love me?"

"How can I not love you? You're my little girl. You'll be my little girl when you're eighty years old."

"You don't even know me."

"You're wrong," he said quietly. "I knew you the first time I looked into your eyes. You're the best part of me."

His words fell into a heavy, tense silence. Toni blinked as if to stop sudden tears, but she didn't repeat his words.

Joe's heart hurt worse. Would his little girl ever love him? Would she ever call him "Dad"? What kind of father was he if he couldn't even inspire love in his own child? What kind of man was he if he'd never been in love?

Now was not the time to worry about his life, or lack of one. He was supposed to be discussing Toni's life, and his worries about the direction she might take.

Joe reached over and took her hand. She started, but she didn't pull away. "I know you think you love him."

"I do."

"Fine, you do. But lives have been ruined for less than love."

"You're talking about sex."

Joe winced, but he didn't look away from her face. He might have learned about sex in the locker room like every other red-blooded American kid of his generation, but he didn't want his daughter learning about it that way.

"Yes, I'm talking about sex. You can get in big trouble playing with fire you can't control."

"I guess you *are* the voice of experience."

Ouch. How was he going to work past her latent anger? All he knew was the truth. So he told her that truth and hoped it would be enough.

"You can be angry at me all you want, Toni. I deserve that. But anger isn't going to change the facts. I took the easy way out. Your mom and I didn't get along, and you didn't seem to need me. I was traveling. I thought I had to make all the money I could before I retired. I was too dumb and too young to realize that I could make money another way, but that I'd never have another chance to be with you while you grew. I'll have to live with that mistake forever, and I doubt I'll forgive myself for it. But I wish you could."

She stared at him and pain filled her eyes. Joe braced himself, figuring his request for forgiveness was going to be tossed back in his face. Instead, he heard something that hurt him more—and infuriated him all over again.

"Mom said you didn't want me. I wasn't a boy, and you were the kind of guy who wanted a son."

"That's not true, Toni."

"Isn't it? Why do you want a new wife, more kids, if not to get a son?"

"Is that what you think?"

Toni dipped her head in acknowledgment.

"Boys, girls—what's the difference?"

"Don't you know?" Her glance and voice were heavy with sarcasm.

"I know there's a difference. What I mean is, I don't care. I always dreamed of a large family, and I wanted to spend time with my kids. That's all I want. I wish I'd had more time with you. But I'm here now, and I'm not leaving."

Her furtive glance and the sheen in her eyes made him frown. "Did you think I was going to leave you again?"

She shrugged, but at the same time she nodded. "Mom always did. She paid someone to be with me. Like she couldn't stand to. Like she couldn't stand to cook or clean."

Joe counted to ten. It would do no good to lose his temper at a dead woman, but oh, how he wanted to. "I'm not like your mom, even though I might have acted that way once. I've been waiting years to have you with me. I'm not going anywhere, honey. I *want* to be with you."

She seemed to believe him. At least, she didn't cry. No wonder she'd been watching him clean and praising his cooking. She figured as long as he did those things, he'd take care of her, too. And when he tired of them, he'd be tired of her. Poor kid.

"Aren't you mad at Mom?" she asked.

Joe glanced at Toni. She looked mad. He didn't want her to be angry with her mother. They had enough problems already. "She had her reasons. I wasn't fair to her. I didn't love her, and I'm sure that made her mad, though I don't think she loved me, either. It won't do any good to keep being angry about what's over and done with. I've got you here with me now, and I've never been happier.''

''I feel sorry for you.''

''Me?'' She switched gears so fast that he could almost hear the grind.

''You've never been in love. It's wonderful. And terrible.''

''So I've heard.''

''Don't you want to love someone and have her love you?''

''Yeah,'' he murmured, thinking of Evie.

Toni got out of the car, then leaned down to glance back in. ''You will someday, Dad. Someday soon.''

Then she slammed the door and ran inside. Joe sat in the car and enjoyed the moment for as long as he could.

She'd called him ''Dad.''

TONI HAD A PLAN, but she needed some help. Adam turned out to be worthless.

''I am *not* going to help you fix up my mom and your dad,'' he said when she called him later that night.

He sounded really mad, but for once she didn't get scared and shy and quiet. This was too important. Besides, Adam had kissed her and told her she was his girl. If he meant it, he would not dump her because she wanted to get their parents together. If he did, then she didn't need him, anyway.

She enjoyed the truth of that thought for a while. She loved Adam, and the fact that he cared about her had shown her she could be herself and that was okay. Now that she knew her dad loved her, the weight she'd carried around for years—the fear she could never be good enough for love—had disappeared. Her dad had *always* loved her, and he always would. He wasn't going to leave her because he wanted her with him.

So Toni was not going to make herself miserable anymore, worrying about everyone else. That was too exhausting. She was worth knowing, worth loving; she made a good friend; and those people who allowed her into their lives wouldn't be sorry. Realizing that truth felt better than anything had in a long time.

She dropped the subject of their parents with Adam. She had a better idea for a helper, anyway. Someone who liked her dad almost as much as Toni liked Mrs. Vaughn.

Her plan involved the Oak Grove Founder's Day Celebration, which would take place next week, near the end of July. There would be a carnival, picnic, all-star games for every level of the league and fireworks. Mrs. Vaughn had made a point of saying how much she loved fireworks and never missed them. Toni was counting on that.

In the meantime, the end of the baseball season approached. Her dad's team was in first place in his division, and Toni's team was in first place in theirs. The interest remained high because of the bet, and the games continued to be packed. Toni no longer worried about her performance. She did her best and that was enough for the team, her coach—even herself, for a change.

She discovered that when she relaxed and let things happen, they turned out for the best most of the time. Having an encouraging smile and a face she adored peeking through the wires of the catcher's mask didn't hurt, either.

One night the team was far enough ahead that Coach Vaughn took Toni out early and let Todd pitch. Toni and Coach Vaughn had had a few discussions on winning and losing and what those things really meant in life. How had Adam's mom gotten so smart?

Though Toni was supposed to sit on the bench and cheer the team, she saw her quarry playing in the dirt underneath the bleachers, and she slipped out of the dugout.

A whisper, a wink, a few giggles, some noogies to seal the deal, and Toni's plan was in motion. Her dad and Coach Mom would never know what hit them.

CHAPTER FIFTEEN

"ADAM, WHERE DID you say you'd be tonight?" Evie loaded blankets, folding chairs and a cooler into the station wagon. Luckily, she had already dropped the twins at the pre-parade lineup, so she didn't have to trip over them while she loaded the day's necessities.

"Tommy's," Adam answered. "He's having a pool party after the all-star game."

Since the temperature had already climbed into the eighties, and the clock had yet to hit ten a.m., the concept of a pool party appealed to Evie a lot. Unfortunately, she hadn't been invited.

"What about the fireworks?"

"His house is right behind the park. We watch them from the pool. It's awesome."

Now that Adam described it, Evie recalled Tommy's party as an annual do. "What about Toni?"

"She didn't want to go."

Evie got into the car and glanced at him. "Is that a problem?"

"No. She said she'd feel funny being the only girl at a pool party."

"I can see her point. Did she want you to skip it, too?"

"No." He put the car in reverse, glanced over his shoulder and backed out of the drive. "She's not like that."

"Good. You *are* going to college next year."

"So?"

"Well, she'll still be here for another year after that."

"Get to the issue, Mom."

"I don't want her to make you feel bad about leaving."

"Why don't you just say it? You don't want her to keep me from going."

Adam's new, and not entirely appealing, attitude was wearing thin. Had she been the one who'd hoped her son would show some healthy teenage rebellion? *Somebody slap me.*

"All right," Evie snapped. "I don't want her to keep you from going."

"She'd never do that."

"Great." Evie folded her arms over her chest and looked out the window, away from her son.

Since their first big argument, relations remained strained between her and Adam. He wanted to be a kid, but he didn't want Evie to be a mom. The two ideas did not compute, so Evie was on shaky ground with just about everything she said and did lately. She wasn't enjoying it.

She'd tried to talk to Adam again since the night he'd locked his door to her, but he had not wanted to listen. For a mother who prided herself on excellent communication with her children, Evie was pretty frustrated.

She had no idea what to say to him to make him understand that without her kids, her life would have been nothing. Certainly, both her pregnancies had been disasters—but that didn't make the children disasters, too. No matter how hard you tried with kids, somehow you always came up short.

The silence between them lasted a few heartbeats too long for comfort, but Evie kept looking outside. They passed the school block. The band stood in position at the front of the parade. Brightly colored jerseys mixed and mingled, as Little and Big League players not participating in the all-star games would march in the parade, wave and throw candy.

"I thought you liked her."

Evie sighed and returned her attention to the problem child of the week. "I *do* like her."

"So why the third degree?"

"I love you. I want what's best for you."

"Toni's what's best for me."

God, I hope so, Evie thought, but she kept her lip zipped.

The weather was perfect to Evie's mind—sunny, hot and dry—and all her troubles and tensions faded as enjoyment of Oak Grove, friends and family took their place. Founder's Day equaled fun and fireworks. What could be better? Though people did bring up the bet here and there, and the fact that both Evie's team and Joe's occupied first place in opposing leagues, the ribbing was good-natured, and folks seemed more excited about baseball than they'd been in years, which was saying a lot.

The all-star games drew huge crowds. Although the most talented players from each team were chosen to play, the kids did not play together until that day, which made the games interesting to watch.

Evie didn't have to coach, so she sat in the stands, drank her Coke, ate her peanuts and cheered. The twins got dirty under the bleachers; Adam and Toni won their game. A harbinger, she hoped, of things to come.

Adam took off with a wave for Mom and a kiss for Toni. Evie sighed. Times had changed. She'd best get used to them.

She called for the twins, needing a hug however dirty she'd get from it, but they were gone. Her heart banged a bit harder and faster. Kids didn't up and disappear in Oak Grove, but then, you could probably say that about the other places kids had disappeared from. Evie preferred to have her kids in sight at all times. Label her paranoid—she didn't mind.

"They're with Dad."

Toni's voice at her elbow set Evie's mind to rest. She turned to smile at the girl at the same instant what Toni had called her father registered. Evie's smile turned into a great big grin. "'Dad,' huh?"

Toni shrugged and looked at the ground. Evie let the subject drop. Something good must have happened between Toni and Joe. Evie was just glad it had. The way the twins worshiped Toni, Evie had figured they'd be calling her "Evelyn" before too long. She needed to spend time curing them of a new bad habit the way she needed another hot dream about Joe Scalotta.

"Where are they?"

Toni pointed to the grass in left field. Joe was on the ground, and both boys tumbled over him. For some reason the twins thought Joe was their personal wrestling trainer. Whenever and wherever they could, the two pulled him to the ground.

"What is that all about?" Evie asked.

Toni shrugged. "They like to jump on him. Maybe they know they can't hurt him."

"Do they do that with you?"

"Nope."

"Me, either."

"Must be a guy thing," Toni observed solemnly.

Evie nodded, enjoying the camaraderie with Toni they'd shared from the first day. Being the only woman in a houseful of men sometimes made Evie feel like the only female on Planet Testosterone.

Benji straddled Joe's chest and Danny his belly. They started bouncing up and down.

Evie put her arm around Toni's shoulders. "Should we save him?"

"Nah. He likes it."

"Go figure."

"Yeah." Toni sighed and shook her head, her attitude so clearly saying "Men!" that Evie laughed and gave her a little squeeze.

Together they crossed the infield and stood shaking their heads at all three of them.

"Boys, get off Mr. Scalotta."

"He says his name is Joe."

"Fine. Get off Joe."

In a sudden and agile move, Joe dumped both of them onto the ground, came up on his hands and knees with a roar and tickled them until Evie feared there would be an accident. Then he climbed to his feet and brushed the grass from his legs.

In khaki shorts and a red tank top, with his hair full of dandelion fuzz and his face flushed from laughter and the sun, Joe was something to see. Evie's breath caught.

Toni went over and started whispering to the twins.

Evie and Joe had not spoken beyond a casual word since the night at his house. Remembering both the truth and her fantasies made Evie blush.

"You look nice," Joe ventured.

She glanced at him in surprise. Her red-white-and-blue short set was worn two days of the year—Fourth of July and Oak Grove Founder's Day. Personally, she figured her star-spangled red shorts might be a bit much, but she'd learned long ago to please herself first, since there was virtually no pleasing everyone.

"Thanks."

They stared at each other. *Now what?*

Joe stepped closer, tilted his head down in a conspiratorial manner, and Evie did the same.

"I talked to her," he said.

"Mmm?" Evie murmured an encouragement.

"I don't think I got through completely, but she seems to have gotten the main point. How about you?"

Evie wasn't sure how to answer that. Adam had said he would not make his mother's mistake, and from his vehemence, she believed he'd meant that. But he'd also said he wanted to be less responsible, more of a kid. Not an encouraging statement to repeat to the very large and intimidating father who waited for an answer.

"I talked to him," she said, hoping that would be enough.

"And?"

It wasn't enough. Brownie point for him. "He knows my opinion."

Joe grunted. "So what do we do?"

"We continue to be good parents."

"How's that?"

"Watch them like hawks. Promises are easy to make."

"And tough to keep."

She raised her eyebrows. "You're starting to get the hang of this dad thing."

His smile was both joyous and rueful. "I think so."

"Mom!"

The twins hit her in the knees. She slammed into Joe's chest. The impact made it difficult to breathe, since the man was built like a brick. He caught her by the elbows before she bounced off and landed on her backside. That would have been lovely. Then he set her on her feet and held her arms a moment too long.

As his size and his scent enveloped her, Evie resisted the urge to fold herself into his arms. Joe made her feel physically safe and emotionally in jeopardy. The combination drove her crazy.

So instead of crawling into his embrace, Evie stepped back, out of reach but not out of range. She pushed her bangs out of her eyes, and her hand shook. Jeez, she had it bad.

He cocked his head. "You all right?"

"Yeah."

"Do those two always love you to death?"

"Every chance they get."

She turned around, and discovered Toni held one boy by each hand. The three of them had their heads together and were whispering furiously. Evie frowned. "What's going on?"

Toni glanced up, and an emotion Evie couldn't quite place crossed her face, then disappeared, leaving Evie with a sense of unease.

The twins grinned and launched themselves at her again, but Toni yanked them back. "Can Toni and Joe watch the fireworks with us? Can they, huh?"

Evie tensed. No help for it now. To say no would be rude. But the thought of watching the fireworks while she shared her blanket with Joe Scalotta made her twitchy. The quilt she'd brought would definitely not be big enough for five.

"Sure," she said. "No problem."

The twins jumped into the air with a whoop and a holler, then gave each other a high five. They missed hands and smacked Toni in the stomach. Benji looked at Danny; Danny looked at Benji. They took off running before Toni got her breath back.

"Hey!" She chased them around center field.

Evie and Joe chuckled and watched in companionable silence.

"She really is great with them," Evie observed.

"Yeah. Amazing, since she's never had any brothers or sisters. You'd think they'd drive her nuts."

"They do me. But they're kind of cute to the untrained eye. Devious—like puppies."

"Puppies? Aren't they always cute?"

She snorted. "You'd think so. Until they go on the rug. Or bark at midnight and again at dawn. Chew up the coffee table, your taupe pumps and the only copy of a Health 4 final exam."

"You've had a dog?"

"Nope. But I have a very good imagination."

"Really?"

She glanced at him, only to find his gaze on her, warm and curious enough to make her heart leap. Did he know how good her imagination was? And that lately it had been occupied mainly with him— naked?

He winked at her and rocked back on his heels. "So the twins do a lot of table chewing, do they?"

She laughed. "Are you always so literal?"

"Not always."

The way he spoke made Evie wonder how good *his* imagination was and how it had been occupied since their last evening together.

"Where's the best place around here to watch the fireworks?" he asked.

"I've already staked my claim. Years of testing have revealed the top spot for optimum viewing capacity."

"You're a professional, I see."

"In more ways than one, buster."

His gaze wandered over her once more. "I've noticed that."

This was fun. "Flattery will get you everywhere."

"Promise?"

Evie just smiled and called to the kids. "Guys, time to eat."

That brought the herd at a run, which saved her the trouble of answering questions she wasn't certain of herself.

JOE HADN'T HAD so much fun since he showed his Super Bowl ring to the president. He didn't want the day to end. He felt at home, part of a community, part of a family.

The day, from eating fried chicken in the sun, to buying the twins ice cream that melted down their faces, arms and legs, then taking them to the portable toilets to wash off, couldn't have been more perfect. As the sun set, and kids started tossing fluorescent necklaces in pickup games of horseshoes and keep-away, he sat hip to hip with Evie, a pink lemonade in his hand and a silly grin on his face. This was definitely the life.

"You seem happy," she said.

He glanced at her. She looked so pretty in her festive outfit, her great legs folded beneath her and one of those luminescent circles on her head. Joe wanted to kiss her, right there in front of God and Oak Grove. He wanted it badly enough that he inched to the edge of the blanket. Sometimes what he felt for her snuck up and scared him to death.

"I am happy." He gazed out over the crowd with a sigh of contentment. "I love it here. Oak Grove is so much like the town where I grew up. One state north, but a whole lot the same."

A band started playing in the gazebo. Big-band music, strains of a time long gone but not quite forgotten.

Joe's parents had often gone dancing. In those days people knew how to dance—together. His mother had taught all her boys, insisting they would be grateful one day. Thus far he didn't think any of them had found much use for the waltz or the fox trot, though the polka had come in handy during college beer parties.

Closing his eyes, Joe remembered how he and his brothers would huddle at the top of the stairs and watch his parents push back the couch and coffee table, then dance around and around the living room.

They'd looked graceful—Mom so lovely and Dad so handsome—deeply in love for always. They would laugh and kiss, then hold hands and come upstairs.

Joe hadn't realized until right this moment how those Saturday night dances had assured him and his brothers of the rock-solid sturdiness of their parents' love—for each other, their children and the life they had built together. As long as his parents danced on Saturday night, all was right with the world.

Joe opened his eyes, swallowed his last sip of lemonade and stood. "Let's dance." He held out a hand to Evie.

Her eyes widened, and she stared at his hand as if it had sprouted a snake's head. "I don't dance."

He hauled her to her feet. "You do now."

She protested all the way to the cement circle in front of the bandstand, where older couples moved in perfect time to the slow beat.

Joe stepped onto the dance floor and pulled Evie into his arms. She stumbled into his chest and stomped all over his feet. "Sorry," she mumbled, though she didn't sound sorry at all.

She came up to his collarbone, and if he leaned down just so, he could rest his cheek against her hair. She smelled like summer and sunshine. "Just follow my lead," he whispered.

"I'll have to."

"It's easy. Listen to the music. Feel the beat. The

box step goes… Step together, back together, side together, front together. That's it, keep going."

"Who are you—Arthur Murray?"

"I've always fancied myself Fred Astaire. The man had grace."

"And class."

"Mmm-hmm."

Evie caught on quick, and as she did, she relaxed in his arms. Joe hadn't danced like this since he'd left home. The combination of the music, and the night, and the scent of her had Joe tingling like a teenager.

"Did you ever think that if people could dance the way they used to, the world might move back toward an age of innocence?"

She looked into his face. "You certainly are a dreamer."

"Or a hopeless romantic."

"Hopeless, for sure."

He sighed and tugged her closer. "Too bad, huh?"

"Yeah. This is kind of fun."

"Don't you teach dancing in gym class?"

"They do square dancing in junior high."

"A useful skill if ever there was one."

She laughed. "They learn rhythm, and cooperation, and following directions. But you might be right. At the next curriculum meeting, I think I'll suggest a ballroom-dancing unit."

"Couldn't hurt."

"Tell that to a fourteen-year-old."

Joe just smiled, and when the music ended, he dipped her. Evie's sharp gasp of surprise, the startled flare of her eyes and the sudden clench of her hands on his shoulders made him lift her back into the circle of his arms. They stared into each other's eyes—long and deep—as the sun slid below the horizon and darkness spread across the land.

"Don't worry," he said. "I won't let you fall."

She stepped closer and leaned her head against his chest, slipping her arms about his waist. The warmth of her body along his made Joe's heart stammer.

"I think it's too late," she whispered.

"I think you're right."

TONI STOOD AT THE EDGE of the dance floor with one arm around Benji and one around Danny. Her plan was working, and she hadn't even done anything yet—except keep the twins away from her dad and their mom. This was going to be so easy, it wasn't even funny.

"Now?" Danny asked.

"In a minute."

"You said that five minutes ago," Benji pointed out.

She ignored them, which she'd discovered worked a whole lot better than arguing. You couldn't win with those two, anyway.

Tightening her hold on the twins so they wouldn't

escape too soon, Toni fixed her eyes on the romantic scene playing out in front of her. Their dance had looked like something from a black-and-white movie. Toni hadn't known her dad could move like that. It made him seem different, somehow. Not like a dad, and definitely not like a rough-and-tough football player. Which was good, because Toni didn't think Mrs. Vaughn liked Joe's old image. But this new one had definite possibilities.

If her dad had been wearing a tux, he could have passed for that suave guy in the movies he liked so much—Bond, James Bond—but the older ones with the Scottish guy who ended up being Indiana Jones's dad. That guy had class and grace.

The band began to play a faster tune, and her dad and Mrs. Vaughn quickly pulled apart. Almost like they felt guilty. *Darn.* Toni had hoped they'd kiss right there on the dance floor.

She gave Benji and Danny a shove. "Go," she ordered, and they were off.

Her dad saw them coming and stepped in front of Mrs. Vaughn before they could knock her down. It was so sweet the way he protected her. But Mrs. Vaughn didn't seem to see it that way. Instead, she frowned and elbowed her way around Joe.

Toni hurried forward to make sure the twins didn't muck things up.

"We're tired, Mom. We want to go to bed," said Danny.

Mrs. Vaughn's frown deepened, and she went

down on one knee, pressing her lips first to one sweaty forehead and cheek, then to the other. Toni watched, fascinated.

Benji and Danny were like twin tornadoes out of control, but Mrs. Vaughn loved them. She was always touching them, even if she wasn't looking at them. Kind of like she knew where they were all the time because they were a part of her. She'd kiss their brows, the way she was doing now, and murmur "I love you" against their hair. The two would smile, as if they'd heard that a hundred times before, which they probably had; then they'd run off to cause more trouble.

Toni gave a sigh of awe, and Joe flicked a considering glance her way, but she pretended not to see. Sometimes, even though she knew it was wrong, Toni wished that Mrs. Vaughn were her mom.

"You guys are hot," Mrs. Vaughn said. "But you don't have a fever."

"How do you know that without a thermometer?" Joe asked.

"I've done this so many times, I can tell by a lip test if their temperature's over a hundred or under."

"We're not sick. Just tired. Can Toni take us home? Can she, huh?"

"No. I'll take you."

Oops. Not part of the plan. Toni intervened. "I can take them. I know how much you like fireworks." She nudged the boys.

"Yeah, Mom, they're your favorite thing. Like raindrops and rosies and whistles and kittens."

"The Sound of Music," Joe muttered.

Mrs. Vaughn and Toni gaped at him. "How did you know that?"

He shrugged and looked away as if embarrassed. "It's a good movie."

Mrs. Vaughn met Toni's gaze, and they shared a grin. Dad was doing okay, even without her help. The image of big, tough-guy Scalotta merrily watching *The Sound of Music* was adorable. But back to business.

"Really, Coach," Toni said. "I don't mind. I'll take them to your house and put them to bed. If you'd drop off Dad afterward, everyone will be happy."

"Everyone except me. I don't want them riding in that red death trap."

"Hey!" Joe's protest nearly drowned beneath the pop of the first firework going off. As the shower of color split the night, the crowd let out a cheer.

Mrs. Vaughn stood, and Toni started talking before she could say no and ruin everything. "I've got my own car now. A very safe and very boring four-door Chevy." She grabbed the twins and backed away. "See you at home! Don't rush. We'll be fine."

Toni ran before either parent could say anything else, dragging the twins alongside her. When they reached the parking lot, she risked a glance back. "Look," she whispered, and the boys turned.

Her dad and their mom walked toward the quilt, hand in hand.

"Jordan fades back," Benji said, as he did just that.

"He flies. He shoots." Danny made motions with an imaginary basketball. "Swish."

"Three points," Toni said. "And that, boys, is the game."

CHAPTER SIXTEEN

"SHE'S A GOOD DRIVER," Joe assured Evie as they settled onto the quilt.

Evie nodded, her unease fading as the fireworks display heated up. "It's just not like them to be tired."

"Ever?"

She rolled her eyes. "You do know who I'm talking about, don't you? Benji and Danny—the brothers of perpetual motion?"

"Ah, them. Yes, I'm familiar with the order. They've taken vows of arguing, wrestling and—"

"Sleeping only when threatened."

"Then I'd grab this break and run with it," Joe said.

So Evie lay back and gave herself over to the wonder and beauty of the light show in the sky. Joe joined her. She tried not to be uncomfortable with him stretched out at her side, hip close, hand brushing hers, then twining fingers with fingers.

"Oh, my favorite," she said as a gold spider, the ends tipped with blue stars, erupted high above.

"I like the worms."

"Worms?"

"Wait. You'll see."

They continued to watch in friendly silence until a particular burst of fireworks lit the darkness and several squiggles of color twirled down, accompanied by a cartoon-like sound that indicated speed.

"There," he said, with suitable awe in his voice. "Isn't that great?"

"Silly."

"So?"

He squeezed her hand and tilted his head toward hers. She could hear the steady, comforting sound of his breath near her ear. The ground at her back was cool, her body warm from the nearness of his. Her kids were safe, and somewhere else for the time being. The fireworks kept up a steady flare of light and sound. Who could ask for anything more?

The finale was loud, long and impressive. As the acrid scent of gunpowder drifted along the night breeze and a final *boom* signified The End, whistles and cheers erupted from the crowd.

"Wasn't that wonderful?" she asked.

"Only one thing could make it better."

She turned her head, and their noses bumped. The tension that had been building between them since he'd dragged her off to dance bubbled up again, stronger than before, and Evie held her breath as she waited for his kiss. On a sigh of surrender, her eyes drifted closed.

"Ice cream." He sat up.

Evie's eyes popped open. Maybe she had imagined the heat, and the want, and the need. She sat up, too.

"You like spumoni?" he asked.

"Love it."

"Let's get some."

She laughed. "In this town? After ten p.m.? You're dreaming."

"I know the exact place." He stood and held out a hand. "You game?"

She put her palm against his. "You bet."

The place turned out to be his house, his kitchen and his freezer. Evie sat at the table and ate ice cream across from Joe, for all the world as though they were a married couple and this was their house, with the kids all tucked snug in their beds upstairs.

But the kids weren't theirs, and the kids weren't here. She and Joe were alone, and the thoughts that kept wandering through her mind were not those of a woman long married to this man. They were the thoughts of a woman fascinated and aroused by the mystery of him.

"Gotta go." Evie stood.

Her chair banged over backward, the sound echoing in the room. Joe looked as frozen as the ice cream in front of him. His eyes were cool and blue, but the heat beneath the ice made Evie's skin moist, sensitive, on fire.

Deliberately, he put his spoon into the bowl, pushed back his chair and stood. He didn't come any closer, but she felt crowded just the same. Trapped in his house, pinned by those eyes, captured by what was between her and him, now and from the very beginning.

She had no excuses left. No children who would bust in. No game to coach. No class to teach. No one who needed her attention—except him.

She could tell herself they had nothing in common. Their goals were so far apart as to be in a different stratosphere. Their futures were divergent; their hopes and dreams at odds. But her body didn't care about any of those things. Her body only cared that his was near, and that the time for fulfillment was now.

Still she hesitated, uncertain, afraid.

Then his hoarse whisper washed over her. "Don't go. Stay with me. Be with me."

She shivered and took a single step forward. That was all he needed to gather her in his arms and kiss her as only he could. He tasted like cherries on snow. She drowned in him, his scent, his heat—his need as overwhelming as her own.

They had done no more than kiss and dance, yet his body was familiar, his touch an old friend. In his arms she would always be safe. She'd been alone so long—a lifetime, it seemed—but she hadn't known how lonely she was. Touching Joe showed her life would never be the same without him.

He flicked the lights, plunging the room into darkness. She sighed with relief from the glare of the light, the heat of the bulb, in a kitchen now cool with silvered moonlight.

She'd wanted to touch his chest since the night she'd seen him in this kitchen, wearing nothing but black pants. She tugged his shirt free of his shorts

and spread her palms across hard planes of flesh and
soft twirls of hair.

His moan filled her mouth, igniting her. His lips
traced her jaw; his teeth scraped her neck. Hands
shadowed the path of hers, touching her belly, fluttering across her ribs, thumb tracing the line of her
bra.

The world dipped and swirled as he picked her
up. Her fingers clasped his shoulders. He stared into
her face. Even in the darkness his eyes shone blue,
his face appeared intense; yet his mouth looked full
and vulnerable, still wet from hers.

"Do you want this?" he asked, and though his
voice was rough with arousal, his words were soft
with uncertainty.

The voice of reason, to which she'd always listened, chattered away in a distant corner of her
mind, telling her to run, hide, go home and save
herself from disaster. She was asking for trouble
such as she had never imagined if she allowed this
man to touch her. He was the enemy of her dream—
a man just like Ray.

But he wasn't like Ray—or, at least, not anymore.
Why did she have to think so much, anyway? Joe
Scalotta made her feel like a woman, and she
couldn't remember the last time she'd felt like anything other than a mom, a teacher or a coach.

The long, contemplative silence hung over them
saying more than words ever could. He shifted as if
to put her down, and the panic that filled her at the
thought of leaving without finishing what had sim-

mered between them for weeks revealed a decision made long ago.

She put her palms on his rough cheeks and yanked his mouth back to hers, kissing him with an abandon she hadn't felt in a very long time. Then she traced her lips to his ear, licked the lobe, blew on the moist heat and whispered, "I want this. I want you."

He didn't waste any more time with talk—she liked that in a man—but strode from the room and up the staircase. She might be short, but she wasn't that light, yet he carried her up the stairs like an oversize Rhett Butler.

Evie stifled a giggle at that image. She doubted Joe would find it funny. He'd no doubt think Rhett a wimp for not dumping Scarlett on her pretty, Southern behind. Evie thought that herself, but she'd always liked the staircase scene. Especially the part where Scarlet woke up the next morning with a great big smile on her face.

A sigh escaped her lips, and she let her head sag to his shoulder, where it fit perfectly into the crook of his neck. She held on to his broad shoulders, enjoying the play of the well-defined muscles beneath her hands.

He stepped into his bedroom and kicked shut the door. The slam reverberated down her spine. He let her legs go, and she slid down his body, cloth against cloth, flesh against flesh, until they stood together, hips aligned to thighs. Then she put her lips upon his.

The darkness made her bold, reminded her of secret sinful fantasies she'd enjoyed many a long, lonely night. His clothes disappeared with a few tugs, and she learned the contours of his body with a scandalous exploration of fingertips, lips and tongue.

From the first, his body had fascinated her—big and hard, smooth and rough. She could not find a spare ounce of flesh anywhere—and she looked everywhere.

He quivered beneath her touch. She closed her palm along his length, and he went rigid, grabbed her wrist and growled, "Enough."

With a quickness that belied his size, he flipped her onto the bed and covered her fully clothed body with his own naked form. "My turn," he whispered. Then his body shifted and stretched, a *tap* sounded and a soft glow filled the room.

Evie blinked and moaned. "No lights."

"Yes, lights. I want to see that body I've been dreaming about every night."

The hum of arousal in her that had become a screech of need as his nude body pressed into hers suddenly went silent.

He kissed her temple. "What's the matter, babe?"

She snorted. "Babe? Please, do I look like a babe?"

He kissed her until she forgot what she'd been annoyed about, then he put his mouth to her ear and murmured, "You look like a babe to me."

His hips flexed, and her body responded with un-diluted lust to the call of his—hardness to softness, hill to valley, man to woman.

She gave up trying to resist the inevitable. "Babe, honey, whatever. Could you turn off the light?"

"Nope." He rolled to the side and busied his hands with the star-spangled buttons of her shirt. She grabbed his fingers, and he lifted his gaze to hers, eyebrows raised in question.

"Uh, you see, well..." She didn't know how to explain that she wasn't a babe, not really, and that his fantasies about her body were going to turn to nightmares when he got a good gander.

"What?" He twined their fingers together. "Tell me."

"All right." She gave up with a sigh that sounded sad even to her own ears. "You're so perfect. Your body is incredible. I love touching it."

"I love when you touch me."

"And I love looking at you."

He wiggled his eyebrows. "I'd love to have a look at you."

How could he joke at a time like this? She was out-and-out terrified, so she turned her head aside, away from his amused gaze. "I look better in my clothes, Joe."

"I don't think so."

"How would you know?"

Fear always made her angry. She pulled her hand from his and would have sat up, but he threw a big, heavy arm across her chest.

"Uh-uh-uh. No running away this time. I'm in no condition to chase you down."

She stared at the ceiling fan above his bed so she wouldn't have to gaze at him. "Have you ever seen a woman's body after she's had a few kids—one pregnancy a set of twins?"

"Can't say that I have—" another button popped open on her shirt "—but I'd like to."

"It's not pretty. I've got stretch marks." She forced her eyes from the lazily turning fan and back to him. "My butt resembles a road map."

His lips twitched. "This I have to see."

"It's not funny, Joe," she whispered, mortified.

"Shh," he said, and the sound soothed her, as did the desire in his eyes.

He still wanted her, and she'd told him the entire ugly truth. But telling wasn't the same as seeing, so she braced herself. No man had viewed her body since she'd hit the other side of thirty.

He held her eyes as he finished unbuttoning her shirt, then flipped the front catch on her bra with an expert twist. The garment flew open, and her breasts swelled free. His gaze lowered from her face to her chest. The slow revolutions of the fan cast a languid breeze across the bed, cooling her heated flesh, making her nipples tighten, then throb.

He stared at her for so long that she wanted to squirm. Then his ice-blue eyes raised to hers. "You mean these silver strands, here?"

His calloused fingertip traced the slope of one breast to illustrate the question. In answer, she shivered. His head lowered, and his tongue traced the path of his finger, along the fullness, then over the peak. His lips closed on a sensitive nipple, and she gasped.

"And here?" His tongue followed another silver trail. "They make me hot. You make me hot." He traced every line, every curve, every mark upon her body, until she forgot what she'd been worried about in the first place.

"We have a saying in my business—marks of the battle make you a man. These make you a woman, Evie. They're something to be proud of, never ashamed. You got them creating life, and there's nothing more of a battle, or a victory, than that."

He left her for just a minute, and the drawer on his nightstand opened, then shut. A second more, and he rose above her, joined himself with her.

He made her feel wanted, needed, cherished and beautiful. He made her feel things she had not felt in a long time—in a lifetime.

Faster and faster, harder, deeper he thrust, and together they shattered, shivering, shaking, sated.

He pulled her into his arms, yanked the cover over them both. Then he smoothed the tangles from her hair, rubbing his fingers along her scalp and soothing her nearly to sleep.

How long they lay there, content in each other's arms, she didn't know. For once, Evie let her worries go and lived in the moment. His bed was as big as he was, comfortable and warm. She stretched out her legs, curled against his side and looked into his beautiful blue eyes.

"You know what I dream?" he asked.

She smiled. "I think you just gave me the X-rated version."

His laugh held true joy, something she had never heard there before.

"I didn't mean that kind of dream. I meant life dreams."

Rubbing her cheek along his chest, she reveled in the texture of his hair along her skin, his heat against her body and his scent filling her soul.

"I've always wanted a houseful of kids. Boys, girls—doesn't matter." Her eyes popped open, and she stopped her explorations. "I like babies. I have this great memory of Toni right after her bath and just before bed, all warm and compact in one of those sleepers, smelling like baby shampoo and powder."

He hugged Evie close, but she just lay there like a lump. He didn't notice. "I love them when they're like that. I want that again. Not that I had it much before. I think at least three—not more than five. Doesn't that sound like fun? How old are you, anyway?"

Evie had gone from sexual satisfaction and happy dreams of a secret affair, straight to shivering, shaking fury. "What am I—your broodmare?" She got up and started searching for her clothes.

"What's the matter? What did I say?"

"I thought you'd changed. The way you've been acting since you came to town...I really thought you'd changed." She found her shorts tangled in the plain, brown bedspread. "But I should have known better. I should have known a guy like you would want to keep me barefoot and pregnant for the rest of my days."

"What are you talking about?"

"You!" She shoved her arms into her shirt and nearly tore the sleeve free. "What you just said."

"That's my dream. Why are you shouting?"

"Don't include me in your nightmare, buster. I've already lived it. I've had three kids, and I've raised them alone. I'm just getting to the fun part, and you want me to go directly to jail, do not pass go, do not collect two hundred dollars?"

"I don't know what's set you off. What did you think this was about?" He made a sweeping gesture to include the tousled bed.

"Sex. Great sex."

"It wasn't just sex, and you know it."

"Do I? Are you saying you love me?"

"I don't know." His voice was as uncertain as his words, but when he looked away, she knew the truth. Why did that hurt so much? It wasn't as if she loved him, either.

"This is what I'm talking about. You don't talk about making babies when you don't know anything about love."

''Hey, don't act so high-and-mighty. You're the one who said this was just sex.''

''I said great sex. And it was. I would have done it again if you hadn't started that baby talk.'' She shuddered. ''What a way to throw a bucket of ice on a girl.'' Evie finished buttoning her shirt and headed for the door.

''You're leaving?''

''You got it.''

''But...but I thought you could stay the night.''

''Are you nuts? This isn't New York or Chicago. Heck, it isn't even Davenport. You don't go sleeping overnight at some guy's house while your kids are home alone.''

''Toni's there.''

''And what would she think if I didn't come home? I'm her coach.''

''I'm her dad.''

The way he said it, all quiet and beaten, took the wind out of Evie's anger. What had she expected? He was just Joe, after all, and he couldn't help what he wanted. But she knew better than to let him think she could ever live in his dreamworld.

''I think it would be best if we forgot this ever happened.''

He sat up. The sheet trailed over his lap, but the rest of him was completely bare. His skin was that perfect shade of bronzed gold that made women's mouths go dry.

Evie swallowed the lust in her throat. That was

all it was, she assured herself. How could she not want to touch him, now that she knew how his skin felt against her hands, how his body felt against her own?

"You think you can forget?" he asked.

"Sure." Her voice did not sound sure at all. "And unless it involves one of the kids or the teams, I think we should stay out of each other's way."

"Why? You going to be tempted?"

To bed—definitely. To labor and delivery—not again in this lifetime.

She sighed. "Joe, please, don't make this any harder than it already is."

"If it's so hard, then why do it?"

"I can't be what you need, and you can't be what I want. I had a marriage like that. I swore I'd never go there again."

"What do you want? Let me try to be that guy."

The way he said it, so eager and sweet, her eyes sparked with tears. If he gave up his dream for hers, he'd wind up hating her. She couldn't bear it. She'd rather not have him at all.

"I'd make you miserable, Joe."

"And you think I'd do the same to you." His shoulders sagged, defeated. "You aren't even willing to try?"

"I'd be willing to try. I'd even be willing to fail—again—if we were talking only about me. But we're not."

"The kids."

"Yeah, the kids. They're my life."

He nodded. At least he understood that.

"Good night," he said.

"Goodbye," she whispered, and slipped from the room.

CHAPTER SEVENTEEN

WHERE HAD HE GONE WRONG?

That question plagued Joe for the rest of the night and throughout the days that followed. He had held her, loved her, offered her his dream. Then she'd flipped out and said she never wanted to see him again—unless it was business.

Toni seemed mad at him, too, and when he asked her why, she just rolled her eyes and muttered, "Men."

What was a guy supposed to do?

His mistake, to his way of thinking, was even to entertain the notion that their uncommon attraction might be love. He'd known from the first that Evie Vaughn could not be the woman for him. She was too much like Karen and not enough like...

Who? His mom? June Cleaver? Joe gave a disgusted grunt. Sometimes he got on his own nerves.

To be honest, now that he knew Evie, she wasn't like Karen at all. The main reason she'd blown him off was her kids. She put them first. So why did she work like a dog—night and day, summer and winter? She'd said his dream was her nightmare, so what *was* her dream? Would she let him get close enough to ask? If he won their silly bet, would she ever talk to him again?

These questions haunted Joe throughout the final game of the season. Unfortunately, his last game and Toni's last game were on the same night, same time, different sides of town. If both teams won, they would face each other in the World Series in Cedar City. An entire season of baseball, and everything came down to one game. Wasn't that always the way?

A sudden cheer rose from the crowd, then the team. Joe jerked his head up in time to see his kids lift the pitcher, who had just struck out a final batter, onto their shoulders.

"We're number one," they chanted as they marched about the field.

Joe smiled and accepted congratulations all around. He was happy for his kids, but his mind wasn't on this game.

His cell phone rang, and he answered.

"Dad? We won!"

"That's great, honey. Congratulations."

"How about you?"

"We did, too."

"Oh." In Toni's voice, Joe heard everything in his heart.

"Yeah, oh."

"Now what?" she asked.

"Now we're off to the big time."

"Goody." She sounded as happy about it as he was.

FROM THE FRONT SEAT of the bus, Evie contemplated fields of rolling corn. "Knee-high by the Fourth of July" went the saying. The calendar read August third, and the corn looked higher than an elephant's eye to her. Must be a banner year.

So why did she feel as though the world was coming to an end, or at least was on a severe downhill slide? Maybe because she hadn't slept well since she'd left Joe's bed. She wanted to be there again. She wanted to be with him again. Every time she closed her eyes she saw him, smelled him, felt him. Would this ever end? She missed him, yet she'd never really had him.

Evie glanced behind her to make sure all her little ducks were in a row, or at least behaving themselves. These newfangled buses that sported televisions with VHS capability and a bathroom in the rear were a chaperone's delight. All her players had their eyes fixed upon the latest in the never-ending saga of James Bond.

Toni had brought the tape, handed it to Evie with a shrug and murmured, "Dad's got them all." Then she'd taken a seat with the twins and promptly started playing road-sign bingo.

What was Evie supposed to make of Joe's fascination with 007? Did he admire the character's heroics—his disregard for life and limb in order to save the world? Or had Bond's suave, martini-swilling, never-aging machismo garnered his attention?

Evie shook her head. It didn't matter. She had to

stop regretting what could never be. She'd been right to put an end to things between her and Joe before someone got seriously hurt.

No one seemed to agree with her. Toni had spent the week avoiding her, and the twins were pouting. The only one who acted close to normal was Adam, and he was as happy as a cat with a bellyful of half-and-half. Which made Evie suspicious. What did Adam have to be so chipper about?

"Grr," she murmured. She was in the mood to stomp on a few happy campers.

"What're you so all-fired crabby about?" Hoyt leaned over the seat. "You've got your wish. You're going to the World Series. Win that, then you're on your way to the state championships and your job is in the bag."

"Yippee." Evie twirled her finger in the air.

"Well, don't that just beat all. What happened to your dream, girl?"

Hoyt was right. Her dream of having the money to send her boys to college brushed the tips of her fingers. All she had to do was reach up and grab it.

Sure, Joe had said he didn't want her job—and he wouldn't take it. But after what had happened at the school board meeting, Evie had no doubt Mrs. Larson and Don would use a loss to Joe as an excuse to keep her from the job she wanted.

Call her slow, but she hadn't figured out until recently that Don didn't think a woman should coach a varsity boys' sport, no matter how qualified that woman was. Of course, he didn't think anything about the men's gym teacher coaching the girls' basketball team. That was just fine and dandy.

Don had done everything in his power to thwart her, without actually telling her no. He didn't want to offend her father, who would come barreling into town being manly and daddyish if he found out his best friend had kept his baby from her dream.

Evie didn't want that, either. She wanted the job because she was the best one for it. That was the only way to keep it, and to change the outdated views of the school board and the rest of the town. She had never been a crusader—she just wanted what was best for the kids and her. But this stuff really had to stop before some other woman, or young girl, got her dreams trampled just because she was female.

Well, no use ranting and raving about Mrs. Larson and the rest of the Oak Grove throwbacks. The only way they were going to change was if they were forced. And the only way Evie could force them was to win the game tomorrow.

"Hey, there's the hotel!"

The peace turned to pandemonium as the bus pulled into the parking lot. Evie stood and held up her hand until everyone quieted down. "You've all got your roommates?"

Murmurs of assent filled the air. Evie glanced at her clipboard. Twelve boys made six rooms. Toni would stay with her dad, the twins with Hoyt. Evie stifled a laugh. He'd asked for them. It had taken her all of three seconds to agree.

Which meant Evie would have her own blessed hotel room. Hotel rooms were few and far between—alone was even farther. So why wasn't she more excited about the little bit of heaven that had come her way? Maybe because Joe Scalotta would be sleeping only a couple of doors down. Evie glanced out the window in time to see the man in question lead his team toward the pool.

His attire consisted of a towel looped about his neck and a pair of baggy, blue swim trunks. Her heart thundered; her mouth went dry. She tore her gaze from the well-defined muscles of his back, only to discover Toni grinning at her and Adam scowling.

"I'll get the keys and the room numbers," she muttered, then got off the bus in a hurry.

But not quickly enough to miss the twins' whoop of laughter and Hoyt's knowing smirk. The universe and everyone in it seemed to be conspiring against her these days.

THE KNOCK ON TONI'S door came before she'd even unpacked. A glance through the peephole revealed Adam scowling in the hallway. She opened the door with a smile, but he continued to scowl as he stepped in and edged a stopper beneath the door to prop it open.

"What're you doing?" she asked.

"Keeping us from getting kicked off the team and me from getting murdered."

"Huh?"

"If my mom or your dad catches us alone in a hotel room, we're toast."

"But we won't *do* anything. Will we?"

"Not with the door open." Adam sat at the desk, and Toni sat on the bed. "What are you up to, Toni?"

Her smile turned to a frown. "Up to?"

"With my mom and your dad. I know something happened, and now they barely talk to each other."

"But they look at each other all the time when they think no one's watching." She gave a sigh at the thought of how romantic it was.

"But my mom mopes around like her best friend died."

"Really?"

"It's nothing to be happy about. If your dad hurts her, I'll—"

"What?" Toni's hands curled into fists. "Who said it was his fault?"

"*What* was his fault? What happened?"

Toni got up and began to pace. She picked up a pillow and hugged it to her chest. "I don't know. That night you went to the pool party—" Adam nodded. "I took the twins home early so my dad and your mom could watch the fireworks alone."

"Are you nuts?"

"I don't know. I thought they liked each other— and all they needed was a little bit of time. I love your mom. I think Joe does, too."

"I don't think Joe knows the meaning of the word."

That made her mad, though Toni had thought the same thing until recently. But her dad loved her, so he might love Mrs. Vaughn. Toni wasn't willing to give up on her dream of having Adam's mom for her very own without a heck of a fight.

"What have you got against my father?" she demanded.

"You want a list?"

Then several things happened.

Someone yelled through the open door, "Hey, Adam, I thought we were going swimming."

Toni hit him up alongside the head with a pillow so hard he fell out of the chair. While she stood gaping at what she'd done, he threw the pillow back into her face.

Then someone else yelled, "Pillow fight!"

Things went downhill from there.

JOE HAD SENT his team upstairs to shower and change. They had practice time at the ballpark right after dinner. Then he swam a few more laps by himself, trying to get Evie out of his mind.

He might as well have told the birds to quit singing, for all the good it did him to try to swim Evie out of his brain. She was in his blood. All he thought about was her. Their one night together had only made him crave more. When he'd held her in his arms he'd known she was the woman for him—forever. But how could that be, when their wants in life were so divergent?

Joe climbed the stairs to his floor. A riot of sound

drifted down the stairwell, breaking into his reverie. He opened the door and got hit in the chest with a pillow.

For a moment Joe stood there and stared. He couldn't believe his eyes. His team and Evie's were out in the hall slamming pillows into one another. A few pillows had torn open, and where in the old days feathers would have been floating in the air, now polyester stuffing lay all over the floor, making the carpet look like it had dandruff.

He squinted through the throng, searching for his daughter, only to find her beating Adam Vaughn over the head. To Adam's credit, he didn't fight back; he just put his hands over his face and let her go. He must have screwed up good to get Toni so mad.

For a moment Joe experienced a flash of camaraderie for the kid. He strode through the mess, grabbed the pillow out of Toni's hand and stepped between the two of them.

"What is going on here?"

Toni lunged for the pillow. Joe caught her around the waist and held her back. Adam peeked from between his arms, saw that she was restrained and lowered his defenses.

"Well?" Joe said. "I'm waiting. What started this?"

Both Toni and Adam clammed up. The rest of the kids were too far gone to be stopped by the mere presence of a coach—even if it was Joe.

He was more concerned with his daughter and the

boyfriend. There was trouble in paradise, and he wanted to know why.

"Toni?"

"Nothing, Dad. It's just kids, you know?"

He did, but somehow he didn't think that was what this was about. "Adam?"

The kid shrugged and wouldn't look at him. Joe could tell they were lying when they wouldn't look him in the face. He hated that, but then again, if a kid could lie and look him in the face, that would be a whole lot worse. Before Joe could pursue the line of questioning, a door opened in the middle of the hall and a whirlwind swept out.

"Knock that off!" Evie yanked a pillow from one kid's hand. "Cut that out!" She caught another in mid-flight. "I want you all back in your rooms on the double. I'm going to count to ten, and whoever is still in this hallway is going to find his or her butt on the bench tomorrow."

The hallway cleared before she hit five, leaving Joe alone with the subject of each of his dreams and every one of his problems.

Evie nodded and made as if to slip back into her room. Joe dropped the pillows and crossed the hall before she could get away.

He cupped his palm around the soft skin of her upper arm. His body went hot and hard at her sharp intake of breath. She went very still, as if she wanted to collapse into his arms as much as she wanted to tear free of them.

"Hey," he whispered, uncertain what to say or do to keep her near for a single moment longer.

Her hair was damp, and she smelled like hotel shampoo—flowers beneath the evergreens—different than usual, but no less enticing. She was still Evie, and he wanted her—for always.

"I've missed you."

She sighed, and her arm slid along his hand. Flesh upon flesh, ice to his heat. They both shuddered in reaction.

"Oh, Joe, don't." Her voice sounded near to tears—kind of the way he felt.

"Stay for just a minute," he begged.

"I need to call the desk. Get a vacuum up here. Grab a few bad boys and make them clean up their mess."

"That can wait a few minutes. The mess won't walk away."

She gave a snort of laughter that held no humor at all. "It never does."

Joe glanced first up, then down, the long hallway. The kids had all disappeared, no doubt hoping if they hid long enough, the storm would blow over them. Someone's television played loud enough for Joe to hear high-pitched cartoon voices sounding much too happy-happy for this world. Joe tuned that out, along with the urge to go rap on the door and make whoever it was turn the TV down.

For the moment he and Evie were alone, and he wasn't walking away from her until they had this out.

"I've been thinking about us."

"There is no us. There can't be."

"You won't let there be. Hear me out."

She shook her head, then backed away from him until her shoulders came up against the wall. He followed, placing one hand on each side of her head. She glanced up, startled, and he couldn't help himself. He kissed her.

Her mouth was open, no doubt to give him a piece of her mind. Instead she gave him access, and he took full advantage—delving within, tasting her, teasing her, tempting her.

Her hands came up, and he tensed, afraid she would push him away. For a long, frightening second she hesitated, then with a sigh that was both sob and surrender she laced her hands behind his neck, and she kissed him back.

Suddenly what had been so damn complicated became really quite simple.

He loved her.

He wanted her, and he needed her, and he admired her, and he liked her. But most of all—he loved her. How could he ever have been uncertain? Maybe because he'd never felt something quite so wonderful, and so frightening, at the same time. Love was exactly the way Toni had described. Only the first moment he'd held Toni in his arms could compare—that utter joy and total terror that made your heart beat so fast you thought you might die right then and there.

"I love you, babe," he murmured against her lips.

"Don't call me 'babe,'" she said, and pulled her mouth from his.

Lost in the novelty of his feelings and the familiarity of her, he took the movement and made it magic, kissing her jaw, her neck, her ear, her eyelids. His lips came away damp, tasting of salt, and he opened his eyes to stare down at her, bemused.

She leaned against the wall, her face sheet-white and her lips passion-red. Tears streaked her cheeks and broke his heart.

He lifted his hand and traced a track with his thumb. "What's the matter?" he whispered. "I love you."

She opened her eyes, and hers were so sad that his own eyes stung. "I love you, too, but it doesn't *change* anything."

"What are you talking about? Love changes everything. I've never loved anyone like this before."

"I have, and it didn't matter. Love wasn't enough."

"My love will be enough. Marry me, Evie. It won't be like before, I promise." He hesitated, wondering if he would embarrass her by giving voice to the suspicion he'd had for a while now. "Are all these jobs because you need money?"

She stiffened. "None of your business."

"It's nothing to be embarrassed about, babe." She kicked him in the shins. "Sorry— Evie. You've taken care of yourself and the kids all alone. Let me in. Let me help. If you marry me, you'll never have to work again."

She made a sound of exasperation deep in her throat. "You don't understand. I want to work. I love my job. Why don't you quit *your* job?"

"Me?" He gave a short laugh. "Why? I've been looking forward to this job half my life."

"Me, too. And I'm so close to what I've always wanted, I can taste it on my tongue every morning and every night."

"But you won't *need* to work. I've got tons of money."

"It's not about money. It's about me. Once upon a time I was alone with three kids and no way to take care of us. I dragged myself and them out of that mess by the skin of my teeth. But I did it."

"And if you marry me you'll never have to worry about going through that again."

"But I will. I'll always worry about that. I need to be what I made myself. What I've dreamed of being. And if you make me into something I was once, and hated, I'll hate you for it. Just like you'll hate me if I take away your dream."

"So what are you saying?"

"I can't marry you. I can't have any more kids. I just can't. I have nightmares about when the twins were babies. I still wake up sweating and shaking, thinking they've been crying for hours while I was passed out from sleep deprivation. Honestly, I can't bear it again."

"You make it sound like torture."

"It was. I remember once when Ray managed to get home and found me crying along with the two of them. He asked me if I loved them, and you know what I said?''

He shook his head.

''I said no.'' She gave a choked sob. ''Right then I did not love them. I don't know why everyone always thinks a mother automatically loves her children as soon as they're born. I'm not saying they don't grow on you, but when you're all alone, and the world caves in, and you've got too many kids— love is the farthest thing from your mind.''

''The world isn't going to cave in on you, Evie. I'll be there.''

''I've heard that before, and words are cheap.''

''You're saying you love me, but you don't trust me. You don't believe I've changed. You don't think I'm going to stick around when times get tough?''

''I'm not saying anything except no, I won't marry you.'' She slipped into her room, but before the door shut he heard her whisper, ''Even though I love you.''

Joe stood there with his forehead against her door and pondered knocking it down. But what more could he tell her? He thought he heard another door click shut nearby, but when he listened more carefully all he heard was silence. Even the loud television had been turned down to a dull roar.

So he went to his room, and when Toni asked what was wrong, Joe didn't answer, because he didn't know how to respond. Then he took a shower and let the hot water pound on his head until it ran cold. But he still couldn't figure out how falling in love had become a bad thing.

HOYT SNORED ON THE BED. Danny slowly shut the door. Without a word, he and his brother held hands and sat in the pretend closet across from the sink. It was pretend because there wasn't any door—only a hanger bar and some hangers attached so you couldn't steal 'em or somethin'.

Danny had never figured out why anyone would steal hangers. Mom always said the things multiplied in the closet dark. Maybe that was why they had to put a lock on 'em here. There was no closet dark without a closet door, so the hangers didn't make babies.

Danny sighed. Makin' babies seemed to be a big problem lately.

"Did you hear what Mom said?" Benji whispered, though Danny doubted Hoyt would wake up just from them talkin', since he hadn't even turned over while the pillow fight was goin' on. Mom would have a kitten if she found out Hoyt had been sleeping all afternoon while Benji and Danny watched cable television.

Danny nodded. "I heard."

He *had* heard, and he was real confused. Mom always *seemed* to love them. She fed them, and hugged them, and punished them when they were bad—which she said was because she loved them so much, though Danny had doubts about the "getting grounded for your own good" rule. And she never, ever did anything terrible to them like he heard about on the news.

"She didn't want us." Benji's voice trembled, and Danny held his brother's hand tighter. Sometimes Benji was a baby, even though Danny had come out last—whatever that meant. "Do you think if she didn't have us, she might marry Joe?"

That *was* what Danny had been thinking, so he didn't bother to answer. Mostly he and Benji thought the same thoughts. People said it was because they were twins, but Danny just thought it was because they were seven. He had a lot of the same thoughts as his friends, too, but no one ever got all excited about it.

"Maybe," Danny allowed.

"What should we do?"

Danny knew what they *had* to do. "If we were gone, Mom wouldn't mind having a baby for Joe. Then she'd be happy, and Joe would be happy, and Adam could go to any college he wants 'cause Joe's rich."

"But I love Joe. I want him to be *our* daddy."

"Me, too, stupid. But I love Mom more."

"Even if she doesn't love us?"

"Even if."

Benji sighed. "Me, too."

"Mom always says if you love someone, you have to sack-the-face for them."

"Huh?"

"That means givin' up somethin' important so they can be happy."

"Like givin' up Mom for Joe, and givin' up Joe for Mom?"

"Yeah, like that."

"So what are we going to do?"

"We're going to go live somewhere else so Mom can have Joe."

"All right. Wh-where we gonna go?" *Sniff, sniff.*

Benji was on the verge of bawling. Danny had to think fast—and it had to be somethin' good. "To Disney World."

That perked Benji right up. "Really?"

"Sure. The place is huge. And it's full of kids."

"When we leavin'?"

"Tomorrow. During the game. They'll never even notice we left."

CHAPTER EIGHTEEN

THE DAY OF THE BIG GAME dawned bright, clear and hot. Evie made sure all the kids had hats, sunscreen and full water bottles. Their game would be from eleven to one—peak sun time. She didn't plan to send any of her kids home to Oak Grove after a hospital stay for heat exhaustion. When these kids were with her, she treated them as she would her own. Up to and including punishments for pillow fights.

Unfortunately, she had been unable to get anyone to squeal on whoever had started the revolt. She had a feeling her culprits were Adam and Toni, who didn't seem to be speaking to each other. She only hoped that whatever had got them in a snit didn't affect their game, but ordering them to make nice wouldn't work, so she left well enough alone.

She'd tossed and turned all night long, her blessed stay in a solitary room becoming a curse, just as she'd feared. Joe's kiss had made her think of their night together, and their talk had made her contemplate all she was giving up by turning him away.

But that wasn't the only reason she couldn't sleep. She felt bad that she'd said the twins' babyhood was a nightmare. Now that she could look back on those years with the eyes of a calmer, saner woman, she was able to recall wonderful times, when before she'd only been able to remember the pain.

Sometimes when one or the other, and not both for a change, woke up in the middle of the night, she could remember sitting in a rocker by the window, watching the moon and the stars, holding a child to her breast and feeling the love wash over her in waves of warmth. Babies trusted you completely. When they fell asleep in your arms with their breath soft upon you, they took hold of your soul, and you became lost to them forever.

By the time dawn lit the sky, Evie had fallen into a fitful sleep filled with dreams of a little girl in a pink sleeper—warm, sweet smelling, compact and trusting, just as Joe had said.

Luckily, once Evie arrived at the ballpark the game captured her attention. The Big League World Series was a big deal in Cedar City. The hotels were filled, the restaurants busy, the stands at the park packed and the concessions doing brisk business. Because of this, the games had a festival atmosphere that was hard to ignore. Not just for her, but for the kids.

While her team warmed up, Evie went over the rules with the twins. "You stay on the bench, out of the way. Do *not* go near the on-deck circle. If you get your brains bashed in, I will kill you. Are we clear?"

"Yep," said Danny.

"Uh-huh," said Benji.

"One soda and one candy is your limit. Here's some money. If you need anything else, ask Hoyt."

They looked sad for some reason, and she couldn't figure out why. Usually they bounced all over the place, so excited for Adam that they could barely stand still. But today they sat on the bench and eyed each other expectantly. Now that she thought about it, they'd been whispering together all morning. Not an uncommon occurrence, considering who she was talking about, but she'd also had enough experience with them to know that whispering followed by uncommon silence meant they were up to something.

"Anything you guys want to share with me?"

"Nope." Danny answered too quickly, and he grabbed Benji's hand as if to keep him quiet.

Evie frowned.

"We just love you, Mom."

"That's nice to know."

"And we'll always love you, forever and ever and ever. No matter where we go, no matter what we do."

Oh-oh, Evie thought. "You guys in trouble?" she asked.

Identical expressions of innocence turned toward her, and they shook their heads, wide blue eyes hiding…something. But what?

"Hey, Coach, need your starting lineup," called the announcer.

Evie glanced that way and raised a hand in acknowledgment. She'd have to get to the bottom of things with the twins after the game.

"Remember what I said." She raised a finger in warning before kissing the top of one nodding red head, then the other.

The game passed like a whirlwind. Evie and Joe shook hands. She tried not to glance at him, but she couldn't help herself. His tight lips and unhappy expression scored her heart.

Her kids were nervous, but once into the game they settled down. Better than she did, anyway. They played like the champions they were.

Because this game was between two teams of equal stature, the score went neck and neck, with first one team ahead and then the other. The talents of the kids were so evenly matched that the game would come down to a mistake, or a gift, or a coach's decision. Neither Evie nor Joe had time for anything but notes on their clipboards and consultations with their assistants or players, as they used everything they knew to coach the kids they'd spent the entire summer teaching. This game was what teamwork was all about.

Evie had stressed throughout the season that her bet with Coach Scalotta was a fun thing, and not really as serious as everyone made out. More a publicity stunt than anything else. She did not want her team worrying that her future rested on their performance in a single game.

Maybe it did, but that wasn't their problem or what was important here. What *was* important was that her team had a good experience, played their best and remembered this game forever as one of the many good things about this particular summer.

Of course, when the ninth inning arrived and Evie's team was down by one run, with Adam on second, two outs, and Toni coming up to bat, Evie got so nervous she felt ill.

This was it. The whole summer, and her future, lay in Toni's hands—and Evie suddenly wanted to call the whole thing off.

Toni came over for last-second instructions, took one look at Evie's face and hugged her. "Hey, Coach, relax. This is supposed to be fun."

Then Toni winked and walked off whistling. Evie's nervousness evaporated on the summer breeze as joy filled her heart. She had never been happier with a kid she'd coached. Toni had gotten the essence of Little League—have fun out there. The world slipped back into place for Evie, and all was right once more.

The *crack* of the bat on the ball, the cheer of the crowd and the voice of the announcer—"Going, going, gone! A home run for Toni Scalotta!"—were anticlimactic to Evie.

Her season had been complete—and a rousing success—before Toni even stepped up to the plate.

She turned around to hug the twins—but they had disappeared.

ADAM WAITED JUST BEYOND home plate and swept Toni into his arms. They kissed amid the whir of cameras. That picture would be front page center tomorrow, Joe figured. It wasn't every day the catcher and the pitcher kissed full on the lips after winning the World Series.

Joe should be annoyed, but right now all he could do was grin. This was probably the most fun day of his life, and he'd lost the game. Winning wasn't everything, or the only thing. It was pretty much nothing—unless it made someone you loved as happy as Toni looked right now.

He had planned on giving a pep talk to his team, though now that they'd lost there wasn't much to be peppy about, but after a quick look at their long faces he decided that they wanted to be alone. So he sent them to the bus with one of the parents and went toward his little girl.

Joe chuckled. His daughter had just hit a home run to win the World Series. Now, that was something you didn't hear every day. Too bad, too, because it sounded darn good.

Toni saw him approaching and disentangled herself from her boyfriend, and her fans, to launch herself into his arms—something she would never have done a few months back. They'd come a long way. They still had a way to go, of course, but Joe believed that they would get there—together.

He swung her around and hugged her tight. "Did you see it, Dad?"

"Couldn't miss it, honey. That was a classic." Joe released her from the circle of his arms. Speaking of happy people... He glanced around, but couldn't find the woman who should be just as happy over this win. "Where's your coach? I need to shake her hand."

Toni frowned and turned toward the dugout. Joe followed her gaze. Evie should have been in the midst of the party. Instead, she and Hoyt were deep in a serious conversation. As Joe watched, she put her hand to her forehead and swayed.

Joe swore and shoved aside everyone in his way until he reached Evie's side. He took her elbow and pulled her around to face him. The fear in her green eyes and the paleness of her face set his heart thumping too hard.

"What's the matter, babe?"

"Do *not* call me 'babe,'" she said absently. "The twins are gone."

"Gone? Where?"

Joe glanced at Hoyt, who shrugged. "They were sittin' there as pretty as ye please. Then the game was done and they were gone."

"They're in the bathroom or on the playground."

"They aren't," Evie said. "I checked everywhere. The popcorn man saw them leave the park."

Panic first fluttered, then burned, in Joe's belly. He changed his grip on Evie's elbow from a clasp to a caress. She folded into his arms with a soft, helpless cry that scared him even worse than her words. Evie was never helpless. But then again, her kids had never disappeared before.

He held her tight and brushed his hand over her hair. "Shh," he murmured. "We'll find them."

"How?" She took a deep breath that threatened to become a sob. "They're so little, and the world's so big, and mean, and crazy." She tilted her head and her eyes glittered with tears. "Joe, I'm scared. Those kids are my whole life."

Adam cleared his throat. He and Toni stood, hand in hand. Adam stared at his mom as if he'd just seen her for the first time. He gave himself a little shake and asked, "What's going on?"

"Your brothers have disappeared," he said.

The initial joy on the kid's face turned to shock. He let go of Toni and went to his mom, but she only moaned and burrowed deeper into Joe's chest.

Adam frowned, glanced at Toni, then at Joe. He looked terrified, and Joe couldn't blame him. His brothers were missing and his usually rock-solid mother couldn't seem to function. But Joe had no time to coddle the kid. He had to find the twins.

"Where do you think they'd go?" Joe asked.

Adam's face was pale, but he didn't fold. He met Joe's eyes, and the two of them exchanged a silent truce. "They wouldn't *go* anywhere. They're a pain in the behind to watch, but they don't wander off."

"Would they run away?"

Adam considered that a moment. "Maybe. But why?"

"That's the $10,000 question I plan to get the answer to once I have the scruffs of their necks in each of my hands. Now, where would they go? Think."

"Iceman, the Wildman, Scalotta!" A microphone

nearly hit Joe in the teeth. "Your daughter has just won the Big League World Series. What are you going to do next?"

"I'm going to Disney World," Joe snarled. "Where else?"

"That's it!" Adam shouted.

Joe tried to look at the kid, but the reporter kept waving the microphone in front of his face. He'd had enough of that for one lifetime. Joe stared her straight in the eye and used his Iceman glare. "Go away," he snapped. She did.

He turned to Adam. "What's it?"

"The twin rats—" Adam winced and glanced at his mother, who had straightened and disentangled herself from Joe's embrace when Adam shouted. "Sorry, Mom. This morning, on the way here, they asked me if you could get to Disney World on a bus. I said you could get to Disney World any way you wanted and a bus was probably the cheapest."

"You think?" Evie breathed, hope lighting her eyes.

"Let's go." Joe took her hand, and they raced for the exit.

EVIE COULDN'T think straight. In fact, she couldn't seem to think at all. Her mind was numb, her heart heavy. Her babies were missing, and she needed to do something to find them, but she couldn't seem to do anything but stare through the windshield of the taxi and try not to cry.

The bus station was within walking distance of

the ballpark, but Joe had grabbed a cab so they could get there quickly. Evie didn't think she'd have been able to run or walk, anyway.

Joe seemed to sense her panic, and he took over. Right now, he held her hand, and she clung to him. He hadn't let her go since they'd left the ballpark. What would she have done if he hadn't been here to help? Evie had always prided herself on handling everything her kids dished out. But this—this was too much for her.

"Here you go," the cabbie said.

Evie was out the door before the car came to a complete stop—breaking her own rule and not giving a damn. Joe threw money at the man and tore through the glass doors right behind her. He bumped into her when she stopped just inside the doorway.

"Thank God," he whispered, and his breath stirred her hair. His hard, capable hands rested on her shoulders, and Evie reached up to twine her fingers through his.

"Thank God," she echoed.

The twins hadn't seen them enter. They were too engrossed in a television bolted to a chair, their noses pressed nearly to the screen.

Toni and Adam walked in. Evie eyed them and shrugged. Adam took one step toward the twins, hands clenched into fists, but Evie touched his shoulder and shook her head.

She approached her boys. They looked up when her shadow fell across the television screen—first joy, then anxiety, filled their blue eyes. They were happy to see her, but they knew they were in trouble.

The two joined hands and waited for the storm to burst, but Evie didn't have the heart to yell. She was too darn glad to see them. Instead, she pulled the twins into her arms and held them tight, breathing in the fragrance of little boy and trying not to sob her heart out.

"Mom, how come you're here?" Danny mumbled against her neck.

"To get you and take you home, where I can ground you for the rest of your natural life."

"Really?" Benji asked.

Evie ignored that. "What are you two doing here?"

"We were watching this great movie." Danny looked up. "Hey, Joe, have you ever watched *Mr. Mom?* You know, with the guy who ended up being Batman?"

"Yeah," Joe said, moving closer.

She welcomed the warmth of his body and the calm in his voice. Sometimes being an adult was too hard. Sometimes you needed someone. She'd done things on her own so long she hadn't realized how much it helped when there were two against the world, instead of one.

"The guy in the movie—he's a stay-at-home daddy. Isn't that cool?"

"Sure." Joe sounded as puzzled as Evie felt.

"We were gonna sack-the-face for you and Mom.

We heard how you want a baby, but how Mom don't want no more 'cause we were so awful.''

Evie's heart did a sickening lurch, and she wanted to cry all over again. "You heard that?"

"We shouldn't have been listenin', we know."

"I was wrong to say that. It *was* rough when you were little. But you guys are my angels come to the earth." She glanced up and found Adam watching her. She held the twins, but she spoke to him. "Things might have been bad, my life seemed ruined, but when I held you in my arms, the world made sense again."

Adam smiled, nodded, and the wall that had been between them dissolved, at least for the time being. Evie could breathe again.

"Weren't we accidents?"

Evie closed her eyes for just a second, took another breath and gave the twins a quick squeeze. "There are no accidents. Only presents we don't know about yet."

"Cool." They wriggled for freedom, but she wouldn't let them go. "Mom, we have to tell you what we found out. You always said that if you really love someone, that means you have to sack-the-face—"

"Are they trying to say 'sacrifice'?" Joe interrupted.

"That's what I said." Danny's nose wrinkled. "Jeez. So we figured if Mom didn't have us, she could have another baby, then Joe and everyone would be happy."

"How could you ever think I'd be happy without my two best redheaded guys?"

"Sack-the-faces have to be made, Mom. We might be little, but we know *that*. Anyways, we saw this movie, and we was thinkin'—you know how Joe likes to cook and stuff, and you hate it, Mom?" Evie nodded. "We never wanted to tell you and hurt your feelings, but you really aren't good at cookin'. But you're the best mom in the world. And the best teacher in town. Everyone says so. So why can't Joe be the stay-at-home daddy?"

"Joe has a job, honey, a job he's been waiting to do half his life. I can't ask him to give that up, just as he shouldn't ask me to give up mine."

"But, Mom, we want a stay-at-home daddy. And we want Joe. Can't we keep him?"

Evie opened her mouth to say no, they could not keep him, but Joe spoke, instead. "Out of the mouths of babes," he murmured.

Her breathing became difficult as hope filled her heart. She stood and faced him. "What are you talking about?"

He pulled her into his arms. "They've got a point, you know?"

"They do? Which point would that be? They've run through so many."

"I'd make a great Mr. Mom."

"Oh, Joe. I don't want you to give up your dream for mine."

"My dream *is* you and the kids. Love and a family—that's what I want. I love you, Evie, and if you really don't want a baby, I can live with that. What I can't live with is living without you."

The fear of the afternoon, and Joe's strong support when times got tough, had shown Evie the truth. Love and a family—that was all that mattered. She couldn't continue to live half a life because of mistakes she'd made what seemed half a lifetime ago.

Somehow, when she wasn't paying attention, Joe Scalotta had crept under her skin and into her heart. His presence gave her peace. He held her up when all she wanted to do was fall down. He made her laugh when tears still threatened her eyes. She didn't want to live without him, either.

"How many babies?" she asked.

Joe grinned. "None? Some? Your wish is my command. One question, though." Evie tilted her head, waiting. "Do you love me?"

"You bet."

"Betting is what got us into this."

"And I won. I guess I get the job I've always wanted. If that's okay with you."

"You'll be great. So, if I sack-the-face, will you marry me?"

Her answer was to jump into his arms, and as he twirled her around and around, she kissed him, long and deep. The twins made smoochy sounds and several spectators inside the bus station clapped.

The *whir* of a camera broke them apart, but it was only the annoying reporter from the ballpark, who had followed them.

Front page center the next morning there appeared a picture of Joe and Evie kissing, above a caption that read Wildman becomes mild man as he pledges future to his Coach Mom from Iowa.

EPILOGUE

One year later

"CALL US when you get to the dorm," Evie instructed, as Adam pulled his car away from the curb.

Joe's arm came across her shoulders, and together they watched their eldest child leave for college.

"One down, four to go," he said.

"At least."

Toni, flanked by the twins, waved until Adam's car was out of sight. Then the boys started fooling around.

"Danny, quit dancing in the street and go get your mom's bags," Joe ordered. "Benji, get your sister's."

The boys hustled off to do just that. Joe no longer had any problem telling the two apart. Living with them kind of cured a person of the double vision. Now whenever someone asked how he did it, he simply winked and said, "I'm their dad. I just know."

"Mom, we better go."

Evie smiled as she did every time Toni called her "Mom." The novelty of that had yet to wear off.

From the force of the love that trilled through Evie every time, she doubted it ever would.

"Here." Evie handed their newest addition into Joe's arms. Maria Scalotta was only a month old, but she was the apple of everyone's eye.

Joe held the baby like a pro, maybe because he was. He had become a stay-at-home daddy after finishing his one-year commitment to OGCC, and he'd taken to his new job as easily as Evie had taken to being the mother of five instead of three.

Not that there hadn't been rough spots. Try having a seventeen-year-old boy and a sixteen-year-old girl who are in love living in the same house. Or having a young man who's been the man of that house suddenly playing second fiddle to his girlfriend's dad.

But truthfully, everything had worked out for the best in the end, just as Evie had always hoped. Though she and Joe had made mistakes in their youth, the example of those mistakes seemed to have impressed themselves upon their eldest children.

Her relationship with Adam had improved. She'd tried to talk to him again, and explain that while his birth had been an accident, his existence was a joy. He had made her life complete, not torn it in pieces. But, after seeing her fall apart when the twins were missing and hearing her words to them in the Cedar City bus station, Adam already understood how much both he and the twins meant to her. Once again—everything had come out all right.

Evie shook her head, remembering the pitfalls of the past year. It hadn't been easy, but with Joe at her side, problems didn't seem half as bad as they had when she'd handled them alone. Even labor and delivery had been kind of fun, since big bad Iceman Scalotta had passed out at the first sight of blood. Evie was laughing when Maria came into the world.

"We'll see you in Pennsylvania?" Evie gave Maria a final kiss.

The baby gurgled and kicked—all sweetness and light—with Evie's dark hair and Joe's startling blue eyes. She already had all the boys in the house wrapped around her little finger—and the girls, too.

"Wouldn't miss it," Joe said. "Maria has a new outfit. And a hat."

"Joe!" Her big bruiser of a husband had turned into a closet clotheshorse where his baby girl was concerned. "We're going to go bankrupt if you keep buying her clothes."

"But they're so cute." He rubbed his nose against Maria's.

Evie sighed. What was a woman to do?

She and Toni took their bags from the twins, kissed both little boys and headed for the car. This year their team was on the way to the national championships. Unfortunately, Adam had to be at college instead of the game, but priorities were priorities. Evie had every confidence in her star pitcher and adopted daughter.

"Rules for the fall season are on the fridge," she called over her shoulder.

The twins groaned, Joe laughed and Maria started hiccuping.

Evie drove toward the airport, watching in the rearview mirror as half her family waved goodbye.

Life didn't get any better than this.

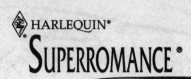

HARLEQUIN®
SUPERROMANCE®

You are now entering

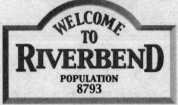

WELCOME TO
RIVERBEND
POPULATION
8793

Riverbend...the kind of place where everyone knows your name—and your business. Riverbend...home of the River Rats—a group of small-town sons and daughters who've been friends since high school.

The Rats are all grown up now. Living their lives and learning that some days are good and some days aren't—and that you can get through anything as long as you have your friends.

Starting in July 2000, Harlequin Superromance brings you Riverbend—six books about the River Rats and the Midwest town they live in.

BIRTHRIGHT by **Judith Arnold** (July 2000)
THAT SUMMER THING by **Pamela Bauer** (August 2000)
HOMECOMING by **Laura Abbot** (September 2000)
LAST-MINUTE MARRIAGE by **Marisa Carroll** (October 2000)
A CHRISTMAS LEGACY by **Kathryn Shay** (November 2000)

Available wherever Harlequin books are sold.

HARLEQUIN®
Makes any time special ™

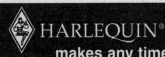

#924 BIRTHRIGHT • Judith Arnold
Riverbend
Aaron Mazerik is back. He isn't the town's bad boy anymore, but some people still don't think he's good enough—especially not for Riverbend's golden girl, Lily Holden. Which is fine with Aaron, since he's convinced there's even *more* reason he and Lily shouldn't be together.

Riverbend, Indiana: Home of the River Rats—small-town sons and daughters who've been friends since high school. These are their stories.

#925 FULL RECOVERY • Bobby Hutchinson
Emergency!
Spence Mathews, former RCMP officer and now handling security at St. Joe's Hospital, helps Dr. Joanne Duncan deliver a baby in the E.R. After the infant mysteriously disappears a few hours later, Spence and Joanne work closely together to solve the abduction and in the process recover the baby girl—and much more!

#926 MOM'S THE WORD • Roz Denny Fox
9 Months Later
Hayley Ryan is pregnant and alone. Her no-good ex—the baby's father—abandoned her for another woman; her beloved grandfather is dead, leaving her nothing but a mining claim in southern Arizona. Hayley is cast upon her own resources, trying to work the claim, worrying about herself and her baby.... And then rancher Zack Cooper shows up.

#927 THE REAL FATHER • Kathleen O'Brien
Twins
Ten years ago, Molly Lorring left Demery, South Carolina, with a secret. She was pregnant with Beau Forrest's baby, but Beau died in a car crash before he could marry her. For all that time, Beau's identical twin, Jackson, has carried his own secret. Beau *isn't* the father of Molly's baby....

#928 CONSEQUENCES • Margot Dalton
Crystal Creek
Principal Lucia Osborne knows the consequences of hiring cowboy Jim Whitely to teach the difficult seventh graders. Especially when Jim deliberately flouts the rules in order to help the kids. Certain members of the board may vote to fire Lucia and close the school. But Lucia has even graver consequences to worry about. She's falling in love with Jim...and she's expecting another man's child.

#929 THE BABY BARGAIN • Peggy Nicholson
Marriage of Inconvenience
Rafe Montana's sixteen-year-old daughter, Zoe, and Dana Kershaw's teenage son, Sean, have made a baby. *Now what?* Rafe's solution—or rather, proposal—has Zoe ecstatic, but it leaves Dana aghast and Sean confused. Even Rafe wonders whether he's out of his mind.